"You do not know what danger you are in when you tempt me like that."

"Tempt you? I didn't—"

Her words were cut off by his kiss. His lips devoured hers and his forceful domination roused her. This wasn't like the tepid kisses from before. She was getting a taste of his unchecked desire.

Striker's fingers moved up and over her breasts to linger at her throat. He laid a finger on her jugular vein and left it there, feeling her heartbeat.

"You are too much of a temptation," he whispered against her lips.

When she opened her eyes, she saw his fangs, extended and gleaming. The look in his eyes should have frightened her, sent her running from the hungry vampire who held her in his arms. But the only emotion she felt was all-encompassing passion....

Books by Connie Hall

Harlequin Nocturne

The Guardian #108
The Beholder #112
Nightwalker #116

*The Nightwalkers

CONNIE HALL

Award-winning author Connie Hall is a full-time writer. Her writing credits include six historical novels and two novellas written under the pen name Constance Hall. She is thrilled to now be writing for Harlequin Nocturne.

An avid hiker, conservationist, bird-watcher, painter of watercolors and oil portraits, she dreams of one day trying her hand at skydiving.

She lives in Richmond, Virginia, with her husband, two sons and Keeper, a lovable Lab-mix who rules the house with her big brown eyes. For more information, visit her website or email her at conniehall_author@comcast.net.

NIGHTWALKER
CONNIE HALL

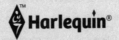

TORONTO NEW YORK LONDON
AMSTERDAM PARIS SYDNEY HAMBURG
STOCKHOLM ATHENS TOKYO MILAN MADRID
PRAGUE WARSAW BUDAPEST AUCKLAND

Recycling programs
for this product may
not exist in your area.

ISBN-13: 978-0-373-61863-7

NIGHTWALKER

Copyright © 2011 by Connie Koslow

Dear Reader,

We all share fantasies of meeting one on a dark night—am I right? But be careful—you may get what you wish for. And the vampire may not be the nice *True Blood*'s Bill Compton type. You may meet up with the Nightwalker.

That's what happens to Takala Rainwater. And let me tell you, Striker Dark isn't named Nightwalker because he's a pleasant sort of undead. He was formed before Christianity. Envision the transformations he must have witnessed, the wars and destruction on which he fed. He could have whispered in Nostradamus's ear, chatted with Einstein, orchestrated civilization to suit his whims and his hunger for blood. Now imagine putting your life in the hands of such perpetual evil....

Oh, yeah, I almost forgot to tell you about Takala's sisters, Fala and Nina. You can read their stories in *The Guardian* and *The Beholder*.

Happy reading!

Connie Hall

Chapter 1

Buckingham Palace

The call came at a most inopportune moment. Striker Dark reached for his phone while keeping his gaze on the queen of England. She cut her eyes at him for a split second, and, without missing a beat, she continued to address the dignitaries with stiff royal aplomb.

After a quick look around, he astral projected out the banquet room's closest exit. He would take the call and get back before the humans present even realized he'd left his seat.

Two of the queen's MI10 agents, a vampire and a leopard shifter, noticed. They were the only Supes (supernaturals) in the room who could follow his departure. They eyed him with distaste. MI10 was a highly classified counterintelligence agency within Great Britain, the counterpart to Striker's own United

States Bureau of Supernatural Phenomena. They both dealt with anything supernatural and kept it hidden from humans, and duties sometimes included protecting royalty and government officials. Two of Striker's own agents were safeguarding the President of the United States right now. But MI10 agents thought themselves a cut above their Yank cousins, and for that reason Striker ignored them completely as he paused in the hallway.

His phone wasn't your typical landline. A crystal, developed especially for him by the tech-support staff at B.O.S.P., drove the gizmo. His clairvoyant powers absorbed the energy it released, and it amplified them. It was like having an omnipresent stalker exploding in his head. Even before he opened the lid he knew something was dreadfully wrong.

His gut flinched, and he couldn't believe the image appearing before his eyes. Hover demons floated and circled five of his agents.

Hover demons could be easily summoned; they killed for pleasure, unlike doom demons, who tortured their victims and demanded payment for their enjoyment. There were as many types of demons as there were types of angels. Angels and demons had their many uses, but Striker refused to summon hovers for anything. They were unpredictable, and in his line of work unpredictability was a detriment.

Black hooded robes covered the demons' bodies and faces, but the flamethrowers and scythes in their hands were clearly visible. His agents were near them, on their knees, execution style. Silver chains crisscrossed their vampire bodies and held them immobile. Striker knew every one of the agents by name. He had trained them himself. They were the elite at B.O.S.P. How could this happen?

In the moonlit background, Striker noticed a wharf. Warehouse lights cast eerie shadows over their faded fronts. Boats rocked against the pier, and he saw the Suter's Marina sign. He knew that place. New Orleans.

A hover paused, the edge of his robe rippling as he lowered the blowtorch and fired. Aquarius, a two-hundred-year-old vamp and one of Striker's OIC's, screamed. A rictus of pain and helplessness distorted his face.

Abruptly, the scythe chopped down on his neck.

His head rolled like a ball and settled near his knees. One blink of recognition from his eyes, and then the life left Aquarius's face forever.

Another demon closed in on the next agent in line. Fizz! Chop! Fizz! Chop! Another shriek. Chop!

Striker wanted to feel sympathy or empathy, but there was nothing left inside to let him feel. He had lived too long on the earth, and it had killed his human sensitivity. It was as if the world had lost all its color and he observed it from an objective, sterile black-and-white environment now. Still, he couldn't look at his own agents, the ones whom he directed and had sent to their deaths, without feeling the injustice. A tiny snarl lifted one corner of his lip, and he felt his fangs extend.

Suddenly the phone's camera turned upward, and a female face he recognized spun into view. Real name: Skye Rainwater, aka Simone Poindexter, aka Lilly Smith. Code name: Culler. She stared back him. Her vibrant blue eyes filled up the screen, the dark, sooty lashes caked with mascara. Eyes so deeply entrenched in his mind that he'd see them the rest of his life.

"Hello, Nightwalker," she said. "Enjoying this little show?"

Striker heard another yell, and it cut the back of his neck like the teeth of a chain saw. "Culler," Striker said. "What the hell are you doing? Help them!"

"I have. Can't you see that?"

So it was real. "How did you set up this blood-bath?"

"Just called Aquarius and told him Raithe was receiving a shipment of girls."

Aquarius should have known better, followed protocol and called Striker. It wasn't the first time Aquarius had broken rank, only this time he'd paid dearly—with his life. "What has happened to you?"

"I'm tired of being out in the field, risking my life and doing your dirty work for the measly pennies you drop my way."

"We invested half a million in your cover. That is a lot of pennies." Striker's voice turned low, soft and quite deadly. He envisioned wrapping his hands around her neck and squeezing…. "How could you betray B.O.S.P. like this?"

"I don't live and breathe the agency like you. I'm a free spirit. And who are we kidding? This is your vendetta, not B.O.S.P.'s. Raithe just helped me see I was on the wrong side."

"I will find you."

"You can try." She cackled, her eyes gleaming bright blue with malice. Then the screen went blank.

Striker thought of headquarters, and Mimi's small

angular face appeared in the screen. Anyone looking at her reflection could tell she was a dwarf. What her looks didn't reveal was her penchant for voodoo. She looked bored until she noticed who it was. A grin spread across her face, and she batted her false eyelashes as she fluffed her curly blond hair. "Anything I can get you, boss?"

Striker knew she was referring to something other than work, but he always ignored her advances. And this was no different. He went directly to the point. "I need the dossier on Culler. Send it right away, and see what aliases you can find that are not in our files. And use the psychics. I do not want one stone unturned."

"You got it, boss."

"Any sightings of Raithe?" Striker had recently upped the bounty on Raithe in the paranormal community, but as of yet no one was brave enough to collect the three million dollars.

"No, sorry," she said forlornly. She knew Raithe was on Striker's top-ten wanted list.

"All right, then. Waiting on the dossier."

He closed the device and shoved it in his pocket. He would apologize later to the queen. He didn't have time for niceties or foreign diplomatic dinner parties. He had to find Culler.

She had been his only hope. What had happened to make her turn? They had been so close to catching Raithe. Striker's lip lifted in a tiny snarl as he thought of his nemesis. Raithe controlled much of the underbelly of the human and vampire races. He dealt in everything from drugs to prostitution to providing living victims for vampires to drain and kill. A real nice upstanding vampire was Raithe.

Striker had been hunting Raithe for hundreds of years, and not once had he been able to get this close to him. It had taken ten years of undercover work, but Culler had finally gained Raithe's trust. Striker didn't want to think about the evils Culler must have endured and participated in to prove her fealty to Raithe. Culler kept assuring Striker that she was okay and didn't need a psychological evaluation. She promised Striker she could locate Raithe's den, but she needed more time. Through the years, she'd given Striker several leads on child-pornography rings and snuff-film makers, mostly throughout Europe, even a bordello filled with werepanthers Raithe tortured for his own amusement, but not the one thing Striker wanted: Raithe.

Then Culler had turned on him and joined Raithe. At the thought of his nemesis, Striker felt his fangs jut out more and scrape his lower lip. He tasted his own blood and realized he and Raithe were more similar than he cared to admit. They were both ruthless in their own way, both unable to stop until the other was eradicated.

Chapter 2

Takala Rainwater stuffed the last bite of a ham and cheese croissant in her mouth as she saw the road sign for the Woodlawn Terrace subdivision. A cemetery name if she ever saw one. Right up there with Pleasant Green and Quiet Acres.

She made an uneasy face as she turned right, finished off a can of Pepsi, and drove her MINI Cooper down the road. The streets of Fredericksburg looked like any other quiet residential neighborhood in February. Neatly groomed houses lined the block. Rows of dormant flower gardens waited for winter to end and spring to begin. Evidence of a recent snow still painted the lawns in a sheen of white. The pockmarked bodies of melting snowmen waved to her from some of the yards. The only evidence of death here was the name of the road.

She grabbed the note lying beside her and looked at the address Blake had given her. Blake Green worked for the FBI's Data and Statistics Department. A friend since high school. He gleaned information for Takala's private investigating agency, and in return Takala sprung for his dinner at a four-star restaurant once a month.

Blake had been searching for evidence of Takala's mother for four years, since joining the FBI. Blake was a bloodhound when it came to finding information, and Skye Rainwater had become one of his obsessions. Finally he'd got a hit this morning. He had flagged the name, and someone must have been researching it, because the flag popped up. He had followed the electronic trail and called Takala all excited, telling her that he'd discovered information in the State Department database on Skye Rainwater. She had two aliases, Simone Poindexter and Lilly Smith. He also gave Takala Lilly Smith's LKA (last known address) here in the States. Surprisingly, it was in Fredericksburg, Virginia, not seventy miles from the Patomani Indian reservation where Takala lived. He also added the usual caveat he did with all the leads he gave her: that the information might be bogus. In this case it could have been planted by the State Department to throw people off Skye's trail. But it was a lead.

Takala wondered how her mother was connected to the State Department, but that was still a mystery to her and Blake. She vowed to worship Blake for the rest of his life and buy his dinner every day for the next twenty years. Blake's ego had seemed worthily pandered to and satisfied, and they had left it at that.

Now Takala felt her heart pounding as she read the numbers. Forty-five was a couple of blocks away. This could be the moment for which she'd been waiting her whole life. Finally, she might meet her mother. Face-to-face. Up close and personal. No room to run.

She had a lot of questions for her, and they were the kind you had to look a woman in the eye while she answered them, like how does a mother just drop three daughters on the doorstep of her mother's home and leave? Even though it was forbidden to speak of anyone who had been abjured from her tribe, Meikoda, Takala's grandmother, had felt Takala and her sisters wouldn't stop asking about their mother until they heard the explanation of why and how they came to live with her. After warning them that she could only tell them once, she had gone on to explain that Skye had left them because she'd refused to marry the man predestined to be her husband—that's how it was for Guardians. They married whomever the Maiden Bear chose for them. But Skye had refused, spit in the face of the creator of her tribe's white magic. Skye had abandoned her family, her preordained station as the Guardian, and her standing in the tribe to marry for love. It had ended badly, and her husband, Takala's father, had died prematurely of lung cancer.

Meikoda said his death was Skye's reprimand from Maiden Bear. And Skye wallowed in her grief, turning to drugs for solace, until she could no longer care for her own daughters. That excuse didn't mesh if Skye had gone to work for the State Department. No, Takala wanted the truth, to hear it from her mother's own lips. That was if she was still alive. This Lilly Smith could be a dead end.

But Takala couldn't dampen the hope stirring in her, or the dread. What if she found Skye, and it didn't go well? What if she offered no explanation and resented Takala looking for her? Takala decided she'd cross that bridge when and if she ever reached it.

She rounded a corner and slowed. Number forty-five was a modest two-story with a white picket fence. Even a Christmas wreath still graced the door. Real homey. Fit right in the burb-style neighborhood. Maybe Lilly Smith had a family of her own.

At the thought, Takala grimaced and spotted the taxi sitting out front. Plumes of hot exhaust billowed from the muffler, condensing as soon as they hit the cold air. Someone was on their way out.

Takala slowed, about to pull over, when a woman appeared at the door, carrying a suitcase. Takala compared the woman's features to the old photo she'd found hidden in Meikoda's hope chest. Her grandmother had said she'd destroyed every picture of Skye when the tribe renounced her, but Takala knew Meikoda couldn't wipe out all the pictures of her only daughter. She had to have kept one, and Takala hadn't given up until she discovered it. Since finding it, she'd only looked at it a thousand times.

The woman on the porch appeared about fifty, tall, with short jet-black hair. She wore sleek brown slacks and a matching cashmere jacket. Her makeup looked flawless on her square face. Lilly Smith glanced nervously up at the taxi driver, and the classic Rainwater bright blue eyes beamed. Yep. Give or take twenty years and about two feet of long, thick braid, this woman was a dead ringer for the image in the photo.

Takala felt her chest swell and a lump form in her throat. Could this really be her mother? She was about to pull over and discover the truth when all hell broke loose.

A woman popped out from behind a hedge in the next yard. The taxi driver leaped out of the car and ran toward the front steps. A black mist appeared, swirled; then the dark mass congealed into the tall form of a guy. Definitely not human travel arrangements. By his pale skin, he looked undead. A zombie maybe. But zombies weren't capable of doing the human-fog-Houdini thing.

Lilly Smith had already seen her pursuers and was leaping over the porch railing. When she spotted Houdini, real fear filled her face.

Houdini must have had the ability to teleport, because he disappeared. Takala couldn't track him until he reappeared at Lilly's back and grabbed her.

Takala jumped into the action. She laid on the horn and stomped on the gas. The car hopped the curb, heading directly for the struggling Lilly. The other two thugs were in her path, and she barreled straight for them.

Seconds before her bumper reached them, they leaped aside.

A fist came out of nowhere and slammed through the driver's side window.

Glass flew and rained down on Takala. A gust of wind picked up the photo and address and blew it out the busted window before Takala could catch it.

She cursed, whipped around and stared into the pink, lizardlike eyes of the person who'd broken her window. The creature looked female, but not all human. Her hair was whitish green, stubbly. A green, sticky ooze covered lips that were so wide they looked like a distorted image in a funhouse mirror. She wore a black jumpsuit designed so that the sticky proboscis that jutted from her belly could pop out unencumbered. It looked like a third hand but with suction cups for fingers. She clung to the car by it, her supple body crouched there like a fly on flypaper. The creature smiled; then her long, grotesque tongue flicked out.

Takala's cheek stung as the creature's hands grabbed her neck.

Takala slammed on the brakes, gasping, "Back off, Freakzilla."

The shifter's sticky fingers stretched like rubber bands, her sharp nails digging into Takala's neck. "Who you calling a freak?" The woman's long tongue flipped out and burned Takala's forehead this time.

Takala could take a lot of two-skins, but gecko shifters just plain grossed her out; so did the little talking green guy on the insurance commercials. But this one was real and had broken her car window and was trying to strangle her.

"Okay, I warned you," Takala gasped past the pressure on her neck. Then she elbowed the shifter in the face.

The blow sent the freak rocketing from the car window. The gecko two-skin hit a cement birdbath with a loud high-pitched squeal.

If Takala had been a normal woman, she felt certain the gecko shifter's gluey body wouldn't have budged. But Takala had the strength of twenty men. Unfortunately, she hadn't been fast enough, and the shifter had raked her reptilian claws across Takala's neck.

"Oooh! Gross." Takala grabbed the bottom of her

T-shirt and wiped the sticky green saliva from her burning cheek, then moved to the bloody claw marks on her neck. That's when she saw Lilly struggling with Houdini.

Abruptly, Lilly's body vibrated into a yellow throbbing orb. She spun out of his grasp and leaped straight through his body like a ghost. When she passed through and out on the other side, Houdini staggered and collapsed.

The atoms of Lilly's body expanded like a rubber balloon, stretching her features into a grotesque ball. Then she blew a cloud of black mist from her mouth, and her body shrunk to normal size again. The dark energy funneled into a small tornado above her head. Then it headed back for Houdini's body.

Takala had overheard forbidden whispered snippets of conversation among her aunts and her grandmother where they had spoken about her mother's power. Skye was a spirit eater, capable of draining the energy from supernatural beings and temporarily paralyzing them. Takala's tribe, the Patomani Indians, had a name for the power: *egtonha*. The power would have been invaluable to an agent. Was this truly her mother?

Takala floored the accelerator, crashed over a pretty picket fence, and skidded to a stop near Lilly, barely missing the downed Houdini. She motioned for Lilly to hop in.

The energy reentered Houdini, and he staggered to his feet. In seconds, he'd gain his full power back.

Lilly seemed to realize this, her gaze shifting between the two Supes coming for her, Houdini, and Takala. Then she leaped inside Takala's car—the least of the three evils.

Takala heard Houdini's icy warning. "You're helping a killer. You'll regret—"

Lilly slammed the door, cutting off his words. She looked over at Takala and yelled, "Drive."

Takala floored it, taking out the other side of the fence and a flower bed. They hopped the curve and sped down the street.

Lilly said, "He set me up and wants me dead. Do you?"

"Nope. I'm riding the white horse at the moment." Honestly, she didn't know whom to trust. Houdini or the woman sitting beside her. Was Lilly a killer as he'd said?

"Thanks." Lilly straightened the lapels of her cashmere jacket in a fussy manner. "Such a mess, isn't it?"

Takala smelled the acrid scent of sulfur and magic on Lilly Smith as she said, "That's an understatement."

Striker felt the power forging a path through his body. He writhed and shook, knowing how it felt to be burned at the stake. He rarely if ever found himself vulnerable, but this was one of those moments. If it had been night, he would have been too strong for Culler to absorb his power. But it was morning, and the sun had drained some of his strength. Not even the tech-support guys at B.O.S.P. could come up with a solution to block that phenomenon. But he still had half of his powers. Culler and her friend would not get away. Not if he could help it.

When he could speak and move again, he rose and sniffed the air. He scented blood, human blood. The predatory side of him could detect the scent of blood from miles away. Not your typical brand, either. This was an enticing smell, different. Too aromatic and potent. The newcomer's blood. He felt his bloodlust stirring—a craving he was certain he had mastered, until a second ago. He felt his world shifting a little out of kilter, and he clenched his jaw in irritation.

He barked at the two B.O.S.P. agents, "Bring in the cleaners, then dispose of this mess." He motioned to the broken fence pickets and tire tracks running through the yards and the next-door neighbors peeking out the window. Cleaners erased the memories of humans and put the world back together in their ordered little universe. There were many types of cleaners in the supernatural world. Those who utilized dark magic caused adverse effects like strokes and Alzheimer's. B.O.S.P. employed cleaners who were trained to use crystal erasers, the only safe type, that actually altered the atomic particles that made up human memory. "And find out who that woman helping her is," he added, narrowing his eyes at the street they had disappeared down.

Tongue looked over at Vaughn, a new recruit. He was so new, no one but Striker knew his code name. "You get the license?" she asked.

Vaughn looked lost and shrugged.

Tongue rolled her lizard eyes. "That's a fallen angel for you."

"D-e-t-e-c-t 1," Striker said, his tone turning soft and menacing, a sure sign he was losing patience with incompetence. His gaze raked both the agents, and that was enough of a reprimand.

They instantly snapped to attention.

Striker looked at them, but his mind was on the license plate, clear in his memory as the image of the driver. Long wavy ginger hair with streaks of golden blond running through it. One green eye and one blue. Dangly hoop earrings. Too much eye makeup and lipstick. Arrogant saucy expression. Didn't seem to show an ounce of fear. Something about her seemed familiar to him, but he couldn't place her. One thing was certain: if she got in his way again, she'd become a casualty. Striker smelled the enticing aroma of her blood emanating from Tongue's fingernails, and he clenched his fists.

"She ain't all human, boss," Tongue said, licking the green sheen off her plump lips as if tasting the woman.

"Thank you for pointing out the obvious." Striker found himself unpleasantly annoyed that Tongue could taste the woman. "Find out who she is and if she's working for Raithe, while I track them." He turned, and his body morphed into a sheet of black mist. When his essence disappeared, a loud clap of thunder followed.

Tongue and her partner looked at each other. Vaughn spoke first. "Man, he's provoked. Never seen him upset."

"Just be glad he's not mad at you." Tongue glowered at him, then pulled out a cell phone.

Chapter 3

Takala checked her mirrors for a tail. Clear so far. She had been forced to stop at a service station and find a quick fix for the driver's side window. They had used Mylar plastic and duct tape. At least it kept out some of the cold air, but the flapping of the plastic was driving her crazy. Takala had the heater going full blast, though Lilly Smith was hunched in a ball as if she was cold.

Takala had found a scarf in her glove compartment and covered the bleeding scratches on her neck. She adjusted it now, still feeling the gecko cretin's nails gouging her skin. If only she had some peroxide and antibiotic ointment. That would have to wait. She grimaced at the neon-pink scarf, but it went okay with her black jeans and black coat. And the blood spots on the scarf actually looked as if they had been added by the designer. For having been attacked, she didn't look half-bad. Wounded or not, she cared about her appearance.

Takala settled back in the driver's seat, aware of the uncomfortable silence between her and Lilly Smith. She felt Lilly's keen eyes studying her. Finally Takala said, "Are you warm enough?"

"Yes, thanks."

"So, where we going?"

"The Richmond airport," Lilly said, uncertainty in the reply.

"Sure." Takala nodded to assure Lilly Smith that she was okay with the drive.

"And thank you. I appreciate your help. They would have killed me back there."

"No problem."

Lilly took Takala's measure for a long, uncomfortable moment, something in her shrewd blue eyes that hid more than just mere intelligence. "You're a brave girl. You don't seem afraid, even after all you've seen."

"I'm not. Supernatural stuff doesn't bother me."

"If you stay with me, you might be more than bothered."

"I'm used to living on the edge."

"Really." Lilly glanced at Takala as if she had no idea what danger was. She lifted her chin a few inches in a challenging, almost condescending way, the smug smile never leaving her lips.

"I'm a detective." Takala swallowed her indignation, and it tasted bitter in her throat.

"A good one, I hope."

"I've stayed alive this long."

"You look young to me."

"I've been in the business for six years."

"Run a lot of background checks, do you?"

"No, I don't like the research end. I'm more hands-on."

Lilly shot her an I-guess-you'll-do-in-a-pinch look.

No matter how hard she tried, her dislike for this woman was growing like a cancer in her gut. She felt as if she were being interviewed for a job and found lacking. Do a stranger a favor, and that's how they repay you.

Stranger or not, was she really related to this woman? The verdict was still out, and she wanted to keep it that way. Two things Takala knew: Lilly Smith had trust issues, and she had a hard time feeling obligated to anyone. Not to mention she wasn't very likable. Takala quickly changed the subject. "Who were those goons?"

"Unfortunately, State Department agents."

So Lilly Smith actually worked for the State Department. One point for Blake. "When did the State Department start hiring paranormal hit squads?" Takala asked, playing along.

"I work—or shall I say worked—for a branch of the State Department…." Lilly paused as if weighing something, then said, "What the hell, I'll tell you. It's called B.O.S.P. Ever heard of it?"

Takala knew of B.O.S.P. Fala's husband, Stephen Winter, a warlock, used to work as an agent there, but she didn't know if she wanted Lilly Smith to know that, so she lied and said, "No, I haven't."

"Not surprised. Most people haven't. They try to keep all humans in the dark about what goes on right under their noses. They'd probably have congressional hearings for the next century if they found out about all the paranormal activities in government."

"The human zeitgeist can't handle it."

"But they got that television series, *Supernatural,* pretty on the mark." Lilly laughed softly, a detectable forced note in her voice.

Lilly seemed to work hard at being sociable. Was this just her standoffish personality? Takala had hoped to find something warm in her, but as yet she hadn't. "Sam's my favorite," she said flatly.

"Dean's mine. So hunky, with that edge of evil."

Okay, she might just have disagreed with her own mother for the first time. She didn't know how she felt about that, so she lapsed into silence.

Lilly broke it. "That strength of yours is pretty impressive—" she considered Takala, her eyes sparkling like shards of blue glass "—but you seem human enough to me."

"I am, in basics." Takala turned the conversation back to Lilly. "So, you can inhale the powers of other creatures. Pretty interesting."

"Only for a few moments. Too bad I can't keep them." A power-hungry glint shifted in Lilly's eyes.

A cold chill gripped Takala. This woman could be her mother, but Takala didn't know if she liked her or trusted her. "Why were those agents after you?"

"They want me dead."

"Why?"

"I was working undercover for them. Some agents got killed, and I was set up to take the fall for it."

"Know who set you up?"

"Nightwalker."

"Who's that?"

"The vamp who just attacked me."

Houdini. Nightwalker. A vampire. The image seemed to fit. "Why'd he set you up?"

"He must have wanted me out of the picture."

"He'd kill his own men just to take you out?"

"You sound skeptical. Believe me, he's capable of a lot worse."

Takala didn't know if Lilly's story was credible. Why not just go after Lilly? Why kill your own men? None of it seemed practical, but then a lot went on in classified government agencies that would probably make her hair stand on end. Not until Fala hooked up with Stephen had Takala found out that witches had infiltrated government positions. Some duly elected officials were possessed by demons. Others were just plain demons. Shifters, too. You name it, and you could find all manner of paranormal creatures in high places. And people thought Watergate was bad.

This Nightwalker vamp could be a real mean dude with limitless power to back him up. She knew little about vampires, other than the ones she'd dealt with in her line of work. Her clients were mostly human with human problems. Occasionally she was hired to protect women from a stalker, who sometimes turned out to be a vampire. She had helped Fala, her sister, the Guardian, the most powerful shaman on the earth, take out a few evil vampires and their dens. Mostly, though, vampires operated below the radar and stayed to themselves. Takala was glad she'd never come up against this Nightwalker vamp. She wondered why Stephen had never spoken of him. When she had some alone time, she'd have to call Fala and Stephen and get the skinny on Nightwalker.

"This Nightwalker dude must be a badass," Takala said. "Never seen a vamp out in daylight. Thought they had to sleep during the day."

"This one's unusually old and powerful. Sunlight only weakens him." Lilly's brows met in a frown, and she said, "So, how is it you showed up when you did? You're not working for B.O.S.P., are you?" Her eyes narrowed to slits as she studied Takala.

Takala took her attention off the road long enough to stare squarely into Lilly's eyes. Then she lied with ease. "I was casing a house—cheating husband." Takala shrugged nonchalantly. "Saw you were in trouble, so I helped."

"I've ruined your case."

"Nothing I can't rectify. He'll probably be there for a while anyway. He's a bigamist."

Lilly chewed that over for a moment, then said, "I don't even know your name."

Takala supplied her usual bogus moniker. "Tonya Richter."

Lilly considered her a moment as if wondering if that was Takala's real name. Then she said, "I'm Lilly Smith."

Only one of her aliases. Takala grinned and said, "Nice to meet you."

Lilly bobbed her head in kind. "Since I've disturbed your case, you have to let me compensate you."

"No big deal."

"I don't like owing people." Lilly thought a moment,

the red of her lipstick making her mouth gleam as if it had been doused in shellac. "How does five hundred sound for your trouble?"

Takala had to find a way to keep Lilly near her. The sign for Interstate 95 appeared, and she hopped onto the highway to Richmond. Finally she said, "I don't want to take money I haven't earned. What about you hire me for protection?"

"I don't know." Lilly tapped her painted red nails on her arm and stared at the traffic ahead of them. "You might end up being more trouble than you're worth."

"I saved your life, didn't I?" Takala sounded as insulted as she felt by this woman's lack of trust.

When Lilly didn't say anything right away, and before she could come up with a reason to say no, Takala said, "I could use the work." She tried to sound more desperate than greedy.

"The economy. It's killing everybody." Lilly shook her head in disgust. "I guess I can hire you. If it doesn't work out, then you're gone. And if you've lied to me about being a B.O.S.P agent, you'll regret it."

Takala ground her jaw together and passed a Corolla blocking her way. Then she said, "Let's get one thing straight here. I'm not lying, and I don't appreciate your threats."

"Noted." A superior grin toyed with the curves of her red lips. "You must understand that in my line of work I can trust no one."

"I get that."

Her tone turned dismissive and businesslike. "I'll only need your services until I get safely to France—if that long."

"Okay. I usually get a hundred dollars a day for expenses, but I'll knock it back to fifty if you pay for my ticket."

"Sounds fair."

This was a no-brainer. Takala didn't have any pending cases at the moment. In fact, a mob boss had tried to abduct her a month ago for testifying in court against him. His thugs had almost killed her. If Fala, her older sister, hadn't used her healing powers, Takala would be dead. She could also spend time with Lilly and see if she really was a murderer, much less someone she could even like.

Takala thought a moment and said, "I'll have to call my boyfriend first and let him know where I'm going. He's about to propose," she added to gain Lilly's confidence. "He just doesn't know it yet."

Lilly arched a dark brow. "Oh, one of those. Isn't it comical that we can make men do anything we want?" She grinned sardonically.

Takala smiled back, but it was only a polite smile. Something told her Lilly Smith enjoyed manipulating more than just men.

Takala didn't like talking on the cell phone while driving, but she had no choice. She pulled out her phone and hit 1 on the speed dial.

A woman's high-pitched giggle sounded in her ear, then, "Oh, Akando. That feels wonderful." Lust filled each word.

Another giggle.

Takala felt jealousy soar through her like a hot poker. "Who the hell is this?" When there was no response, she yelled, "Hello! Akando!"

A deep, sexy voice melted over the phone. "Hey, babe."

"Don't *babe* me. Who's with you?"

"No one."

"You're lying through your teeth. I heard a woman's voice." Takala wished she was standing before him, because he wouldn't have any teeth when she was done with him. "Who's with you?"

"Just a friend."

Another giggle, then a smooching, sucking noise. Takala felt a hole opening in the pit of her stomach, and her heart began being sucked down through it. Her chest ached as if he'd just put his foot through it.

She'd really thought Akando was the one. The love of her life. No! No! No! This wasn't happening. "Just tell me the truth," she said, the need to cry burning the back of her throat. She wouldn't cry. Not over him.

He paused as if summoning his courage. She'd never thought Akando was weak until this moment. "The truth is, you're sweet, and we've had a good time, but I want to date other women."

"You told me you loved me."

"I never said that."

"You did."

"I didn't. I made a point of not telling you that."

Had she heard only what she wanted to hear? She could have sworn he'd said it at least once. When she couldn't remember the exact moment, she said, "You implied it."

"I can't help what you let yourself believe."

"Let myself." How could she have been so oblivious?

"Yeah, you got carried away."

"Only because you made me believe you loved me."

"Don't blame me, babe. You came up with that notion on your own."

Another feminine giggle near the phone.

The sound cut through Takala like fingernails on a chalkboard. "I guess we've both been deceived," she said.

"No, I pretty much knew what I was getting into with you."

"What does that mean?"

"You're just too intense."

"So that's why you're breaking up with me?" she asked, hating the whiny and weak sound in her own voice.

The woman spoke in the background. "Just hang up on her."

"Don't you dare," Takala said. "Explain *intense*."

"Insecure, clingy. You're sweet, but…"

"But?"

"You scare me."

The woman chuckled softly.

The knot in Takala's throat grew baseball-size as she said, "You didn't seem too scared when we slept together." She heard her voice crack.

"That was different. You're a good lay."

"That's all I am to you?"

"No, I mean—"

"Forget it!" Takala slammed the phone shut. Tears streamed down her cheeks in earnest, so much so that she couldn't see to drive. She slowed and pulled the MINI over onto the shoulder.

"Everything okay?" Lilly asked softly.

"I thought he loved me. I thought he was the one, but he's still in love with my older sister."

"You're rebound material?"

"I guess so." Takala wiped at the hot tears on her face, smearing them across her cheeks.

"And you didn't see it coming?" Even Lilly sounded surprised that Takala had been so unaware.

In all honesty, Takala had considered it. Akando had been betrothed to Fala, Takala's older sister and the current Guardian since birth. It almost destroyed Akando when Fala chose Stephen Winter over him. Takala had been angry at Fala at first for hurting Akando; she'd had a crush on him since childhood. But it had not worked out because Takala had been there to nurse his emotional wounds. And she believed she could make Akando love her. Who would put balm on her own wounds?

Takala hiccupped and said, "I should have listened. My baby sister warned me not to get involved with Akando. I just didn't want to hear the truth." Why hadn't Takala seen what was so obvious to Nina? Why was it Takala could read people in her line of work, knew the moment they were lying, but when it came to her love life, she was clueless? She thought of Fala and Nina. Both happily married to men who worshipped them. Why couldn't she find someone? What was wrong with her?

Lilly Smith patted Takala's shoulder. "Heck with him. You don't want someone like that. There's plenty fish in the sea."

"I'm sick of trolling for them. I always end up getting the pointy end of the hook. Men are pigs." Takala banged her head on the steering wheel, making the whole car shake.

"Tell me about it, honey," Lilly said.

Takala felt Lilly Smith's comforting hand on her shoulder, the hand of the woman who might possibly be her mother, and her sobs became uncontrollable.

Chapter 4

"You can't take those."

Striker shoved the sunglasses down onto the bridge of his nose and eyed the kid who'd just accused him of stealing. He looked about sixteen, with freckles and red hair, too young and naive to know he was annoying a vampire. Normally, Striker would have stopped to purchase the sunglasses and baseball cap, but he couldn't let Culler and the woman out of his sight. He held the boy's gaze while his will seeped into the young man's conscience.

"I have paid for these," Striker said, hypnotizing the kid with his eyes.

"Right, sorry, sir." Like a puppet, the boy moved back behind the counter of the little gift shop.

Striker shoved the glasses back up on his nose, made sure the cap covered his hair, then he picked up a *USA*

Today on his way out. He stepped into the flow of people moving toward the various airline ticket windows.

He spotted Culler and her friend about fifty yards ahead. It was hard to miss her companion, not because the scent of blood was all over her and his predatory sense of smell could find her in a twenty-story building in seconds, or that she was tall and head and shoulders above the crowd, but because she dressed like a rock star. Thick ginger-blond curls hung down past her shoulders. Her long legs were stuffed into tight black hip-hugger pants. Several spike belts of varying widths hung around her slender hips. She wore a tie-dyed T-shirt that left three inches of her flat belly showing. A pink scarf, dotted with blood, draped her neck. And over it a black leather bomber jacket. Silver studs spelled "Virgin" across the back of the coat. Black cowboy boots covered her feet and calves. Lethal silver points jutted from the tips of her boots. She held a small carry-on suitcase, and she kept scratching at the scarf around her neck. He didn't much care for women who dressed ostentatiously or had an I-own-the-world air about them. The modest feminine medieval fashion for women was his favorite style, but that look was long gone, obsolete, just like that part of his life.

They went through the line, and Culler bought Rock Star a first-class ticket to Paris. On their way to Gate 5, they stopped at a row of shops.

Rock Star turned and looked nervously around. Striker was leaning on the wall near a water fountain, pretending to read the newspaper. She glanced past him as they paused at Arlene's Tid Bits, a woman's clothing boutique.

He zoned in his sensitive hearing and listened to their conversation.

"Let's go in," Culler said. "I need a toothbrush and makeup and clothes. It's not fair. You carry an overnight bag in your car. I had to leave home with nothing."

"Sorry." Rock Star shrugged her shoulders. "Hazards of my job. When following people, you have to be ready at a moment's notice to leave."

What was her job? How deeply was she connected to Raithe? Rock Star could be higher up in his organization. What was the connection between Rock Star and Culler? Maybe Rock Star was the ticket he needed to find Raithe. By the enticing odor of her blood, he knew vampires would kill to have a taste of her. He'd like to see below the scarf. Was she just covering the scratches Tongue had left on her neck, or was Raithe's mark on her neck? The thought brought a sadistic grin to Striker's lips. He'd like nothing more than to find leverage with Raithe by using one of his own blood slaves. If she had been just a regular human, Raithe could easily replace her, and she would be useless to Striker. But this woman was a cut above, her blood like manna. Striker could only hope she was one of Raithe's obsessions. An object Striker could definitely use.

"I suppose so," Culler said.

"Look, I'm just gonna pop across the hall there, to the fudge shop. I can still keep an eye on you."

"Don't let that cretin make you fat. He's not worth chunky thighs."

Culler actually sounded like she cared. Striker thought she was the most talented liar he'd ever seen. She had to be to fool Raithe.

"This isn't breakup eating. I'm just hungry."

"Keep telling yourself that."

Striker watched them part, Culler stepping into the clothing shop and her companion heading for the candy store. He kept an eye on Rock Star while she watched Culler. Kids and parents lingered in the store. The kids begged for everything. The parents picked and chose for them. Rock Star walked down the cases and found the fudge. She pointed to almost every type.

The clerk's eyes widened in disbelief. He asked if he'd heard her correctly. She wanted three pounds of peanut-butter fudge, along with everything else.

"Yes, eating for two." Rock Star patted her slender belly.

"Sure it's not twins?"

"Sometimes I think so." She smiled at the clerk, a dazzling white-toothed grin that mesmerized the man for close to half a minute, causing him to drop several pieces of fudge on the floor. Stunning didn't come close to describing her face at that moment. It appeared she knew how to wrap men around her little finger with just a smile.

Even with all the airport noise, Striker could zone it out, tune his hearing into the blood pumping through her veins. He could detect the minutest abnormality, and he didn't hear the heartbeat of an unborn fetus. She was pulling the clerk's leg. Why that slightly amused him, he didn't know.

His phone buzzed, and he pulled it out. Mimi's smiling face met him. "Hey, boss. Got the info you wanted. This new player is one Takala Rainwater. She owns Rainwater Detective Agency in Richmond. She's full-blooded Patomani. Her sister is Fala Rainwater, the Guardian." Mimi paused for effect.

Striker knew of Fala Rainwater. Who in the supernatural realm hadn't heard of the Guardian? The Guardians were legendary in fighting evil; even his own kind had suffered at their hands. Striker had let Meikoda, the previous Guardian, operate as long as she had stayed out of his way. Fala could prove to be more of a problem. He'd read the dossier on her, an ex-police detective, generally considered a hothead. Striker hadn't had a run-in with her yet, but she already had one strike against her in his book: she'd stolen Stephen Winter, one of his best agents. Made the idiot believe he was in love. At the thought of love, Striker lifted one corner of his lip in a snarl.

Mimi continued. "Her youngest sister, Nina Rainwater, has phenomenal psychic powers. She recently wedded Kane Van Cleave. These three chicks are loaded with white-magic power. Takala, the middle sister, has off-the-charts strength. The seer assures me she's not involved with Raithe."

"He could have had her charmed, and the seer's eye blocked."

"Got a point there. The seer said Takala's searching for her mother, Skye Rainwater."

The name hit him. Culler aka Lilly Smith aka Simone Poindexter's real name was Skye Rainwater. She'd changed it when she entered B.O.S.P. So, were mother and daughter both killers? Both involved with Raithe. Or was Takala Rainwater really just searching for her long-lost mother? If so, she'd wish she had never found Culler.

"I want this on high priority. Dispatch two teams of our most competent agents to Paris, and have them standing by at Charles de Gaulle Airport. And send two more to me now—not Tongue or Vaughn."

"Right."

Striker glanced up just as Takala Rainwater was leaving the candy store. Her arms were laden with a grocery-size shopping bag and her carry-on. She must have bought ten pounds of fudge, but she carried it beneath her arm as if it weighed nothing.

Striker caught a whiff of the fudge, and it mingled with the sweet metallic scent of her blood. Blood was his candy, or poison, depending on how one looked at it. The potency skated through his senses. He took a deep, shuddering breath. His desire to taste Takala Rainwater was becoming more and more a forbidden temptation. But he would overcome it. He knew what happened if he didn't. He could become like Raithe again, and that he would never let happen.

She paused at the door of Arlene's Tid Bits, one eye on Culler, then rummaged through the shopping bag. She came out with a chunk of fudge. She licked it and moaned softly at the pleasure of the taste.

Striker imagined something very similar, only involving her neck or, better yet, the femoral artery that pulsed at the top of her thighs. The unbidden daydream dissolved when two of his agents appeared at his side. One was Katalinga, a lynx shifter. She had dark brown short hair, upturned feline eyes, and wore a brown spandex pantsuit that sheathed her body. She always looked as if she'd stepped out of the sixties. Brawn was a wizard. Tall and built like a wrestler. He had short-cropped auburn hair and deep, serious green eyes. He wore blue corduroys, a pin-striped oxford shirt, and a gray blazer.

"Hello, sir," Katalinga purred. She had a Swedish accent, which only accentuated her *r*'s. "Reporting for duty." She sniffed the air. "What's that delicious aroma?"

"That would be one of our targets standing in front of that clothing shop behind me."

"Her blood really smells delish." Katalinga licked her lips. "We should get a copy of that for the lab so they can reproduce it."

"Our techs are talented, but I doubt they can invent anything close," Striker remarked.

He and the B.O.S.P. blood-dependent employees injected themselves with a serum that sustained them for twenty-four hours between feedings. It helped them when they were out on a mission. The serum left an aftertaste in the mouth, a "flavor" as the techies called it. Yet it could never come close to human blood. And he felt certain never equal the taste of Takala Rainwater's.

The serum supplemented Striker's usual diet of freeze-dried animal blood that he reconstituted. It was the worst-tasting substance imaginable, but he only drank it for survival, not pleasure. He couldn't remember the last time he had enjoyed anything or found joy in anything but his work.

He'd had enough small talk and said, "Keep them safe and in view at all times."

Brawn had been studying Takala Rainwater as she ate the fudge, and he appeared enthralled. "You mentioned two targets?" he said without taking his eyes from her.

"The other one is in the store at the register." Striker felt a sudden pang. Was it possessiveness? No, more a feeling of familiarity. What seemed so familiar about Takala Rainwater? He couldn't lay his finger on it. Other than her aromatic blood, she was nothing to him but a problem. Why should he care who looked at her? "We'll switch off. You both are on now. I will check out the gate and make sure it's clear."

"Affirmative," Brawn said.

Striker walked down to Gate 5, glad to have some distance between him and Takala Rainwater. He didn't need distractions at present. What he needed was a moment alone with Culler, to discover what she knew about Raithe and if she was still in contact with him. And he would, tonight on the flight, when he had his full power. If she was charmed, he could break through it. He'd never underestimate Culler again. And Takala Rainwater… Well, he'd enjoy that encounter, probably overmuch. He looked forward to luring her into isolation, discovering her weaknesses and her needs, all the elements of hunting targets at which he excelled.

His fingers reached instinctively for the tiny vial of soil hanging around his neck. Still there. Over the years it had become a compulsion to check it. He was forced to carry it with him at all times during the day. It was the soil that enabled him to stay awake during the day, the earth of his vampire birth, the same ground in which his casket was buried. It was the one thing he shared with Raithe. Over the centuries it had turned to dust from age. He'd been forced many times to go back to Rome and dig up more soil. He had always hoped to corner Raithe there, but never had. One day and soon, he promised himself.

Chapter 5

Takala hardly felt the vibration of the Air France plane in the luxurious seat in first class. It beat being sandwiched into those tiny coach seats where she never had enough room for her long legs and she felt like a canned sardine. If you had to fly, this was as close to heaven as you would get.

She glanced over at Lilly. She had finally dozed off. She wore eye covers, and her blanket had fallen down to her waist. Takala bent and tucked it back up around her shoulders.

Then she reached for another piece of fudge. She'd lost count of the number of pieces she had eaten. It wasn't only Akando's defection bugging her; it was Lilly. She knew the longer she waited, the harder it would be to tell her the truth. The only proof Takala had that Lilly was her mother was the photo that she'd lost. She just didn't trust her own instincts or Lilly right now. She really needed to know if Nightwalker had been right about Lilly. More than likely he was the killer, but she had to be certain.

Since leaving the airport, Takala had felt eyes on her, and it hadn't subsided. The sensation caused a prickling on her neck that refused to go away.

She glanced behind her at the only other person in first class. The woman wore a knit brown pantsuit. Her dark brown hair was cut in a boyish bob. She was sleeping. Takala decided the jumpy feeling had to be the product of her imagination.

Earlier she had heard a few voices come from coach class, but now the only sound was the distant throb of the jet engines. The whole overnight flight must be bedded down for the evening. She hadn't seen a stewardess in an hour. What time was it? She looked at her watch. Two o'clock in the morning. They must be somewhere over Europe.

She didn't know if it was nerves, or the sugar buzz she'd gotten from eating so much chocolate, but she just couldn't sleep. The light on the complimentary cell phone blinked green, and she snatched it up and left her seat so she wouldn't wake Lilly.

The Boeing 747 was a wide-body with three aisles. The coach section was full to capacity. She chose the left aisle and walked back to the restroom. As she suspected, most of the passengers were sleeping, but a few glassy-eyed insomniacs were watching movies or listening to music through headphones. She dialed Fala's cell-phone number.

A sleepy voice said, "Yeah."

"Fala, it's me," Takala whispered so as to not wake up anyone.

"Where are you, and why weren't you here to welcome us home?"

"Sorry, on a case." Takala paused at the door to the head.

"You know Nina ran away and got married?"

"Yeah, she told me."

"She told you before me?" Fala sounded a little disappointed.

"I think she thought you might disapprove."

"Well, he's a shifter. That's not too bad."

"Rich, too. That always helps."

They both chuckled at that.

Fala was the first to speak again. "So, what kind of trouble are you in?"

"I'm not."

"Then why is Grandmother in the prayer cave? She says she needs to pray for you. What have you done?"

"Nothing." Takala hoped Meikoda knew nothing of her current adventure and was only cleansing her soul. She didn't want to tell her older sister about Lilly. She knew she'd be angry for trying to find their mother. She, like Nina, believed that their mother wanted nothing to do with them. "Can you put Stephen on the phone?"

"For what?"

"I just need to ask him about someone he might have worked with at B.O.S.P."

"Oh, all right— Wait, I have to tell you this. Nina told me not to say anything, but you should know. I saw Akando with a strange redhead today—"

"I know all about it."

Fala said, "I'm sorry."

"I don't care anymore." A lie. His cheating still hurt like a giant was stepping on her solar plexus. What really smarted was how quickly he'd moved on and how blind she'd been to believe he had cared for her at all. She forced more conviction than she felt into her voice. "We're history."

"Sure you don't want to talk about it?"

"No, he's shown his true colors. I don't know what I saw in him. Be glad you didn't marry him."

"Believe me, I found the right guy. Stay in touch, sis, okay?"

"Okay. Now put Stephen on, please." Takala made a face at the tan door of the toilet as she heard Fala say, "Here, honey, for you."

A lot of rustling in her ear, then Stephen's deep voice. "What's the problem?"

"What do you know about someone named Nightwalker?"

"He used to be my boss." Stephen's voice seemed to clear of sleep. "Stay away from him."

"Too late. What I need to know is, can I trust him?"

"You can't trust any vampire," Fala said in the background. The phone must be on speaker, Takala realized.

"What if he warns me about someone. Can I trust his word?"

"I'd say so unless he has an ulterior motive," Stephen said. "Basically his scruples are intact. He's only malevolent if you get in his way. What's this all about?"

She ignored his last question and asked, "Is he the type who would kill his own men to set up another agent?"

"Not if the agents were loyal."

"Would you trust him with your life?"

"If we were both on the same side—what's going on, Takala?"

A whoosh of icy breath brushed her neck and ear. It was like opening a refrigerator door. She panicked, even as cold hands snatched the phone from her grasp. She heard Stephen shouting her name until the phone clicked off, then someone pushed her through the bathroom door.

She stumbled inside. Before she could turn to ward off her attacker, hands caught her elbows and shoved. Her hips hit the sink as she wheeled and looked into Nightwalker's face.

His eyes were inches from her. For a few heartbeats, they faced each other, breathing heavily, eyes locked.

Up close, his pale skin glowed with a pearly luminescence that didn't seem to have clear-cut lines, the edges of his features just a tad blurred, as if his power strained at the physical boundaries of his body. Purple eyes peered out from under thick blond lashes, the intelligence in them almost palpable. He had a rugged roman nose that fit perfectly in the handsome planes of his face. His glossy blond hair was slicked back in a ponytail, adding a roguish quality to his features. The ruthlessness of his sunken cheekbones fought with the dimple in his chin and added a pleasant edge to his face that couldn't be trusted. He wore a perfectly tailored black suit and a starched white shirt without

one wrinkle. Not even his tie had been pulled out of line
during the struggle. And his cologne smelled like spicy
butter rum, a scent that might have made her mouth
water…if she hadn't been feeling threatened.

His eyes steadily turned the color of blackberry wine.
The depths looked bleak and endless, like a long, empty
tunnel. Because vampires didn't have to blink, his stare
had a relentless piercing quality, like that of a falcon, as
if he hovered above her ready to dive.

All her self-preservation bells rang at once. Her
heart felt like it had parachuted out of her chest and
was dropping fast.

Then his eyes changed. The whites were disappearing,
the pupils dilating.

She felt his will batter her. It was a thousand-pound
weight throbbing in her skull. She tried to move, but
the undertow of his trance-inducing eyes trapped her.
Fear slithered along her shoulders, hummed down her
spine.

The black orbs probed her, reached deeper, grasped
for control. The edges of his form seemed to shift and
blur from his unearthly force.

Then something inside her rose up like a wall, and
she suddenly had a fighting chance. His underworld tug
was strong, but it struggled to penetrate her white magic,
the source of her strength. She locked gazes with him,
aware she might lose this battle at any moment, and she
hated losing a fight—especially to a vampire who had
attacked her first.

The tiny bathroom seemed to shrink in size, and all
she could feel was his chilly breath on her face. He had
both hands on the sink, trapping her between them. He

wasn't physically touching her, but he might as well have been. His dark aura was steadily drawing over her like an iron blanket, his will lashing at her own.

"Look, bloodsucker, you can't glamour me." She found her voice, but it was strained, uneven. "Got that?"

The lids of his eyes flicked ever so slightly in surprise that she had fended off his power this long. Then a slow, ruthless grin twisted up the corners of his mouth, exposing the tips of his fangs. "But your sweet words only provoke me into wanting to try and glamour you." His voice was slick and silken and echoed in her mind like he was inside her head with a bullhorn.

"I warn you, don't try it!" Takala knew if she didn't break this mind lock, she wouldn't stand a chance. She knocked his arms away and aimed for his jaw.

He caught her hand with superhuman speed. They arm wrestled midair as he said, "You can't resist me."

"Wanna bet?" Takala was surprised by his strength. Vampires might be able to move faster than she, but one-on-one they weren't much stronger. But this one was. It felt as if her fingers were set in solid granite. Her whole arm trembled as she strained against his strength. He wasn't struggling at all, and she knew he wasn't using a quarter of his strength. If he chose to, he could crush her hand and send her down on her knees.

"That was unwise." His voice softened to a deadly hiss.

"Sometimes you just gotta take risks." She went for him with her other hand.

He grabbed that one, too, jerked both hands behind her back, and kissed her.

His will invaded her in a huge gush, sweeping into her like a windstorm, crashing into every crack and crevice. She had lost this round.

For a second, the full brunt of his power held her muscles, her bones, her veins. It was like radioactive dye being breathed into her, burning at first; then his darkness oozed inside her and she felt herself becoming powerless and groggy in his arms. She grew aware of his cool lips, rough and pressing. Then they absorbed her human heat, and they were hot and ruthless and mesmerizing. That was her last thought before he claimed her mind.

Striker wanted to continue the kiss, to subjugate her, to savor the heat of her lips and body engulfing him, but he couldn't allow himself to take advantage of her in that way. No, it was bad enough he'd given in to the desire to kiss her. He could have forced his will on her by just touching her. No doubt about it, Takala Rainwater tempted him, a morsel for the taking. But he had only one resolve, and that was to find out if she worked for Raithe.

He broke the kiss and stared down at her face, at the strong curve of her jaw. His fingers itched to touch her square chin, and he gave in to the desire.

At his touch, her closed eyes fluttered.

He traced the line of her jaw as he stared down at the ginger-blond lashes, a little darker than her coppery gold hair. They formed thick crescents on her high cheekbones. Her full lips were swollen from his kiss, the sweet scent of chocolate still on them. He couldn't draw his gaze from her tanned face; it had a reddish golden glow that mesmerized him. He didn't think he'd ever seen more beautiful feminine features assembled in one package.

Something about her seemed familiar. What was it about her that tugged at him, that reminded him of someone? It was there, buried in the eons of his life. He just couldn't retrieve it.

Takala moaned seductively and pressed her shapely pliant body against him. He hadn't noticed it before now, but there wasn't an ounce of extra flesh anywhere on Takala Rainwater. She was all hardened, lean muscle. Her back and shoulders rippled with it. She had the physique of a female bodybuilder, slender hips, indented small waist, and high rounded breasts, all held together by sinew. Strong, yet so intoxicatingly woman. He felt his body responding, and he cursed.

She inflamed dormant desires and sensations that he had controlled for two centuries. He thought he had evolved past all that, exorcized those demons. But there was no denying it: he wanted her right now. And the danger of being near her was growing by the second.

He forced his mind back on the mission and his resolve to stop Raithe. He quickly propped her down on the toilet and rested her head back on the wall. Then he unwrapped the scarf from around her neck. He inhaled the overwhelming scent of her blood, and he had to fight the desire to place his lips against the pulsing jugular vein.

You have her under your power. Taste her blood. Take what you want and need. He heard Raithe's old voice in his head, tempting him.

No, he wasn't like Raithe. He wasn't a monster.

He used to be. For hundreds of years now, he'd led a monastic life of self-denial, atoning for his past evil transgressions—that is, until Takala Rainwater crossed his path. He reminded himself he had more willpower than to let a piece of tempting human baggage destroy all he'd worked so hard to accomplish.

He felt a tremor of sheer will run through him as he made himself concentrate on the task at hand. He half expected to find Raithe's puncture marks on her neck. When he saw only Tongue's claw prints slashing sideways across her skin, slightly swollen and red, he felt relief. Though he wasn't entirely convinced that she wasn't one of Raithe's minions. He had to invade her thoughts to be absolutely certain of it.

He didn't have to verbally ask her questions, all he had to do was probe her mind. He immediately detected a brain animated by magic; the insidiousness of it grinding and scraping the edges of his mind. And her thoughts were surprisingly an open book, not obstructed by dark forces as Striker had first suspected.

Takala had arrived at Lilly Smith's house from a lead she had received from a friend. She wasn't certain she trusted Lilly. She hadn't told Lilly they were mother and daughter yet. He was getting recent feelings of love and hate for someone named Akando. So, she was above suspicion. He had expected the opposite, hoped for the opposite.

Now he had an innocent to take care of, and he'd seen evidence of how selfish and manipulative Culler could be. But weren't those the very characteristics of a first-rate undercover agent? And not any agent, but one who had infiltrated Raithe's organization. Her deceptive and malicious talents had to be second nature to her.

No doubt Culler would use Takala Rainwater, then get her killed. He had to make sure Takala continued to suspect Culler, so he whispered in her ear, "You will under no circumstances trust Lilly Smith or anything she says to you. You understand?"

"Yes."

"Now, you will wait here five minutes, then return to your seat and forget everything about this encounter."

"Okay." She spoke without opening her eyes, in a lazy, dreamy voice.

He picked up the phone and hit the redial button. He heard Stephen's voice say, "About time you called back. Fala and I were worried sick."

Striker didn't want the whole Rainwater clan destroying his chances of catching Raithe, so he decided to put their minds at rest. "It's me, Winter," he said.

"Nightwalker. Where's Takala?"

He stared down at her. She was sprawled across the toilet, her eyelids closed but pulsing behind the lids. "She is indisposed at the moment."

"You better not let anything happen to her," a husky female voice said. "Or I'll find you and rip your head off."

"I suppose that is your new sweet bride."

"Yeah, and I'll show you just how sweet I can be if you hurt her," Fala said.

"Be quiet, Fala," Stephen said. "Listen, Dark, is Takala mixed up in something bad?"

"Not really. I know she is innocent. I will make sure she's unharmed and see that she returns home"

"You better," her sister said.

Striker clicked off. He didn't much like domineering females who threatened him, even if she was the Guardian and could probably back up her threats.

He put the phone in Takala's hand and wrapped her fingers around it. Then he exited and warped up to first class. The speed at which the jet was flying only enhanced his ability, and he felt a little lightheaded when he paused at the doorway. He'd never get used to airplane travel.

Katalinga perked up from pretending to sleep and she nodded to him. She motioned with her eyes toward Culler, who sat across the aisle from her, sleeping quietly, her mouth agape.

He moved in behind Culler. As he looked down at her, the image of his agents being murdered surfaced. He had to hold back a desire to exact retribution for them as he touched her shoulder.

She woke with a start and pulled off the sleeping mask. Instant recognition. She leaped to grab him, but he already had made contact. He languished in her fear for a split second, then he took control of her thoughts.

She slumped back in the seat, and he probed her mind. He could only find her most recent memories, of being attacked at her home, hiring Takala to accompany her to Paris. She, too, was afraid of something, but that was a gray area, and he knew he'd hit a charmed part of her brain. He concentrated, fully pouring all his force into her, but he could not break the weaver spell. He'd never come up against such powerful magic. Raithe had outdone himself. Striker would just have to wait and see who she was meeting in Paris.

He erased her memory of their encounter, then he left her. He acknowledged Katalinga on his way back to his seat. Then he spotted Brawn in coach, watching a movie. He sat between two elderly women, who were asleep, one snoring like a jackhammer. Striker had used astral projection, so Brawn hadn't been able to follow his movements, but he could see Brawn clearly now, and they exchanged a glance.

After another section, he found his aisle seat. A woman with a young daughter slept in the seat beside his, the little girl nestled up next to her mother.

Striker put back on the cap and sunglasses and sat down. He heard the bathroom door open, then smelled the scent of Takala Rainwater's blood before she walked past him. It was a brand of O positive that he would never be able to get out of his mind. She looked perfectly normal, oblivious to him. She kept gazing at the phone in her hand as if she couldn't quite figure out why she was holding it.

She moved past him with an air of graceful invincibility, and he fought the desire to follow her. He had remained desensitized for so long, this sudden attraction was more than unnerving. He watched the sway of her slim hips and remembered the heat of her lips and body, the pulsing of her jugular beneath her lovely skin. He wrestled with the desire to extend his fangs, but instead turned and looked out the airplane window. All he could see was darkness and hints of the moon drifting in and out behind clouds. No reflection of himself, only a cap and glasses floating in open space. But he knew if he had one what he would see: a vampire fighting for control. He gripped the arms of his chair so hard he heard the metal crunching. He let go and frowned. Somehow he would conquer this attraction to her.

Takala noticed that Lilly was still sleeping, and the one other passenger in first class hadn't moved positions. The lady had the seat all the way reclined, and she slept on her right side. Harmless enough. Takala sat down as quietly as possible and put the phone back in the cradle. Her hands were trembling. What was up with that?

She felt odd, too. Shaky. Her heart beat wildly as if she'd just run a marathon. Her lips felt strange. She touched them and flinched. They were sensitive and swollen as if she'd been kissed. Something had happened to her back there in the bathroom, but what?

She concentrated, trying to recall her last memory. Talking to Stephen…suddenly losing the connection. What had he said? Stay away from Nightwalker. Could she really trust Nightwalker's word if he had warned her to beware of someone? Well, she didn't have much confidence that Lilly wasn't a killer. She couldn't get close to Lilly or reveal who she was until she was certain of her character. And something told her Nightwalker would stop at nothing if he wanted someone dead. And he was a vampire, for heaven's sake. Even Fala had warned her not to trust a vamp. So, at the moment, she had no faith or trust in anyone but herself. And her memory was playing tricks on her.

She wished she had her Glock, but after Homeland Security put her through an hour of rigorous red tape, scrutinizing her background, her concealed permit, and her private investigator's license, they still made her check the weapon. It was in the cargo hold under lock and key, and she'd have to wait until touching down to get it. She hoped to get it past French security.

Something about not having her weapon made her nervous. She reclined her seat and closed her eyes, trying to remember those moments she'd lost. For some reason her mind conjured up the image of Nightwalker. Something about him nagged at her. She gave up trying to think about it and felt wide awake.

She pulled out a piece of peanut-butter fudge from the bag and one of the tiny bottles of rum she had stashed from the last stewardess round. If she couldn't sleep, at least she could have a snack. When she opened the rum, the smell of it wafted through her senses. She took a long, deep sniff, and the scent brought back a feeling of terror. Must be her nerves working overtime. She downed the bottle.

Chapter 6

They caught a tailwind over Greenland and made good time. At three in the morning, the 747 set down on a Charles de Gaulle runway. The airport was about twenty miles from Paris, so the pilot had told them, but on the landing approach Takala hadn't been able to see the lights of Paris for the cloud cover, a major disappointment. All she could see was opaque darkness out the windows and her own reflection in the glass. Not good.

Her hair was greasy and probably had remnants of slime in it, compliments of the gecko shifter. And her eyes looked numb from being sequestered in an airplane for hours and from sleep deprivation. They were wide open and staring. She was a zombie with bad hair.

She pushed the errant strands of hair back behind her ear and applied some lip gloss. At least she looked a little more human.

She desperately wanted to breathe fresh air, see sky overhead, walk on terra firma. Maybe it would help her jet lag and this antsy feeling crawling through her. She hadn't been able to shake the strange sensation that someone was watching her and Lilly. Nor could she account for the lost time in the bathroom.

She glanced behind her. A stewardess was helping the other first-class passenger pull down an overnight bag from the storage compartment.

Takala flanked Lilly as they debarked and headed up the gangplank. The pilot and stewardesses were lined up, saying goodbyes, tired smiles plastered on their faces.

Takala stayed on Lilly's right side, keeping her body between the crew and her newly acquired client. Takala had been hired as a bodyguard, and she hoped she was impressing Lilly with her skills—at least enough so that Lilly would keep her around.

She still didn't trust Lilly, even though she looked like her mother in the old photo and had the same powers. Hadn't Nightwalker warned her that Lilly was a killer? But hadn't Lilly accused Nightwalker of being one, too?

Takala needed to find out for herself if Lilly's character was as bad as Nightwalker had said. She was also interested in learning why Lilly had chosen France to escape Nightwalker, and the real reason Nightwalker was after her. Takala didn't understand why he would set up his own agents to frame Lilly for their murder. Even Stephen didn't think that was possible, unless they were dirty. She could believe it if one agent was corrupt, but five? Highly suspicious.

"I hope you enjoyed the flight over," Lilly said, smiling over at Takala. "Nothing compares with first class."

"Yeah, it's nice, but they scrimped on the meal portions."

"Dinner was four courses." Lilly's dark brows met over her nose, and she seemed to take the remark as a personal affront.

"Oh, and really good. They just didn't give you very much."

"They were normal portions. I ate so much I must have gained two pounds." Lilly eyed Takala with distaste. "That fudge you ate didn't seem to harm your figure. How can you eat so many carbs and never gain weight? If I ate all that fudge, I wouldn't be able to button my pants." She eyed the almost empty bag of fudge Takala carried.

Takala whispered so the people behind her couldn't hear. "It's my metabolism, part of my strength. Sampson had his hair. I have food." She shrugged.

"Oh, a curse."

"I don't know. Eat anything you want and never gain weight. Some people would kill for that kind of curse." Takala heard the defensive tone in her own voice, and she changed tracks. "So, what's next on the agenda?"

"As soon as I'm safely in a taxi, I'll pay you. Then you'll be free to catch a flight back to America."

"You won't need my services any longer?" Takala tried to come up with a reason to be near her, but she didn't want to seem too obvious.

"No, I'll take it from here. As soon as I'm certain we weren't followed."

"I'm not going back right away. I've never been to Paris. I'm gonna hang around and sightsee." Takala hoped that gave Lilly a segue into inviting her to tag along.

"It's lovely. You'll have great fun," she said with an airy tone of dismissal.

Takala wondered if Lilly had ice water in her veins or was only interested in getting on with the business of murder. She was nothing like the person of Takala's hopes and daydreams. She had always seen her mother as a replica of her grandmother, Meikoda. Meikoda was exacting and severe, but she could also be loving and kind, with a heart of gold. But Takala felt little warmth in this stranger. Well, they couldn't part just yet. Lilly left Takala no choice but to follow her.

The airport didn't seem quite so busy in the early morning. A few people were awake, sitting at food counters, or reading, but most were sleeping, slumped in their seats as they waited for flights.

Takala couldn't shake that feeling of eyes on her, and she glanced around. Only passengers on the flight. Several women struggled with tired, crying children.

She and Lilly hopped on the shuttle that took them past the baggage-claim area. They passed through customs and had to wait for Takala to get her Glock. At first they wanted to keep the gun while she was in Paris, so she had called Blake. He used his connections to contact someone in charge of airport security. After a fifteen-minute wait, they handed her the Glock with a warning not to use it. It helped to have good friends in high places.

She thanked them for the advice. Then she and Lilly

headed for the taxi pool. They stepped through double glass doors and out into a covered portico. It stretched from the main airport to a parking garage across the street. Moths fluttered around yellow fluorescent lights. Beyond the lights, Takala could see only darkness.

She turned to look for the porter and saw an empty desk. Strange. Most airports kept porters on duty all hours of the night. Late flights or not, passengers always demanded help with their luggage. No one home here.

She couldn't see one taxi visible in the four lanes, either, but she smelled remnants of car exhaust lingering in the air. It mingled with the dense humidity of impending rain. But there was also something more tangible weighing the atmosphere down, something that made the skin at the back of her neck crawl.

"I don't like this," Lilly said, voicing what Takala felt.

"Me, either. Smell that sudden stench?" Takala sniffed the air.

"Rotten eggs?"

They both looked at each other and said simultaneously, "Demons." Some demons had a decaying odor that accompanied their dark magic and signaled their arrival.

Unfortunately, the warning came too late. Eight hover demons materialized, floating right out the side of the brick parking garage. They lifted their scythes in unison.

"Nightwalker strikes again," Lilly murmured. "He really wants me dead."

"Not if I can help it." Takala decided she had a lot of questions for this Nightwalker vamp—if she ever met him face-to-face. "Run, Lilly!" Takala turned to face their attackers.

"Too late." Lilly took up a fighting stance behind Takala's back.

The hover demons separated, circling them. Drooping hoods obscured most of their faces. All Takala could see were dark, indistinguishable features and two glowing green eyes.

One grew bold and lunged at Takala.

She grabbed the scythe before it struck, then whipped the weapon back at the demon like a javelin.

The scythe careened through its body, the blade's tip protruding out the other side. It squealed and buckled. Green goo, demon blood, spewed from the gaping hole left in the demon's body and robe. As soon as the blood hit the air, it left only green smoke in its wake. The hover's dead spirit coagulated and frothed into a green gelatinous mass. The wool of its mantle, like the green blood, disappeared in a poof of gray smoke. Takala watched as the hover's spirit whirled out of the portico and up into the air. She knew it would be sucked back to hell's dimension and reappear again in some other noxious form. Like angels, demons' spirits never died; they were just recycled. Made killing demons frustrating.

At the death of their brethren, the other hovers let out a loud, piercing shriek that deafened Takala. She had heard that the demonic war cry of hovers could actually deafen a human. She hoped her ears stopped throbbing and ringing soon.

The battle turned ugly.

Hovers attacked simultaneously. Four hovers moved

in on Lilly. Takala tried to help her, but she had three of her own to battle. She knocked away a scythe that came at her side, then somersaulted, avoiding another blade. Instinctively she reached for her gun, but she realized it was useless. Bullets couldn't kill hovers anyway; only the hell-mined metal of their own weapons and magic worked on them.

She saw Lilly couldn't get near the demons to siphon their power. They slashed relentlessly at her with their scythes as she ran for her life. Takala rarely admitted defeat, but she knew they didn't stand a chance.

"The demons attacking Takala Rainwater are mine," Striker said.

"We have the others." Brawn and Katalinga fell on the demons chasing Culler. She had ducked behind a long line of empty baggage carts and was using one to fend off the hovers.

Striker suspected these were the same demons who had killed his agents, so he would show them as much mercy as they had bestowed on his men.

He materialized near one, grabbed the scythe and shoved it into the demon's gut.

Green blood ejected in all directions, disintegrating as it reached the earth's atmosphere.

He wheeled to attack the demon who had cornered Takala on the ground, hacking recklessly at her. She managed to stay ahead of the blade by rolling and tumbling. In seconds he was on the demon and caught it from behind in a chokehold.

A hover could conjure fire, and its body became a

burning green torch. But it couldn't hold on to the scythe, and that fell to the ground with a loud thump.

The demon thrust both flaming hands into Striker's face. Striker leaped back and lost his hold. The hover turned into a blur of attacking flames. Striker teleported to stay out of the demon's reach.

"Demon spawn, take that!" Takala had picked up the scythe, and she thrust it into the hover's flaming back.

The demon shrieked, then exploded into green ash.

"Demon spawn?" Striker raised a brow at her.

"If the shoe fits." She eyed him boldly up and down as if she'd spoken about him, her mismatched eyes radiant with a suspicious light.

A hover attacked from the side.

Takala still held the blade, and she stood her ground. For a moment it was a struggle of who could hit harder and faster. Metal sparked red as they clashed. It surprised him how agile and strong Takala was. Striker found an opening, grabbed the blade from Takala, and sent it straight through the demon.

It screamed and dissolved.

Takala rounded on him. "Hey, stay out of my way— unless you want to get hurt."

"You needed help," he said.

"I handle my own battles, thank you very much."

"You are welcome."

"I wasn't thanking you." Something dawned in her face, and her expression turned serious as she said, "I know you. You're Nightwalker?"

"At your service." To his dismay, he realized he hadn't erased all her memories of him, only the one in the bathroom. She'd seen him at Culler's home. Culler must have given her an earful of lies about him. He wished now he had cleared all her recollections.

A whirling fireball of energy sailed past them and they ducked.

They both looked up at the same time to see Brawn and Katalinga. Katalinga's arm was sliced open, and Brawn fended off two attackers by throwing magical balls of blue energy at them. But he was getting tired, and the demons were advancing, easily evading them.

Before Striker could stop her, Takala leaped to help. He had to admit, either she was the most courageous female he'd ever met or she had a death wish.

He searched for Culler. Nowhere in sight. Had she escaped?

Takala lured a demon from Katalinga, protecting her, while Striker and Brawn fought the other foe.

Striker could hardly keep his mind on dispatching his adversary for worrying about Takala's safety. But Katalinga wasn't going to stand by and do nothing, and she shifted into a lynx and leaped up on the demon's back, hanging on the robe by her claws. It was the distraction Takala needed, and she grabbed the scythe and drove the handle back into the demon's midsection. It screamed and gusted into a green cloud.

Katalinga fell to the sidewalk, landing on her feet.

While Brawn distracted the demon with his fireballs, Striker seized the handle of the scythe and used the demon's own hand as he propelled the scythe into the hover's side. It shrieked at its own death; then its gel-like soul warped upward.

When they were done, and everyone save Striker was

catching their breath, Brawn said, "That was close. What a bunch of devil spawn."

Striker and Takala shared a private look. She fluttered her brows at him as if to say, "Told you so."

Striker found himself grinning. He'd smiled more since meeting Takala Rainwater than he had in decades. He didn't like this influence she had over him, and he forced his mouth back into a stern line. He noticed that the magic spell that had kept the area clear of humans had dissipated, and people were gawking at them through the glass doors. Striker pushed a button on his phone and thought of where he was; then the cleaners appeared.

They looked like normal businesswomen and men in black suits. They held what looked like tiny cell phones but were in reality devices that erased human minds. Striker nodded toward the humans behind the glass. The cleaners began zapping them with a white crystal ray.

"Nifty," Takala said. "My people clear human minds, but with magic."

"This is easier and more efficient," Striker said. "And doesn't harm humans."

"Our white magic doesn't hurt them." She looked offended.

Striker found himself wanting to run his tongue along her lips and taste them as he said, "Yes, but at B.O.S.P. we don't need to cast spells. We've moved past spells, hex bags, and the stone ages."

"Stone ages!" She snarled at him. "I'll have you know our magic is timeless. And it's environmentally friendly. We don't need to mine or grow crystals."

He'd give her that one concession. "There you have us."

Takala hadn't heard his reply, for she had seen Katalinga down on the sidewalk and she was already hurrying to help her. The agent was still in lynx form, lying on her side. Blood smeared her chest and paw from a gash on her shoulder. Takala had taken off her jacket and was about to throw it over the cat, when Brawn stopped her.

"Pardon me, but she's my partner. I'll help her." He shot Takala a proprietary look.

Takala stepped back and waved to Katalinga. "Sorry, just trying to help."

"Thanks, but I got it." Brawn's brows narrowed in concern as he gently scooped Katalinga up in his arms, her lynx form growling in pain. He addressed Striker. "We lost Culler."

Striker had his gaze on Takala. He could see the cogs behind her eyes turning as she blurted, "Wait one doggone minute. Lilly Smith has another alias?"

"Culler is her code name," Striker said.

"So she told the truth when she said she worked for the same agency as you?"

Striker swept his hand toward Brawn and Katalinga. "We all work for B.O.S.P."

"Well, isn't that cozy." One of Takala's brows shot up; then she spoke to Striker. "And are all of you trying to kill Lilly Smith—I mean, Culler?"

Striker said in an unnervingly calm voice, "If that were the case, she would already be in a body bag."

Takala narrowed her gaze at him, her thick ginger lashes only giving her beautiful eyes a sexy bedroom look. "Well, I guess G-men can tell the truth, *sometimes*."

"It is rare." Striker watched her eyes flame up; the

blue one lightening and turning almost green, and the green one darkening to a seawater blue. He liked vexing her, he realized ruefully, but not as much as he enjoyed seeing the myriad colors of her eyes. It was like looking into a kaleidoscope.

"So, is she a killer?" Takala asked.

"Yes, and she can lead us to a larger fish."

"Who's the fish?"

"You are on a need-to-know basis."

"I need to know."

"We do not discuss state secrets with civilians."

"Even if she could be my mother?" Takala stepped up into Striker's face. She had to be all of five feet eleven, not as tall as his six-two frame, but she could look him in the eye. And she wasn't backing down.

"I'm sorry to hear it," Striker said without an ounce of sympathy.

"You can't use her like that. Arrest her and get her somewhere safe."

"She's been undercover for years. She's my only lead. I shall deal with her as I see fit."

Silence tightened every muscle in her body. She crossed her arms over her chest and splayed her legs. Her gaze narrowed, steadfast, resolute, daring him to defy her. Scalding steam shot from those eyes.

He watched her face go through countless expressions: mulish obstinacy, dogged determination, suspicion. Not one hint of submissiveness. Most human women sensed the threat in being near him when he was angry and kept their distance. Not this one. She openly courted danger by standing as close as she could to him and defying him by looking straight into his eyes. Worse, she didn't seem to care about the risk. He'd never met a woman like her. He wanted her to be afraid. Wanted to grab her and overpower her and hold her until he felt her soften and tremble with fear in his arms.

"I won't let you." She finally spoke, openly defying him.

"Let me give you some sage advice, Miss Rainwater. Forget this need to reconnect with her. Forget you ever found her."

"I can't."

"Then let me help you." He made a move to touch her shoulder.

She leaped back as if a spider had almost bitten her. "Keep those vampire fingers off me. I mean it."

"Then do not tell me how to run my investigation."

Takala glared at him. "Fine, run your show, but you're not pulling rank on me. You may think you can order everyone around, but I don't work for B.O.S.P. I've got a stake in Lilly Smith, and I'm going to make sure she's okay."

"She is a wanted killer, and she will destroy you. For your own benefit, let it go."

Stubbornness and doubt flitted through her face. Then her eyes glazed over in confusion. "I want to believe what you say, but she told me you set her up to take the fall for those agents dying." Her fists tightened at her side. "I don't know who to believe."

"She lied to you." Striker kept his eyes on her hands. He'd seen what she could do with them. He knew her confusion came from the suggestion he'd given her last night to not trust Culler. "She was the one who planned their deaths."

"How do I know that?"

"Because I'm not in the habit of terminating agents with extreme prejudice." Striker stared at her lips and wanted to kiss the pout off them.

"Wait one minute." Stress lines formed on her brow as she sniffed his collar and fixed him with a distrustful stare. "Butterscotch rum. This isn't the first time we've been up close and personal, is it? You were on our flight." She turned and looked down at Katalinga's feline face. The upturned golden eyes hadn't changed. They looked the same as when she was in human form. "Hey, I remember her. She was sitting in first class with us." Her gaze whipped over to Brawn. "And you. I saw you in coach." She made an angry circle in the air that encompassed the room. "All of you were there." She glowered at Striker. "Did you glamour me last night? That's what happened, isn't it? I knew it."

Striker didn't explain his actions to anyone, and it was beneath him to argue with pushy, overbearing females. He grabbed her shoulder and plowed into the barrier of her white magic. For a second, her dogmatic resolve fought his own. He rarely met an enchanted human who could resist him, and he could feel annoyance swelling inside his chest.

"If you want to live, don't do that juju thing again. I mean it." Her fists shot up to push his hand away.

His power broke through before she could fend him off. He gave her the subliminal suggestion to relax.

Her arms fell at her sides, even as her eyes lost their luster, the gaze of someone who had spent too long in a bar with a bottle of cheap gin.

"Now I'm the only person you can trust," he said.

"You'll do exactly as I command." He enjoyed this little victory more than he should. He had a feeling Takala Rainwater rarely lost contests of will. What she didn't know was that he never lost them. "We're going to walk through this airport without incident, and you follow my commands to the letter. Is that clear?"

"Right, chief," she repeated in a toneless robotic voice.

Striker received a call on his phone. He recognized Hacker, a young vampire and B.O.S.P. agent. He must have been on the team Mimi had dispatched to the airport ahead of them. "Yes?"

"We have the target. She's getting into a taxi."

"Stay out of sight and do not engage. I repeat, do not engage. I want ten-minute updates on her movements."

"Yes, sir."

Striker shut his phone, grabbed Takala Rainwater's elbow and escorted her through the airport. "Ten minutes?" she asked distractedly, staring over at him. "We could lose her in ten minutes."

"I did not ask for your advice, Miss Rainwater."

"It's free, so take it." A flaunting smile lit up her face.

"Free or not, keep it to yourself." Striker tried not to look at her lips.

Her brows rose slightly, as if she was having a hard time with that command. Then she said, "Okay. Where are we going?"

"That remains to be seen."

"I don't like this."

"That makes two of us."

"Gosh, I'm hungry. Can we get a burger?" she asked in a candid, almost childish entreaty. She batted her long lashes at him innocently.

Striker thought she was way too alluring when she was subjugated and compliant. His expression darkened. Now that he had her, what could he do with her? Culler knew what Takala looked like and her identity. She might want to tie up loose ends. He couldn't just put her on a plane back to the States; she could be in danger. No, he'd have to keep her with him. He heard her whine again for food, and he frowned so hard his forehead hurt.

Chapter 7

"Get in," Nightwalker pointed to the backseat of the Saab.

"Sure, then can we eat?" Takala nodded a greeting to the driver sitting behind the wheel, a female with red hair and freckles. She looked all of sixteen, the girl next door, save for the pale luminous skin and the fangs that had jutted just below her upper lip when Takala sat down behind her. Takala was certain she didn't like or trust vampires, but she wasn't used to being rude, either, so she said, "How's it going?"

The woman said something in a foreign language. It sounded Russian, and the tone was not at all cordial. Nightwalker said something back that sounded like a reprimand, and the girl leaped out of the driver's seat.

"Move up front," Striker said to Takala as he hopped out and took over the driver's seat.

"She one of yours?" Takala asked as she got in and

closed the door. She watched the redhead disappear into a huge parking lot.

"I do not like to hire them that young, but she was a waif and needed structure and purpose in her life."

"Didn't peg you for a humanitarian."

"I'm not."

A loud ringing began in her ears. Something was pushing its way to the top of her mind. She leaned back against the headrest and closed her eyes. It felt as if a tooth were being extracted from her brain, and if it didn't let go soon it might implode.

"Are you all right?" he asked.

"Just tired," she lied.

Suddenly a bright light blinded her vision, the origin coming from inside her own eyes. What was happening? When her vision cleared, so had his chains on her will. They crumbled like old bread. Without a doubt, she knew she was in control again. It was like reaching the surface after having your head dunked below the water. She almost cried out from the sensation, but Nightwalker had his razor sharp gaze on her. At the sight of him, memories burst into her thoughts.

What had he done to her so far? She remembered his glamouring her, first in the bathroom. That kiss. It hadn't been bad, but the audacity of him to think he could control her like she was a puppet. Then he'd done that mind-bok-choy trick again in the airport. They'd been arguing about Culler or Lilly Smith or whatever her name was. It still didn't change the fact she could be Takala's mother, and she was in this one for the long haul.

Why hadn't his influence over her stuck? She'd been

really mad at him both times he had controlled her with thought transference. Maybe that's what made her magic strong enough to resist his power. Maybe being angry helped her build up a tolerance to it. She really didn't care how it happened, only that the light bulb was on again.

Oh, yes, she'd play along. He was getting calls from his agents. They knew exactly where Culler was, and as long as she stayed with him, she'd have a better chance of finding Culler and discovering if Nightwalker had been right about her. Takala didn't trust Nightwalker, though he had saved her life. But maybe that had been for nefarious reasons of his own, or to let Culler escape so she could lead him to Raithe. Then Striker could kill her on his own terms. Culler was in trouble, and no matter how rotten a person she was, Takala couldn't leave her to the sharks. That's what it felt like, swimming with sharks. And Nightwalker was the Daddy Jaws of them all.

She gazed at his profile, his wide shoulders almost touching her seat. The dash lights cast an eerie blue shadow over his deep-set eyes and cheeks, and he looked even more deadly. He had a way of sitting so still he didn't look alive. Even driving, his movements looked mechanical, reflexive. She found herself wanting to pinch him and see if he reacted.

His phone vibrated. He pulled it out of his breast pocket one-handed. "Yes. I see. Keep her in sight. I'll be there in…" He checked the satellite guidance system. "Eight minutes."

He sped up and flew around a corner.

"Hey, do we have the target's location?" she asked, worried now for Lilly Smith's life.

"Yes, and she could be in trouble."

Takala tried to hide her emotions and look like the brainless robot he thought she was. It took all of her willpower to remain silent and not ask more questions about Lilly.

They drove down a street lined with bars. Hookers of all sizes and descriptions stood on corners, drumming up business by waving at traffic and passersby. Some were made up to look like Goth vampire impersonators, but Takala had a feeling they might be the real deal.

"What's this place?"

"Among my kind, it's known as Bloodstroll."

"Bloodstroll?"

"A street to find a meal while taking a leisurely stroll."

"I'll make sure to avoid it—if I'm ever back this way, Nightwalker."

"Please call me Striker." He gave her one of his pointed disarming glances, those purple eyes as hard and sharp as tacks.

She quickly glanced back out the window, feeling her pulse speed up from his scrutiny. "Okay, Striker," she said, trying the name out. "I'm Takala," she added for his benefit. "Is our target here?"

"Yes, in the Petite la Belle."

Why would Lilly come to this seedy part of Paris? They had just passed the Petite la Belle. It was a sleazy pink bar with a huge naked neon woman sitting over the front door, her legs and breasts moving. Takala had seen something very similar to it in Vegas once, but it hadn't been so tasteless.

He killed the lights and pulled up into an alley. In seconds he expertly squeezed the car between two motor scooters with inches to spare. It was like having the car driven by remote control. No contemplating, no mistakes, just park it.

He cut the engine and said, "Stay here."

"Please let me go." Takala hated the pitiful begging note in her voice.

"I will not have you harmed. Stay. Keep the doors locked." He left without a backward glance; then he shifted into that speed-travel hyperdrive all vampires used and disappeared from sight.

Takala still felt the sting from having been spoken to like a child. Well, he'd learn that she didn't obey so well. One of the cleaners had picked up her carry-on at the airport and given it to her. She searched it for her gun.

Gone.

He must have taken it. Sly, arrogant dog that he was! She slipped out of the car, still cursing him.

Cold air nipped at her face and body, but she had such a high metabolism she was always hot, and the fresh air felt good.

The smell of oily food, dirty garbage bins, and city soot permeated the walk.

Two men approached her and blocked her way. One had bad teeth and greasy ocher hair. The other wore taped black glasses and sported a crew cut.

They spoke French. She caught *bonjour* and the way

their gazes raked her body. Obviously they wanted more than just a friendly "Hello."

"Sorry, not interested." She tried to step around them.

One grabbed her arm.

"Shouldn't have done that." Takala lifted him with one hand and tossed him on the hood of a parked car like he was a rag she was tossing away.

The other one quickly backed off, wide-eyed with disbelief.

The hookers and drug addicts huddled nearby catcalled to her their approval of dispatching the men, giving her a host of thumbs-ups.

She waved and smiled at them. After a backward glance to make sure the two men weren't following her or bothering anyone else, she continued down the block and reached the Petite la Belle. The smell of cigarettes and the sound of techno rock blared from the entrance. The bouncer, a tall muscular woman sporting pixie-short pink and orange spiked hair, guarded the door. She wore a rhinestone-studded white pantsuit that could have made an Elvis impersonator jealous. Two rings rung down from her nose and at the end of each eyebrow. She whistled and winked at Takala and said something that sounded a lot like a flirtation.

Takala couldn't tell exactly what the woman was implying, but she was certain it wasn't very nice. She stopped and tried to go inside.

The woman blocked her way and pointed to a sign. It was in French, but an English translation below it said No Admittance Without a Membership Card.

How had Lilly entered the place? Was she a member?

That gave Takala a greasy feeling in the pit of her stomach. And Striker? He must have just vamped his way through. She didn't have that luxury. Takala nodded that she understood and was glad to get away from the front door and the bouncer. She could feel the woman's eyes following her as she kept walking.

A taxi stopped near her, and a group of men hopped out. They looked as if they were in the throes of a bachelor party. They flashed their membership cards and entered the Petite la Belle, distracting the bouncer's attention.

Takala ducked down a tiny alley that ran the length of the building. She waded through trash and smelled the overpowering scent of urine. Several rats scurried out of her way, chittering at being interrupted. Nothing frightened Takala more than rats. Wererats were on her "yuk" list, too. Nina, her younger sister, liked rats because she could communicate with them. Takala had no desire to talk to rats or anything resembling them. She froze until she was certain they were back in their holes; then she hurried down the length of the building until she reached a back alley.

It was narrow, the walls of old buildings crouched together. Several dim yellow bulbs cast creepy shadows over the line of an overflowing dumpster. Beyond the sphere of lights, darkness and shadows loomed.

All she could think about was Lilly's safety. Why would she come to such a place? She wondered where Nightwalker was inside and how she could avoid him.

Takala tried the back door.

Locked.

She easily twisted it until the lock broke; then she

slunk inside. She stood in a pantry with a large freezer. A rack held a line of dirty aprons. Near it were what looked like six employee lockers.

Takala peeked through the swinging door and glimpsed a kitchen. Four cooks were busy slinging food and yelling over the music while a busboy emptied out a dishwasher. Bare-breasted waitresses came and went among the ordered chaos. The male cooks didn't even seem to notice. Business as usual.

Takala donned a dirty apron and slipped through the hustle and bustle of the kitchen unnoticed. She grabbed a French fry off a plate and ate it. Actually, it wasn't bad.

She ducked into a hallway near the bathrooms and slipped off the apron, tossing it into a tall ashtray. Then she stepped out into the packed bar.

She had been in many strip bars before, getting dirt on cheating husbands mostly. The European strip joints seemed similar to their American counterparts. The cheap speaker system, the disco ball, the center runway, poles on the bars where the women undulated, doors behind which patrons and waitresses disappeared for a short time in pursuit of drugs, sex, or both.

She surveyed the crowd. No Nightwalker. Where was he? She spotted Lilly at the bar. She sipped a pink daiquiri and was speaking to the guy sitting next to her. Lilly looked comfortable, completely at ease, at home in this place. Was she in her element? It hit Takala that there were a lot of sides to Lilly Smith's character that disturbed her. She could imagine telling Fala and Nina about this. Fala would blow a gasket, and Nina would just say, "I told you so." Nah, she'd spare them the ugly details. In fact, she might not even mention this whole episode. It would only hurt her sisters to know the truth, and Takala would never intentionally do that. Who knows—she wasn't even sure she would make herself known to Lilly Smith. What would be the point if the woman was a cold-blooded killer? But one thing she couldn't do in good conscience was leave Lilly in danger.

She watched the disco lights shining off the top of Lilly's companion's bald head. He wore blue hexagon sunglasses pushed down on the end of his pug nose. His mottled skin took on the hue of his sunglasses. He had small slits for eyes and a tongue that darted out as he kept licking his lips. A serpent two-skin? They were almost as bad as wererats.

Takala scanned the room for Nightwalker, and that's when she felt an arm lock around her waist. She lifted her elbow to strike the person, but she hit a brick wall: Nightwalker's midsection.

He didn't even flinch, merely dug his purple eyes into her face and glided her over to a shadowy corner. Takala didn't struggle. She knew it would be useless against his strength.

"I see you have a problem with authority," he said into her ear.

She felt his cold breath against her sweating skin, and it sent a shiver down her neck. "I was certain you needed my help."

"If I had, I would have said so."

She opened her mouth to shoot back a response, but he said, "Shh!" Then he was pulling her close and kissing her.

Chapter 8

Striker forced himself to not think about kissing Takala. He felt the moment she stopped fighting him and grew pliant in his arms, her breasts a seductive weight against his chest. Then she was responding to him. Her warm hands reached around his neck and grabbed his ponytail, her lips softening. Her hands twined in the back of his ponytail, shooting hot vibrations along his neck. It took all of his concentration to shift his attention back to Culler and her contact.

Striker opened an eye and glanced over Takala's head. He had successfully diverted the serpent shifter's attention, and he and Culler huddled together at the bar, deep in a serious conversation. Striker tuned in on their words.

"Philippe, I need to get in touch with Raithe," Culler said, speaking in French.

"You know the rules. He contacts you."

"But he hasn't called, and I'm being hunted. Night-walker wants me dead. He hired hover demons to kill me. Please ask him to contact me right away. He can't leave me hung out to dry here. He owes me."

"Raithe owes no one anything, Lilly. People are indebted to him. You should know that. When he found out you were a snitch, he let you live, didn't he?"

"He made me set up those agents so he could get off on tormenting Nightwalker. We're more than even. The least he could do is help me now. I need protection."

So, Raithe knew Culler worked for Striker. The killing of his agents had been masterminded by Raithe. Raithe had to prove that he was one step ahead of Striker, that he would always be superior. Well, Raithe wasn't perfect. He would slip up one day, and Striker would be there. He felt Takala squirming in his arms, and he realized he was crushing her. He loosened his grip, aware of her long, lean warmth against him.

She seemed content now, and he continued his onslaught of her mouth, letting the total awareness of her assuage his need to destroy something at the moment.

"I'll see what he says," Philippe said.

"Please, tell him I'm desperate." Culler finished off the drink.

"Aren't we all, sweetheart."

Culler shot him a petulant glare, then weaved her way to the door.

Philippe shook his head at Culler's back, as if she had just signed her death warrant. Then he stood and walked toward the front door. His gait weaved a little, a sure sign he wasn't comfortable with human legs.

Striker broke the kiss, saw the dazed look in Takala's

eyes and knew she felt the same sexual attraction he was feeling. He didn't need that particular complication right now. Forcing his mind back on his responsibilities, he pulled out his phone and said, "Follow the target. But do not intercept."

"Affirmative, sir."

Striker closed the phone and pulled Takala toward the front door. "We have to go."

"Wait a minute! What about Lilly?"

"She's gone."

"Gone?" Takala glanced frantically toward the bar.

"You should be more observant."

"Stop kissing me and I might."

"Are you saying I distract you?" A smile turned up his lips while he guided her through the crowd.

"Not on your life. It's just damn annoying." She jerked her hand out of his.

"I needed cover while I listened to their conversation." He reached the door and forced her to wait a second or two; then they stepped out. This was the closest he'd ever been to finding Raithe, and he couldn't let Philippe out of his sight.

"What did they say?"

"Culler blamed me for the attack, when she knows full well it is someone else's doing. I think she's playing some kind of double-crossing game to pit us against each other and come out smelling like a rose."

"Nobody wins in this deal."

"Very true." He laced his hand in hers and wondered if he had already lost.

She let him steer her down the street while he kept his eyes on Philippe, who was getting into a Tesla.

They were losing too much ground, so Striker picked her up and fast-forwarded them to the car. They moved so quickly her equilibrium hadn't caught up, and she staggered when he set her down near the car.

"Jeez, I'll never get used to traveling like that. My head's still on a merry-go-round."

He had to hold her, and her body brushed his. Desire flared through him again, and he cursed under his breath.

"Did you say something?" she asked as he opened the car door and stuffed her inside.

"No." He jumped into the driver's seat. In seconds he was in the flow of traffic, keeping a safe distance from the Tesla.

"You're following too close. I always keep four car lengths behind a target."

Striker glowered at her. "Thank you for the advice, but I was shadowing suspects before you were born."

"Did you lose any?" She cut her eyes at him.

"I always get what I go after." Striker shot her a pointed look. He didn't know why, but it annoyed him that she questioned his efficiency.

"So do I." She stared back at him, straight into his eyes.

In order to drive, he had to glance away first. He found himself wanting to grab her and kiss that superior look off her face. She really didn't know how close she was to danger.

His voice came out sharp as he changed the subject. "You put us both in danger by not staying in the car. Next time, obey my orders. Do I make myself clear?"

"Perfectly."

Her voice wasn't as compliant as he would have liked. In fact, he detected willfulness in the one word. Was she growing resistant to his power? He could hardly fathom it. No, it must be her pugnacious strength of character that affected her suggestibility. He had never known a human, charmed or not, able to resist his hypnotic intimidation. But then he had never met a woman as reckless and as physically powerful as Takala Rainwater. And he disliked it immensely. If she continued to defy him, she would get them both killed.

Silence fell between them, the only sound the purr of the engine. Irritation still nagged at him, and he knew why: his own weakness. That kiss. Twice now he had made the same mistake. And it was not because he hadn't had alternatives. He didn't have to kiss her in the plane. And in the bar, he could have pulled her into a shadow and not been seen. He had to stop touching her, smelling her, feeling her blood pumping through her veins. No one knew better than he that desire could destroy him and anyone near him. He had to get a handle on it. He would, he promised himself.

"How long are we going to sit here?" Takala shifted restlessly in her seat. They were somewhere in the Monnaie area of Paris. They had followed the two-skin to a four-story brownstone. The house looked well cared for, its black iron railings and fence sparkling beneath a streetlamp.

"A while, I think." He hadn't bothered looking at her as he spoke.

As she stared at his attractive profile, replays of that last kiss repeated in her head; Striker's powerfully built body touching hers, the aroma of butter rum mixing with the starch on his dress shirt and assailing her senses, his permanent five o'clock shadow abrading her skin in an oh-so-masculine way, making her shiver and want to feel that roughness move down to lower parts of her body. She could still feel his hands splayed on the small of her back, his powerful lips working their magic on her mouth. And she had turned to mush in his arms, kissing him back in a wanton way. Totally embarrassing.

Why had she responded to him? To a vampire, one she didn't trust? Okay, he was one of the sexiest vamps on the planet—a blond Hugh Jackman with fangs. And his golden hair was as soft as it looked—she'd found that out when she ran her hands through his ponytail in the bar. She kept wondering if he ever wore his hair loose. She'd like to see it down. And something about those pristine suits he wore made her want to rub her hands over every inch of the fabric and wrinkle it. Damn it, everything about him drew her to him, except the cold, distant expression in his eyes. It frightened her. Held every sin imaginable. Something about them was obscenely knowledgeable, able to pry the darkest secrets from her soul.

Hadn't she learned yet? All men were risky. Hadn't she promised herself after breaking up with Akando that she was done with men for good? Somehow she would stick to that pledge. All she had to do was think about all the breakups, the agony men had put her through. No, she was definitely over them.

She shifted in her seat, and her eyes strayed back to Striker. He sat so still. Hadn't moved a muscle since they parked the car, nor had his dogged gaze shifted from the brownstone. He seemed preoccupied.

His stillness fascinated her. She didn't think she'd ever get used to his undead motionlessness. Was that the way it was with all vamps? Either they were stone statues, or they moved at light speed? No wonder they had proved to be man's most adept predator. How many women had Striker snacked on? A tiny shiver went through her as she considered that question.

"What are you doing?" she asked, hoping to get her mind off the fact that she was fighting an attraction to a guy who could kill her with one bite. "You seem centered on something in the house."

"I'm listening to our target take a shower."

"Wow, I didn't know vampires hear that far away."

"We like to surprise humans." A wicked half smile toyed with the corner of his mouth.

It turned butterflies lose in her stomach. "Humans that know about you," she added, trying not to think about the kiss again.

"Consider yourself one of the fortunate ones."

"I don't know if it's so good knowing what prowls the night."

"Vampires aren't as bad as some of the things out there."

"Yeah, but they aren't candy stripers, either." She folded her arms over her chest and stared at the brownstone.

"In my line of work, I've seen worse," he said, his voice full of ennui, as if the world bored him.

"I bet you have. You've probably got a few of them working for you, too."

"Like Lilly Smith."

"Don't talk about her like that."

"You need to realize the truth. She'll get you killed."

"See! That right there is annoying. You don't know if that'll happen."

"She's been programmed to kill. She lacks a conscience. She'll have no compunction in having you killed." His deep purple eyes didn't show a glimmer of emotion, but his words spewed venomous truth.

"I don't care. I can't just walk away, so stop warning me about her. I wish we weren't working together." She heard the frustration in her own voice. "I work better alone, anyway."

"Unfortunately, we're stuck with each other until I put you on a plane to America."

"But you won't, not now."

"Only if you follow orders. I know it is hard for you."

She hadn't meant to argue with him, but he was infuriating. "What does that mean?"

"You have a problem with authority."

"I guess I do when you're calling all the shots." Takala realized she had raised her voice, but his tone had stayed at the same even keel. She bit back all the rejoinders she had for him. It wouldn't do to ruin her chances of keeping him close. At least she would know where Lilly was and that she was safe.

"My case, and I am in charge, but if you wish to leave, I can have you taken to a hotel." He spoke to her as if he were humoring a child.

"Why do I have a feeling you'll have me watched?"

"I will not have this case compromised."

"I know what I'm doing."

"You are out of your league on this one. You should be grateful I'm offering you protection."

"Gee, thanks. What about Lilly? Can you say the same thing about her?"

"For the time being, my people will see that she remains safe."

"Do you trust your agents?"

"Absolutely."

"You've already had one defection with Lilly herself." She saw him flinch, which was a miracle.

He drew in a long, patient breath and said, "It happens with undercover agents sometimes. Unfortunately, they turn."

"So why are we following this creep?"

"At the moment, he's my only other lead to Raithe."

Takala felt her gut clench at the name. "Is this Raithe an old vamp?"

Striker nodded.

"Is his nickname Aconite?"

"One of many."

"Then I've heard of him." She didn't want to mention that her knowledge of Aconite's evil notoriety came from stories of previous Guardians, her ancestors. The less he knew about her background, the better. "So, Lilly Smith is involved with Raithe?" Takala wanted to believe her mother had more integrity than that.

"Deeply."

She frowned and said, "You and Raithe have a history?"

"A long one."

Takala picked up on the brutal overtones in his voice.

She hesitated a moment, then said, "You're settling old scores, and Lilly's caught between you."

"She chose to betray and kill my men. I wouldn't say she's caught."

"Maybe she had no choice."

"You try to justify her actions?" His voice dripped with scorn.

"There's no justification for murder. I'm just saying Raithe might have forced her. You are assuming the worst."

"Could someone force you into killing five innocent men?"

"No." Takala pouted. She had reached the end of the line. Out of excuses for Lilly Smith. But she had to keep her out of harm's way. Striker obviously didn't care about Lilly's safety. He just wanted Raithe. Takala was all Lilly had, and she couldn't just abandon her own mother, even if she was a killer and had abandoned Takala and her sisters as children. Two wrongs didn't make a right.

She realized she was tired and hungry and sick of being ordered about and kissed by an arrogant vampire. Well, the kissing part really wasn't so bad— No, no, no! She was off all men. She leaned back in her seat and closed her eyes. Then she was sleeping and dreaming of vampires attacking her from all angles.

Chapter 9

Takala startled awake and realized the car was moving. "Where are we?" She blinked at the unfamiliar streets. The sun had risen, and she was forced to hood her eyes with her hand to see.

"We're following our target." He motioned with a finger at the traffic. "The Tesla, four lengths ahead."

So he had been paying attention. She found herself smiling at him and said, "I see it." It was a black bullet, zipping through traffic.

Striker followed expertly behind, not letting the car get out of sight.

"Have to say, you are a good driver."

He shot her a quick glance, a ghost of a smile on his lips. "Was that a compliment?"

"Be careful, you're ruining the chances of another one."

They looked at each other and chuckled. She liked

his laugh. It was a deep rumbling bass that shook his whole body. It also seemed rarely used.

He sobered and asked, "Sleep well?"

"How long was I asleep?"

"It's noon."

"Good grief! Why didn't you wake me?"

"You looked as if you needed the rest."

"Don't you ever sleep?" She took his measure. Not one blond hair had escaped his ponytail. His tie was arrow straight. No wrinkles in his wool suit. No tired lines under his eyes. The same debonair air that seemed to be starched into him. He hadn't changed. In fact, it looked as if time hadn't touched him at all. James Bond Vampire, at your service. Still handsome, disarming, and not to be trusted.

"Not while I am on a case."

"How do you do it?" She stared at his profile in awe.

"What?"

"Look so together in the morning. It's totally irritating." Takala pulled down the visor and stared at her reflection in the mirror. Her hair was all over her head, and her eyes looked as if she'd been partying for a week. She pulled out the scrunchie holding her braid and shook her hair lose, finger combing it.

"I try." He grinned at her, a breathtaking sexy smile that revealed a fluorescent aura shining beneath his white translucent skin.

Or was that the sun playing tricks on her eyes? Either way, he looked mythical, Apollo-like, and way too sensual. She forced her gaze back to the mirror. "By any chance, you wouldn't have lipstick or toothpaste in here, would you?" She checked out her teeth in the mirror. They looked in need of a good brushing.

"We do not equip our vehicles for human primping." He cut his gaze at her, and a teasing light extracted an emotion in the purple depths that she couldn't name. "You do not look as bad as you think."

"Really. Was that a compliment?"

He looked at her, and they grinned at each other.

At his close scrutiny, she felt the sheer force of his eyes pulsing against her. Her stomach did a little flip-flop, and she chided herself for letting that devilish face get to her.

He frowned back at the road and asked, "Hungry?"

"How did you know?"

"Your stomach has been loudly protesting lack of food for the past two hours."

She frowned at him. "A person is really exposed around you, aren't they? You read minds. Hear every body function. Is there anything you can't sense about me?"

"Not much. You are human, vampire prey. We have survived by hunting you." His eyes glistened almost black as they landed on her neck. "Naturally, we are attuned to your every nuance."

"See your point." She instinctively laid her hand on her throat. What would a vampire bite feel like—no, what was *his* bite like? Was it as remarkable as his kiss? Takala breathed deeply, inwardly yelling at herself to get over him. It wasn't good, or natural, nor would it end happily—just like the rest of her relationships; it was doomed from the start. Even more so, because he was a ruthless vampire who didn't care about using Lilly or anyone else for bait.

He turned back to the road and drifted into silence. It was a heavy, still kind of tension that poured over the whole car's interior, ending their few moments of light banter.

She swallowed hard and noticed the streets filling with housing projects. Clothes wafted on lines four and five stories up, looking like multicolored flags waving in the breeze. Screens were broken or nonexistent on windows. Bags of trash sat along some walkways. Youths hung out on corners, probably selling drugs. They were entering a not-so-desirable suburb of the city again.

"What area is this?"

"We're on the Left Bank, south of the main city." As if he could read her mind, which he probably could, he said, "It gets worse up ahead."

"I know Paris is one of the most beautiful cities in the world, City of Lights and all that, but you couldn't prove it by me. I've only seen her worst side. I'd sure like to tour the Eiffel Tower or the Arc de Triomphe. Where are they?"

"The Tower is north of us at the moment, at the Champ de Mars park. The Arc is on the Right Bank."

"You sound like you know the city."

"I lived here at one time." His voice deepened and his expression turned to stone, as if the memories were not all pleasant. "Do not be fooled. Paris is like a rose, beautiful soft petals with enticing aromas, but beware of le thorns."

Had he been one of the thorns? She tried to imagine him prowling the city in search of his next feeding. She remembered his strength and decided she wouldn't want to meet him on a dark street at night. Fear tightened her shoulders as she changed the subject. "Is this an area Raithe would hang out?" she asked, taking in the locals and the sidewalk vendors.

At the mention of Raithe's name, his fingers tightened on the wheel, every knuckle showing. "Yes," he said, a barely perceptible frisson of excitement passing over his face.

"Listen, I have to tell you up front, if you put Lilly in danger to get Raithe, I'll stop you."

"Are you threatening me?" Anger rode his eyes, and he blinked several times.

Clearly, he was used to having his every whim obeyed. "Just warning you. If she's in danger, I'm going to help her."

"Admirable, but I am not the one putting Lilly in danger. She has single-handedly managed that on her own."

"What do you mean?"

"The moment Raithe found out she worked for me and used her to kill my men, that signed her death warrant. She is dispensable to him now. Eventually, he will get around to disposing of her. He never leaves trails." He fixed her with a smoldering look. "Rather than throw idle threats at me, your best course of action would be to stay out of my way and let me find Raithe. She might have a chance if he is stopped."

He had a point. Takala sighed and decided she hated when he was right. And he was right more times than he was wrong. She refused to speak to him and stared out the window, feeling her stomach churning from hunger.

The Tesla whipped down a street toward a river. A no-swimming sign denoted it was the Seine. Takala could see the sun shimmering off the green opaque surface. Gulls flapped along the edges of the quay, picking at trash and debris. The car pulled into a parking spot, across the street from a sign with the international symbol for a subway pointing to a descending staircase.

Striker said to himself, "I thought so."

"What? You know this place?" She looked at the pedestrians going up and down the subway steps. They looked tired and bored.

He sighed loudly and said, "Unfortunately, yes." He parked half a block away, near a tiny shop selling art paintings.

Why couldn't he give her any details? She had to pry everything out of him. So she sounded annoyed when she said, "So, spill."

"Ancient tunnels, caves, and catacombs run beneath Paris. Particularly here. We have dossiers on several malevolent vampire groups that plague the underground in this area."

"Do you know the tunnels here?"

"Yes."

"Good, we won't get lost."

"There is no 'we' involved. I am going in alone," he said in that annoying I-control-the-world way of his.

"Why?" Her fingers curled into fists, and she brought them down near her sides.

"You lack an extraordinary amount of prudence in all areas of your life."

"You don't know me. You can't make judgment calls like that."

"I saw how you ran toward danger to protect my agents at the airport without thought for your own life or limb. How you disobeyed my orders and came into the bar." He grimaced. "Now you wish to follow me into a den of vampires."

"I can handle danger."

"You have never seen anything to match what could be in those tunnels. Did you not see how you affected the young girl who delivered this car?" he asked, his voice polished yet teeming with the promise of something dark and scary and totally unbending. "Your blood sent her over the edge. That is why I dismissed her. If they should smell your blood…"

She wouldn't look in the deep purple pools of his eyes, because she could feel them sucking her in. "What about you? How do you handle it?"

"I have more willpower than most, and I am one of the nicer ones." An undercurrent of something dangerous swam below the surface of his voice.

Takala remembered something Lilly had told her and said, "Doesn't sunlight weaken you?"

"Somewhat." Striker frowned and pulled his attention back to the serpent shifter.

Their mark was heading for the stairwell.

She started to say something, but Striker held up a hand to silence her and opened his phone.

A foreign-accented agent's voice said, "Yes, Director."

"Subject is heading down into Underground 23. Going

in. I need backup." Striker closed his phone and hopped out of the car.

"Wait, you need me. You're not operating at full power, you just admitted it. Let me go with you. I'm not helpless."

He held the door open a moment, gazing at her, his conscience clearly fighting with her suggestion, hating it. Then he said, "Since it's morning, and they are probably sleeping, and you will just disobey my orders to stay put, I'll concede this one time. But you must do exactly as I say."

She saluted him with two fingers. "Right, chief," she said, stepping out of the car.

She didn't even hear him close the door, only the chirp of the locks. Then he appeared at her side.

They trailed the shifter down two flights of stairs into the subway, melding into the flow of people.

Takala saw the guy check behind him once, but he looked right past her and Striker at the crowd around them.

"This den—do you think all the vamps are sleeping?"

"I hope so," he said, his gaze on the shifter. "They are young vampires."

"Like how old is young?"

"Two hundred years."

Funny how what was young to a vampire was so old to a human. "With all your B.O.S.P. intel, got any idea who our boy is going to see?" Takala asked, wondering if he knew more than he'd told her.

"Could be one of the families we've been monitoring, or an entirely new group who moved in."

The shifter opened a door marked in French and below, in English, Do Not Enter, Subway Personnel Only, and slipped through.

They let their target get a safe distance ahead. Then Takala and Striker followed, leaving several crying children with their father. He had little patience and was berating them. If Takala hadn't been in a hurry, she would have stopped and told the guy to read a parenting book.

Striker moved the door so the hinges didn't creak as they stepped through. Darkness surrounded them, and she had to wait for her eyes to adjust.

Striker seemed to sense her uncertainty. He clasped her hand and guided her through the darkness. His hand wasn't warm and comforting, just solid strength, and she felt safer holding it. A new feeling for her. She'd never been in a dangerous situation in which she didn't feel confident and bold and in control. She didn't know if she liked someone else leading the charge. It made her feel spineless. But then she'd never met a guy stronger than she, who made her feel protected. Either way, she was glad Striker was beside her.

They followed the sound of the guy's footsteps through the tunnel. They echoed, muffled and distant.

Takala leaned over and whispered, "Is this an abandoned subway tunnel?" She inhaled his butter-rum, starchy-wool scent, mixing with the dank, musty smell around her, and it made her feel oddly comforted.

"Yes."

She felt his cool breath on her ear, and a tiny shiver went through her.

"Be careful here," he whispered, putting his arm

around her waist and easily steering her over an old rail that ran along the tunnel floor.

A man had never led her around by her waist, and she decided she liked it, especially since she could feel his hard tensile strength brushing her side. She found herself wanting him to do more than put his arm around her waist. Not good at all. In fact, it was relationship suicide. And she'd had enough of that.

"Thank you," she said softly, brushing out of his grasp.

He caught her hand again, and she decided to let that ride. Holding hands was safer than an arm around the waist. And she had to own up: the hand-holding didn't feel threatening.

Taking care not to make a sound, they moved deeper into the tunnel. The scent of heavy, moldy earth and bricks and industrial grease grew stronger. An icy breeze whipped down the tunnel and set the hairs on the back of her neck standing on end. A door opened ahead of them, and the shifter walked through it.

Striker guided her to the door and went through first; then he cautioned her forward.

She entered a tunnel that looked as if it had been hand dug with pickaxes, the granite sides gouged and jagged in places. Torches burned on either side of the walls. Water dripped down the sides and collected in puddles on the ground. Lime and chalk deposits formed ugly tribal masks on the walls, their misshapen eyes following them. This place gave her the creeps. They must be close.

That's when the scream pierced her ears.

Chapter 10

Takala took off running, but Striker pulled her back. "Could be a trap. Let me go first."

"I'm not a fluff ball that will fall apart at the first gust of danger." She met his gaze. They were close, nose to nose. His rapid breaths brushed her cheeks, glided across her neck. Her nipples hardened instantly. She cursed her body and said, "Stop worrying about my safety.

"You are under my care. Therefore, I am your protector."

Another blood-curdling scream split the air.

"Are we going to argue about this all day?" Takala asked.

He turned and did his disappearing routine. One minute there, the next warping through space and time.

Takala ran down the tunnel, but she knew he'd reach the screamer way before she could. Didn't seem fair.

The tunnel forked, and Takala followed the constant screaming to the right. The passage opened up, getting taller and wider and more cavernous. The metallic scent of fresh blood mingled with the fetid odor of rotting flesh. She put her hand over her nose to keep from gagging.

She spotted Striker, crouched behind a huge wall of rubble, probably debris left there by the tunnel builders. He peered around it and waved her forward. She crept up behind him and glanced past his shoulder. Then her jaw dropped.

Charnel house could not describe the ghastly sight before her. Naked humans of all sizes and descriptions were bound throughout the cavern, fang marks in every conceivable place on their bodies. Blood splatter all over them and the walls. Some were still alive, their eyes empty, begging for death. Others had been drained of blood, their rotting bodies left to hang by chains and rope. She quickly counted twelve alive and forty dead.

She had seen death and violence in her lifetime. When your grandmother was the Guardian, and she had raised you, you saw every type of carnage and bloodshed in the fight against darkness. Usually Meikoda would take care to draw evil away from home and dispatch it, but there were always unpredicted surprise attacks on Takala and her sisters, or on Meikoda herself. So Takala was no stranger to the manifestations of evil. Yet the helplessness of these victims tore at her and angered her. She looked at Striker, and his face was blank, solid granite. He had probably seen this all before.

She spotted the serpent shifter. He stood in front of a

girl who looked about fifteen. She was screaming, her eyes frantic with madness.

"Don't worry, I won't torture you like the others did," he said, his voice a hiss.

This only made the girl scream louder.

"Shut up, shut up!"

Then it happened. The guy morphed. His eyes narrowed to slits. Pupils turned bright yellow and vertical. His skin elongated and stretched, leaving his clothes in a heap. His face flattened as the thick boa-constrictor body took shape, at least forty-five feet long. He slithered up the girl's leg, his forked tongue shooting out, tasting her skin.

Fear gripped every part of her body now. Her mouth opened wide, but she couldn't form a sound.

Takala and Striker both ran out at the same time. Striker went instinctively for the boa's head, locking onto the back of it. Takala grabbed its tail.

Fortified by magic, the creature was stronger than a normal snake, and Takala felt its body curling in on itself, twining around her legs and waist. Takala couldn't imagine how people could own pet boas. They needed to tangle with a serpent shifter.

She glanced at Striker. The snake had twined around his neck and chest, picking him up and slamming him onto the cave floor like a rag doll. He wasn't faring any better than she was.

The snake's body curled around her neck, squeezing until she thought her esophagus would be crushed. Takala looked over at the chained girl, saw the fear and death in her eyes, and that was all the impetus she needed. She channeled her anger into her hands and yanked them loose from the muscular clenches of the snake's body. Instinctively she curved her fingers, forced power into the tips, then speared them into the snake. She drove them up to her wrists. Bone cracked. Flesh crunched. Pain flared through her raw hands.

The creature growled, a monstrous reptilian sound. Then it rolled over and over, dragging Striker and Takala with it. Takala felt her head pound the rocky floor again and again, but she kept her hands buried in the snake's writhing flesh.

Striker managed to grab the creature's head, and the thrashing stopped for a moment.

With one quick trust, Takala ripped open the snake's underbelly. Surprisingly there was little blood, mostly writhing and twitching muscle. She managed to wiggle free and ran to help Striker.

Striker still had a death lock on the head, but the snake's coiled body trapped him.

She caught his shoulder for leverage, then drop-kicked the snake in the head, driving the tip of her boot into its eyeball.

The snake growled and thrashed again.

She rolled down onto her feet and wheeled around to attack again, but Striker ripped off the jaw of the snake…and half its head.

It flipped one last time, then lay there, muscles still jerking in the throes of contracting. Striker crawled out from beneath the heavy body.

Takala helped him stand and asked, "Are you okay?"

"Of course." He wore the expression of a vampire who had just felt his own mortality and couldn't believe it.

She heard the slight waver in his voice and saw that he'd torn his tie in the fight. It was the first time she'd seen him a little rattled, and he kept staring at her bloody hands. "Aren't you glad I came along?" she asked.

In one slick move, he extracted the handkerchief from his breast pocket, shook it out, and handed it to her. He kept his gaze from her hands. "We just killed the only lead I had to Raithe. Glad doesn't describe how I feel at the moment."

"It was either kill him or he'd kill us." Takala wiped her hands and flinched as the material met the gouges on her fingers. "Thanks." She held out the kerchief.

"Keep it." He waved it away. His eyes took on a frantic, ravenous appearance. The pupils dilated, the whites quickly overtaken. They were wide black holes, swallowing everything in sight. The humans. The bloodbath in the cave. His gaze landed on her.

He swallowed hard, his Adam's apple working in his throat. "I have to get some air."

Before Takala could answer him, he fast-forwarded and disappeared.

She had found the chink in his armor. Blood. She tossed the handkerchief to the floor, then moved toward the chained humans, who called for help.

"Don't worry, I'll untie all of you," Takala said. "Please, someone tell me who did this to you?"

"Don't move." An elderly man with a thick gray mustache and salt-and-pepper hair spoke in broken English. "There's a trap. On the floor."

Takala froze, holding up her right foot. She saw it now. An area four-by-four feet. At first glance it looked like the rest of the floor, but on closer inspection she noticed the rock had been cut and replaced. Directly above it, she saw four AK-47s mounted to the ceiling, aimed at the spot. One step on the floor and she was Swiss cheese.

"These guys are real humanitarians," she said snidely. She gingerly backed up and called to the elderly Frenchman, "Thank you for saving my life, sir."

"Please, just get us out."

Takala kept her distance from the booby trap and approached the elderly man. "Who did this to you?"

"Vampires. Never believed in that stuff before being forced here. Oh my God, we're all going to die! They'll kill us all!" Hysteria clutched him, and he rocked his head from side to side, as if the motion helped him cope with all he'd experienced. "You have to get us out before they wake up. Please, please let me out of here!"

"Do you know where they're sleeping? Did they mention it?" Takala asked as she broke the ropes with her bare hands, aware of the stinging rawness of her skin.

"No. They just leave." The man staggered, then gained his legs and ran out of the cavern, still naked and shaking his head. Takala was certain Striker would intercept him.

She moved to the girl next. She fell into Takala's arms. Takala gently set her down and propped her against the rocks.

"Did anyone hear the names of the vampires?"

"Laeyar was one," a young man bound next to the girl said, his accent so thick Takala had to really concentrate to understand him.. "He's the leader."

Takala kept her eyes on his face, for she didn't want

to embarrass him by looking at his naked body. "Did this Laeyar let the serpent shifter come here to feed?"

"Yes. Laeyar let him. He's killed one of us every three days. Laeyar goes out hunting and brings more of us."

"Please, let me out," a woman of about fifty pleaded. She was a bleached blonde and spoke perfect English. Her eyes were swollen and encrusted from crying. Takala counted five bites on her neck alone.

After freeing the young man, she worked on the ropes of the blonde and asked, "Have you heard the name Raithe mentioned among them?"

The woman looked too beaten and frayed to do more than nod.

The young man was supporting the girl, probably his girlfriend, as he said, "Laeyar brags that he dines with this Raithe person."

Abruptly, a blinding light appeared and B.O.S.P. cleaners materialized. Striker must have called them. She noticed that one of them held the hand of the elderly man who had tried to leave. The agony and fear had vanished from his face. He looked only content and dazed. He was fully clothed now, too.

The victims cowered, frightened.

Takala said, "Please, they won't hurt you. They're only here to help." She left out that they wouldn't have a memory of this horrible event in their lives. Definitely a good thing.

When all the humans were untied, one of the cleaners, a man with buckteeth and chubby cheeks, who looked an awful lot like a beaver shifter, approached her. "We can take care of that for you." He nodded to her injured hands.

"Any aftereffects from those crystals?"

He grinned. "Only that you'll feel great. Pure crystal energy does that. No ill effects."

"In that case, knock yourself out."

He held up a small clear tubular apparatus that looked like a wide wand. Weird glowing pink gel and tiny pyramid-shaped crystals bubbled inside. He hit a button on the end, and a lilac-colored light sprayed over her hands. It felt like a scrub brush going over her skin, uncomfortable but not unbearable. She grimaced; then it was over. No pain. The wounds cauterized in seconds. Her skin miraculously healed right before her eyes.

"Wow, I want one of those." She pointed to the wand. "Can you put me on the B.O.S.P. Christmas list?"

His grin widened and he checked her out. "No, but you can be on my own special list." His lips twitched with a rodent tic.

She didn't think she had led the guy on, but obviously he thought otherwise. Male testosterone, be it Supe or human! Who could figure it out? Not her; she stayed lost.

"Thanks, I gotta go." She hurried away and saw one of the cleaners zap the booby trap.

The molecular structure of the AKs shifted, blurred, then disappeared. Just like that. Booby trap annihilated. Too bad cleaners weren't available to fix her love life.

She went in search of Striker and found him in the subway tunnel. He was talking on the phone, his form all in shadows. His phone light cast an eerie yellow radiance over his pale face and neck, making him look like a handsome ghoul.

When he noticed her, he closed the phone with a

quick snap and stood there, a motionless monolith in the shadows.

"State-secret stuff?" she teased, staring at his shadowy face.

"Something like that."

The gloomy darkness seemed to amplify the tension between them, and she could actually feel his presence prickling the nerve endings of her skin. She stopped a safe four feet from him and said, "So, what happened back there?"

"Nothing."

"Yeah, right. Know what I think? I've found your one true weakness."

"Really? Enlighten me."

"Human blood."

One moment there was plenty of distance between them; the next he was up in her face, his cool breath brushing her lips. "Not *any* human blood, just yours." He bent, picked up one hand and sniffed it. "I can still smell it, *bonne bouche,* ambrosia, nectar of the gods." His lips brushed the back of her hand, sending tingles up her arm, into her breasts.

Takala wanted to pull back, step away, but she just stood there, entranced by his nearness, caught in the vibration of his voice.

He stroked her hand with his thumb while he used his other hand to capture her chin and raise it. He stood staring into her eyes while he gently traced her jawline, her lips. Hot yearning poured down her throat, into her belly, and settled between her thighs. God, she wanted him to touch her all over.

He stroked her lips for a moment and heaved a loud sigh. Then he whispered, "You are so lethal."

A second ticked by, her heart pounding. Any moment he'd close that two inches and kiss her. She could feel the sexual longing between them draining the oxygen from the air. Abruptly, he dropped his hand and stepped back.

Why hadn't he kissed her? Sad thing was, she had wanted him to, dammit! When her heart settled down and she had her resolve to stay away from men squarely in place, she said, "That's right, and don't forget it. And the blood in my body, I like to keep there. Got it?"

"I promise you, Takala, I will never drink your blood." His voice held that dangerous facile edge that hid all his emotion—if he felt any to hide.

She couldn't tell if he was being serious or not, or if this was one of the ways he captivated and charmed female victims. She heard the nervous catch in her own voice as she said, "And I can promise to never let you."

"Good. Then we are in agreement."

"Miracle of miracles. First time for everything." She couldn't see his face in the shadows, but she could feel his smile.

Had he meant that bit about her being lethal and never drinking her blood? Like she was just a nuisance he had to fend off? She should feel glad about it, but she found herself taking exception to it. For some reason, it made her feel worse than the loser she already was when it came to men. She heard Akando saying, "You scare me." Now she had a vampire on the run. Maybe it was her pride, but she could feel a need building in her to seduce Striker, bring him to his knees, make him take back those words.

"This Laeyar dude," she said, her voice cool. "We have to find his den before sunset. Is it around here somewhere?"

"I've had my agents searching for it with no luck. Every vampire knows better than to keep his den near his food source, but we had to make certain. The danger of being killed by enemies and vampire hunters is too great."

"There are really vampire hunters?"

"Plenty. B.O.S.P. alone has bounties on over two hundred that I know of."

"Oh." Takala had never met a vampire hunter. They were a loner breed, evidently. But at the moment, she thought they each deserved a Medal of Honor. She hated to ask her next question. "Are there other dens like this one?"

"Unfortunately, yes. Some vampires are unscrupulous when it comes to feeding."

Revulsion twisted inside Takala. Just the thought of humans being treated and slaughtered like cattle made her sick.

She asked, "You got any idea how we can find him?"

"The only thing we can do is come back here at dusk when he returns to feed. Let's go."

"Where are we going?"

"To a hotel."

All sorts of lurid unbidden things popped into Takala's head…and they all involved a bed. No, no, no. He was just dropping her there to get rid of her. He grabbed her hand, and Takala felt dizzy as the world sped by. But it didn't stop those lurid images from coming back, and she ground her teeth.

Chapter 11

"This isn't a hotel," Takala said as he zipped the car into a parking spot.

"You need calories more than sleep."

"How do you know?"

"Your stomach growls like a den of lions. There is a sidewalk café here that is the best in Paris. Perhaps we can silence your hunger for a while."

"Sorry to be a nuisance." Takala smelled the delicious scent of fresh-baked bread wafting through the heater vent and realized she was starving.

"Nuisance doesn't quite cover it." He cast her one of those unreadable guarded glances that gave nothing away.

She made a face at his shoulder as they got out and walked down a busy block. Icy February wind whipped past her face. The smell of city exhaust mingled with the tempting scent of French cooking. She could almost taste the pounds of butter.

This must have been Café Row, because she counted six cafes before he paused at one. It was small and quaint, Bella la Table. A yellow and blue awning waved over a circle of wrought-iron tables. Despite the cold, people huddled down in seats, drinking espresso, eating, reading papers or books, or chatting. The restaurant's inside dining area looked as busy and full as the outside. Behind the etched plate-glass windows, harried waiters cleaned tables and took orders.

"You mind the cold?" he asked in that commanding tone of his as if he knew the answer and only asked the question out of politeness.

"I certainly wouldn't come to a Paris sidewalk café and not sit outside. So, no, please let's sit here." She motioned to the outdoor tables.

Striker nodded his approval and snapped his fingers at a waiter. He motioned them to sit anywhere. Striker chose a table beneath the awning and sat in a chair where the sun couldn't touch him.

She said, "I thought sunlight didn't bother you."

"I can function in it, but if I have a choice, I prefer not to get a tan."

"Ha, you *do* have a sense of humor."

"Only since meeting you." He grinned, and it warmed the empty depths of his eyes, charmed his irresistibly attractive face.

The warmth in his expression tugged at her chest as he pulled the chair out for her. Then he pushed her up to the table. Always the gentleman vampire. She bestowed a thankful smile on him.

A waiter dropped two menus on the table and left abruptly, saying something she couldn't catch. The menu was written in French, and she tried to pick out the few Parisian foods she knew, like crêpes, boeuf bourguignon, chateaubriand. Something called poulet à la diable sounded good: deviled chicken in fried butter. She felt Striker watching her, and she glanced up to see he hadn't picked up his menu.

She realized he didn't eat food, and he'd stopped here for her benefit only. "I'm sorry," she said.

"For what?"

"You don't eat."

"Oh, I eat." He stared hard at her neck as if it might be a morsel on his plate.

"You know what I mean."

"I do." His brows moved a quarter of an inch as he frowned. Then he picked up the menu and glanced down at it, ennui settling over his face.

"Don't you miss the taste of food? I'd rather be dead if I couldn't enjoy eating."

"One adapts and finds pleasure in other things." One of his intense stares reached across the table and caressed her.

A tingle warmed her belly, and she felt herself being drawn to him. No, she wasn't feeling anything for this vampire. Was she?

Thankfully, the waiter returned at that moment and leveled an impatient look at both of them.

Striker ordered an espresso, and Takala started with a ham and cheese crêpe, poulet à la diable, a baguette with plenty of butter, an espresso, and she requested the waiter return for a dessert order.

The guy looked at her like she'd lost her mind if she thought he was ordering all that food. Then Striker said something to him in perfect French and he hurried off, completely chastened.

"What did you tell him?"

"That you were my wife and pregnant."

Takala found herself grinning. That was her favorite excuse for her appetite. She felt obliged to say "Thank you."

Silence settled between them. Takala inhaled the scent of the baking bread and something delectable and sugary, like chocolate cream pie. She wondered what it was so she could order it. She drew in the smell and said, "I wish they could bottle this. It smells like my grandmother's kitchen. She's a great cook."

"She bakes often?"

"Oh, yes, it's her therapy, I think. She raised me and my sisters. We were a lot to handle." Takala grinned at the memory. "Well, I guess I was the real problem."

"Rebellious, were you?"

"When I thought I could get away with it, but my grandmother always found me out. When you have the Guardian raising you, it's pretty tough getting away with anything. It makes you ingenious." She grinned.

"I can see you pushing the limits. Tell me, what did you do?"

"Everything." Takala rolled her eyes, then said, "I remember casting a magical spell once to block her extrasensory powers. I burned up my room instead. A candle got out of hand—boy, did I spend a long time in the sweat cave." Takala grimaced at the memory.

"Sweat cave?"

"Our prayer cave and my punishment. I spent a lot of time there as a kid, fasting and praying, contemplating my bad behavior. I can see my grandmother now. All she had to do was point to the door, and I knew my fate."

"But I can tell by your voice that you do not resent it very much."

"No, I know now she did it for my own good. I respect my grandmother—love her. She was there for us when we needed her. She wouldn't have left us like my mother did." Takala heard the resentment in her own voice. When she saw his steady gaze boring into her, as if he were probing her for more information, she realized she'd said more than she wanted.

Suddenly she felt self-conscious, a rare happenstance in her life. She stopped talking and observed the couple next to them. Middle-aged and bored with each other, their noses were buried in the morning paper. She envisioned herself and Akando in those very same chairs. It probably would have ended that way if she had forced him into a loveless marriage. How many affairs would he have had by the time they were fifty? Would she have been so dense she wouldn't have known he had cheated on her? Tears came to Takala's eyes, and she had to blink them back.

"What is wrong, Takala?" His brow creased slightly in concern, and he reached across the table to touch her hand.

"Nothing." She liked when he spoke her name. It added a smooth flair to it, and right now she needed to hear her name on another man's lips. She grew aware of his touch, his wide hand covered hers, the weight of his long fingers curling around her own.

When she gazed down at their touching hands, he seemed to grow uncomfortable and pulled back.

Takala felt the loss of his touch right away, and it left an empty sensation on her skin.

A pregnant pause settled between them, and they gazed everywhere but at each other.

Then he said, "Does your grandmother know you have been searching for your mother?"

Takala studied the menu, staring blankly at it. "No, and I'm not telling her. My people disowned my mother. It is against our laws to even acknowledge she exists."

"But you are breaking the laws?"

"I just wanted to locate her, get her side of the story." Was he trying to make her feel guilty about wanting to meet her mother?

"Did you ever stop to think that those laws are in place to protect others from the person who has been abjured? Perhaps it is for your own safety that you follow them."

"I don't need a lecture from you." She gripped the menu so tightly it trembled in her hands.

"Then why have you not yet told Culler who you are?"

"How do you know that I didn't?"

"I read your mind."

Takala snapped, "Stay out of my head. This is personal."

"I hoped to spare you some pain."

"Too late." Takala stood up and slammed the menu down on the table. "Where's the restroom?" Before he could answer her, she found the universal sign pointing inside. "I see the way."

Without another word, she strode off, boots pounding the concrete tiles. What right did he have to lecture her on how to live her life? Maybe she would never tell Lilly Smith. Takala wasn't absolutely certain that Lilly was her mother. Yes, Lilly looked like the picture and exhibited the powers of an *egtonha,* but Takala just couldn't believe the woman who shared her blood was so reprehensible. And until she was absolutely convinced Lilly was her mother, she'd keep the truth to herself. Still, even if she were certain, she might not ever tell her. But it was her decision to make, and she didn't need Striker's advice.

After following the signs to the back of the restaurant, Takala found the bathroom. She locked herself in a stall and had a good cry. Jet lag was really getting to her.

Striker waited and grew impatient. The waiter had brought the food, and it was getting cold in the crisp air.

Earlier, because of his sensitive hearing, he had heard her crying in the bathroom. Several times he started to go to her, but he thought better of it. Obviously, her mother was a touchy subject.

He hated hearing Takala weep. There was a slim chance he had been too harsh on Takala, but she needed to stop looking at Culler with blinders on. She had to face the truth.

He couldn't remember the last time he'd cared enough to involve himself in another person's life or to consider another's feelings. He thought he had lost the human ability to sympathize, but he couldn't deny the guilt he felt right now, or this need to comfort her.

It was dangerous, he knew, to feel anything for her. It was imperative he remain detached from all stimulus, particularly emotion. It had kept him from losing control, kept him from the bloodlust that could destroy him. He couldn't let unbidden emotions get out of hand, but there was no harm in opening her eyes to the truth, was there?

Takala's outward appearance gave off an aura of invincibility and overconfidence, but he now knew she was utterly defenseless when it came to her heart. Yet he needed her to understand that she was better off leaving Culler out of her life. And if the truth hurt her, then so be it. Better he destroy these maternal ideals of hers than Culler taking Takala's life.

He was about to go and find her when she walked through the door and back out onto the patio. Her two-colored eyes were puffy and red. Remorse stabbed him again, and he wished she were more receptive to the truth about Culler.

As she made her way across the restaurant, he noticed several male waiters stopped in their tracks and watched her. Jealousy flared. It was all he could do to stay in his seat and not teach the oglers a lesson. But he could forgive them their fascination, for Takala drew his own gaze like a moth to a flame. Her ginger hair fell around her shoulders in waves, the blond highlights glimmering in the café's lights. Her black leather pants poured over her long, shapely legs, hugging them in an alluring way. The long boots that came to her knees. Her leather coat undulated around her slim hips. And in the front he could see her flat belly exposed by her short T-shirt. That confident stride of hers wasn't feminine at all. Her hips didn't sway with it, but her chin was high, her shoulders and back fencepost straight, which uplifted her sensual full breasts and showed them to advantage. It was the most alluring female walk he'd ever seen. Something about it made him want to cover her, dominate her, make her his.

He hadn't felt a need for a mate in hundreds of years. And he wouldn't turn Takala into a slave whom he could command only to quench his thirst for blood and sexual pleasure. He thought he had conquered all physical desires. But no, he could feel an overwhelming craving erupting inside him just looking at her, burning through his body, pushing at him, tempting him to let go. His heart raced. A tremor shook his hands, and it took all of his willpower to force his gaze down and examine the iron scrollwork on the table until he gained control again.

She sat, refusing to look at him, and began eating the ham and cheese crêpe first.

She swallowed, then spoke. "This is really good," she said, making small talk as if nothing had happened between them.

Introduction of food seemed to have lifted her spirits more than anything he could have said or done. With some females it was roses. With Takala it was food. If he ever needed to bribe her, he'd have to exploit her weakness.

"Yes." He sat back and watched her cut the ham crêpe into three more pieces and bring an enormous bite to her full rosebud lips.

She shoved in the mouthful, chewed and closed her eyes in delight.

He didn't think anything had fascinated him more than watching her eat. She licked the béchamel sauce from her lips, and his body drew up like a piano wire.

"Let's make a deal. We'll start over. You don't tell me how to live my life, and I won't tell you."

He was glad she didn't seem to hold grudges or was one of those females who pouted for days. "Fair enough. Tell me about your sisters," he said.

"They're great." She talked in between bites. Now that she was eating, she seemed animated and demonstrative. She lowered her voice to a whisper, leaned across the table and said, "Fala, she was always good at magic. Always had shaman powers. Becoming the Guardian just made her more powerful. Nina, my baby sister, she can talk to any kind of living or dead thing. She's the quiet one, nothing like Fala and me."

"What about you? What talents do you possess?"

"Me, just my strength. It's only brute force, nothing life-altering or meaningful." Takala shrugged, leaned back and started consuming the poulet à la diable.

Striker, amazed at the speed with which she ate, said, "Strength is an admirable quality." He felt his charismatic, confident mask slipping into place. Was he trying to charm her?

"I don't know." She shrugged as if her strength were nothing.

"But I do. We would be in the belly of that serpent shifter at this moment if you had not intervened. You truly amaze me."

She brightened at the compliment, and her eyes twinkled. "That makes us even. You saved my life at the airport, and I kept Snaky Jakey from eating you alive." She gave him a winning smile. "Enough about me. What about you? You told me you were old, so spill your real age." She looked bluntly at him.

He ran a finger around the lip of his mug and said, "That is a prying question."

"Well, if talking about it bothers you…" Her voice trailed off as she finished the last piece of chicken.

He frowned at her. "It doesn't."

"Then you won't mind telling me." She shot him an all-too-unyielding look.

"I suppose you will not stop asking until I reveal it."

"You know me too well." She batted her beautiful eyes at him, enjoying this excessively.

"I was a gladiator in Rome." He watched her face for a reaction.

Her expressive eyes widened in disbelief. "You serious? Like BC serious?"

He nodded.

"Did you fight in the Coliseum?"

"Yes."

"Did you use a trident and a net, or a sword?"

"Trident."

"Wow! That must have been a horrible existence."

He nodded, feeling his facial muscles hardening around his lips. "Most of the gladiators during my lifetime eventually ended up vampires."

"Why?"

"It was their only way out, and Raithe was their keeper. He sent them from one hell to another." Striker heard the hatred in his own voice.

"How long did he do this?"

"Centuries, until he got bored with it."

"So he turned you?" she asked, her expression softening with compassion.

"Yes." The warmth of the coffee cup drew him, and he cupped both hands around it, feeling the heat seeping through his fingers.

"If he's your maker, do you have to obey him?"

He laughed bitterly. "Do not believe what you see on television."

"I don't."

He let his gaze bore pointedly into her face.

She amended her statement. "Okay, maybe a little. Other than popular culture and rarely running across them in my line of work, I don't know much about vampires. They're not in my quilting circle." She grinned, her eyes twinkling, making her whole face glow with life and beauty.

He smiled, and it warmed him all over—no, *she* warmed him all over. "Good. I would keep it that way."

"You don't sound like you like your kind very much."

"I have lived too long and seen what they can become. So I guess you are correct—some vampires disappoint me." Flashes of humans, chained like animals, dead and dying flooded his mind. He felt almost self-conscious about her having seen the depravity of some vampires.

They lapsed into silence, and the waiter paused and looked down his nose at her and asked if she wanted dessert.

She ordered a cheese course, crème brûlée and tarte tatin. The waiter shook his head; she grinned at his back and said in a conspiratorial whisper, "I'm beginning to like French waiters."

Striker watched her dive into the bread, butter it and eat a large piece before she said, "Surely as your maker, Raithe must hold some power over you?"

"None." Striker's lips lifted in a sardonic smirk. He guessed that wasn't completely true. Raithe was the only person in the world who could rouse him to murder.

"At first?"

"Yes. I was his child." He drew out the word through clenched teeth.

"But now?"

"He hasn't been able to influence me for a thousand years. Other than enemies, we are nothing to each other."

"So, what was your human name?"

"You mean the one I was born with?"

"Yes."

He contemplated the question for a long moment, staring down into his cup. There was no reflection, only the watery image of the canopy flapping overhead. It was like his memory, thousands of faded pages. "It has been so long. I've had so many names since then." He thought hard, then finally said, "I remember now. Domidicus."

"Nice Latin name." As a way of explanation, she said, "I took Latin in high school. It actually comes in handy sometimes, but obviously not in Paris." She waved to the customers around them speaking rapid-fire French.

"True." He nodded, unable to take his eyes off her.

"What do you remember about your life as a human? How did you end up a gladiator?"

He felt himself drifting back through those ancient

memories. "I was a physician in Rome. A nobleman died under my care, and my penance was the ring."

"I'm really having a hard time picturing you as a healer."

"I wasn't very good at it, obviously," he said, his voice flat.

"You look more like a dangerous and polished predator now. That should heal your ego."

"Tremendously." He cocked a brow at her and sipped his espresso, eyeing her over the cup.

"Were you married in Rome?"

"No."

"Did you have a family?"

He ignored her question and looked so hard into her eyes that she squirmed a little in her seat. Then it hit him. He knew why she looked familiar to him. "I have it."

"What?"

"Who you remind me of."

"Who's that?"

He studied her face as if seeing it for the first time. He could not believe the resemblance. "You're the spitting image of Calliope."

"Calliope?"

"My sister." Sadness crept into Striker. He hated remembering his past—especially the early years. It was the reason he had a hard time recalling his first name and why he had tried to wipe away those memories.

"You loved her?" Her eyes held his.

"Love?" He paused over the word, trying to give it meaning in the horrifying chronicles of his life. Love was something he had given up on long ago, but he felt it now, that sting when he thought of his sister and parents. The thoughts of them still poignant and painful, like having his mind dredged with a pitchfork. Striker's fingers inadvertently tightened around the cup, and it shattered.

He watched the dark liquid drain down his fingers and hand, not feeling the hot fluid. No, all he could envision was the bloody face of his sister. Raithe standing over her mutilated body, smiling his innocent yet wicked grin, an expression of an egotistical god who held the power of life and death, and he always chose death.

"Oh, golly!" She reached across the table and dabbed at the spill with her napkin.

Her touch brought Striker out of the memory trance, and he took the napkin from her, holding her hand a little longer than necessary. "Thank you," he managed to say, his voice sounding distant even to his own ears.

He drew back, and the bleak hollowness that had kept him alive for eons settled back over him. He felt comfortable there, alone save for himself and his need for revenge. With methodical strokes, he wiped his hand and the cuffs of his jacket.

"Are you okay?" She laid her fingers over the back of his hand.

"Quite." He absorbed her skin's heat, allowed it to seep into his stone-cold body. It somehow anchored him to the moment, oddly soothing the savage part of him that wanted Raithe's blood.

Then her phone rang and spoiled the sensation.

Chapter 12

Takala felt his fingers grasping lightly at her own as she pulled her hand back and reached inside her coat pocket. She was glad for the interruption, because she wanted to haul Striker off somewhere private, hold him and kiss him and make the rawness and isolation she'd seen in his eyes go away.

"Excuse, me," she said, without looking at the number. "I need to take this." She leaped up and walked out of the patio and onto the sidewalk. "Yes." She watched the cars pass by as she spoke.

"Takala."

She heard Akando's voice, and her stomach dropped to her knees. She slapped the phone shut and was about to stuff it into her pocket when it rang again.

"Don't hang up."

"Why?"

"Because I've been thinking."

"Really? I thought the only way you could think was with your dumb stick." A low blow, but he deserved it.

"Takala, I mean it. I don't want to lose you."

"Too late, bucko, you already have."

"No, Takala, I'm certain that was a fluke. I'd been drinking. I picked that chick up at a bar, and I couldn't get rid of her."

"Ever heard of the words 'Get out'? 'Leave'! 'Vamoose'! 'Scram'!"

"You know what I mean."

"No, I don't. You would have kicked me out if you didn't want me there."

"It's not that. It's just…"

At his hesitation, she said, "What? Spit it out."

"Well, you're never around much, always working on a case. I got lonely."

"I saw you when I could. You know I have to work."

"I know, but it wasn't enough for me."

"For once, be honest. I thought it was my scaring you that turned you off. Now you're saying I needed to spend more time with you. Which is it?"

"You caught me at the wrong time when I last talked to you. I'd had too much to drink. Didn't mean what I said at all."

"I don't have time to listen to this."

"Please, Takala, I love you."

"For how long? Until the next bimbo comes along?"

"I swear, I'll be faithful."

Takala couldn't stand the groveling tone in his voice. It caused her insides to churn. Just hearing his voice put her back in the car talking to him while another woman shared his bed. He was crushing her into pieces. "Don't call back."

She slammed the phone closed and stared up into the bright sunlight. She felt like screaming at Maiden Bear, the bringer of white magic, to give her some insight into the male mind. A road map. Anything, so she wasn't floundering around. When she got home, she was going to the prayer cave and wasn't coming out until she felt enlightened when it came to men.

She ground her teeth together and was about to turn, when hands touched her shoulders. She whipped around to look into a pair of fathomless purple eyes, inches from her.

"He doesn't love you." There was an enraged look on his face she had never seen before.

"You heard us?"

"I couldn't help it."

"I can't deal with this right now. I'll meet you at the car—and please tell them to put the rest of my meal in a to-go bag."

Takala hurried to the car, not looking back. She felt Striker's gaze boring into her back and didn't care. She just wanted to curl up somewhere with her sisters and talk to them. But she couldn't call them, because they'd ask why she was in Paris and she wouldn't be able to lie to them. No, she had to endure this alone—no, not really alone. She had Striker to talk to. That was a joke. She couldn't open her soul to a vampire she just met. Maybe she already had. She shook her head and jogged the rest of the way to the car.

Takala watched as Striker pulled the car into the alleyway of the La Montague Hotel. A laundry truck and food-service vehicle sat in the delivery bay, and he parked behind them.

They hadn't spoken since the Akando incident, and she broke the quiet bond between them. "Why are we going in the back?"

"Culler is staying in the penthouse, and I don't want to ruin our cover. We'll take the back stairs."

"Any activity from her?"

"Hasn't left her room."

On cue, a parking attendant in burgundy and gold livery came through a door and walked to the car. The guy looked human and unremarkable except for a pot belly that hung over his trousers. Takala wondered how Striker managed to coordinate the minions who took care of his needs.

Striker exited and handed him the keys. He spoke to him in French.

Takala got out and grabbed her overnight bag and her to-go bag from the backseat. She followed Striker through a door with an exit sign over it, hearing the parking attendant drive away.

They walked up six flights of stairs in silence, Takala lagging five steps behind him. His movements seemed stiff, and she knew he was brooding. Well, she didn't need advice on love from a vampire who couldn't remember what it felt like.

When they reached the next level, he held open a door and waited for her to go through first. His eyes were so dark purple and distant, she couldn't stand it any longer. She said, "Okay, I'll listen to what you have to say."

"No, I overstepped my bounds. I should not have eavesdropped on your conversation."

"It's okay. Tell me what you want to tell me." Now he was making her want to hear his advice.

He strode beside her, looking straight ahead. "It won't help matters. You are not receptive to constructive criticism."

"I take it as well as the next guy." She leaped in front of him, blocking his way. "So tell me."

His eyes bored into hers with that soul-stealing look of his, as if he could reach down inside her. "He is not right for you."

"No man is." She hugged her carry-on tightly to her chest.

"Love will find you when you are not looking for it."

"Can you get any more cryptic?" She rolled her eyes.

He blinked, a sure sign he was annoyed and struggling for patience. "Did you set your sights on this Akando, or did he court you?"

Takala wanted to say Akando hit on her first, but she had gone after him with her feminine guns loaded. She had loved him—or so she'd thought. But there was no use lying to a guy who could read her mind, so she said, "No, I went after him."

"Have you asked yourself why you feel so insecure that you need to be in a relationship, even if it is only one-sided?"

"You heard what he said. He said he loved me."

"He says that now, because he lost you. He doesn't love you. He only wants you as a possession. Once he gets you, he'll pursue his passions elsewhere."

"Thank you for your insight." Takala heard the

material of her carry-on stretching and popping, and she had to stop squeezing it.

"You want honesty, I offer it. Has it been this way with all your relationships?"

"They end badly. I push them all away or something," she said, forcing out the truth. "I think it's going okay, then wham-o, they break up with me, and I'm standing there hitting my head against a wall."

He touched her chin, running his hands along her jawline. Takala felt tingles shoot down her neck, and she gazed down at his tie, no longer able to make eye contact. She felt suddenly light-headed, her legs and arms prickling like they had gone numb and the feeling was just returning. The jet lag was really taking over.

He stared at his hand as if realizing he was touching her, and he stepped back and said, "You are looking for love and acceptance. You have abandonment issues. Until you accept that you are worthy of love and you do not need to force men to love you, you'll not find happiness in a relationship. You will only drive men from you."

Had Takala wanted love so much that she pushed all men away? Was he right? She didn't want to admit it, but he could be. He wasn't being smug about it. He looked pensive and sincere, and he spoke with the authority of two thousand years of living experience. It was hard facing her own character flaws, hearing it from a stranger, a heartless vampire. He could be wrong about Akando. He had said he loved her. But hadn't he cheated on her?

She swallowed hard and said, "I'll think it over." She fell back in at his side and they walked to Room 723.

He pointed at the door and handed her the pass card. "This is your room."

She felt a tinge of disappointment that they weren't sharing a room, but she didn't say that. Logically she knew that was a horrible idea, but her body was disagreeing with her. "Where is your room?" she asked, hoping it was in a different hotel, a safe distance away.

"Across the hall."

Takala gulped and looked at the door to 724. It was about four steps away. Great!

"Now rest. I'll wake you before sunset."

She turned to say thank you, but he'd already disappeared, the door behind her shutting with a final click.

Takala used the card key and stepped inside. Why did she feel as if she had somehow connected with Striker? That advice. She would have resented anyone else telling her that, but she felt bared to the bone when she was talking to him, raked over the coals. He could be right about her. A scary thought, indeed.

She walked into the bathroom, found her toothbrush and paste and brushed for a good ten minutes. Then she turned on the shower and disrobed. She needed to bathe, crawl into bed, and hope that he was wrong about her. But she had a gut feeling he was right. And it was her mother's fault. All of it. This woman of whom she couldn't let go. What if Lilly was her mother? All signs pointed to it. Striker had warned her about Lilly. Takala had all but decided to let it go, not tell Lilly a thing.

Still, she couldn't go home without making sure Lilly was safe. She wasn't about to let her mother get caught in the crossfire between Striker and Raithe.

No, she couldn't allow that. She'd have to find a way to warn Lilly and get her to safety. But after seeing the handiwork of Laeyar, she was torn between stopping him, possibly finding a lead to Raithe and helping Lilly. Raithe needed stopping; she was on that wagon, but not at Lilly's expense. She just had to pick the right moments and make them both happen. Somehow.

Takala stepped into the hot shower, and as she soaped up her body, the memory of Striker kissing her came back full force. She groaned, trying to force it away, but it was impossible. He had kissed her twice. The first time on the plane seemed like a dream, but bits of it came to her, the shiver of excitement, his will forcing her to succumb to him. The second time in the bar she had given in to her passion and she had wanted more. No denying it. She craved a taste of the danger she felt, that overpowering sense that he would devour her whole. She'd never experienced that with a guy. Never. It was always her passion that consumed the guy she was with. What would it feel like to make love to a vampire who felt more desire than she could even dream about? Thoughts of it sent chill bumps through her, and she turned the water to a hotter setting.

Across the hall, Striker listened to Brawn and Katalinga updating him on Culler's movements. Thanks to the cleaners, Katalinga was her normal, healthy, efficient, accommodating self.

"She ordered room service twice and hasn't moved," Katalinga said, staring down at her phone with her cat eyes.

"Called anyone?" Striker asked.

"No," Brawn added.

"Very well. Keep up the good work, and no slip-ups."

"Right, sir." Brawn couldn't draw his gaze from Katalinga's butt as they left his room.

Striker made a mental note to switch the partners. Sexual attraction among agents was dangerous, not to mention it ruined their efficiency. If he was going to track down Raithe, he needed all his agents working at one hundred percent.

He found himself drawn to the door, mesmerized by what was going on in Takala's room. He could hear her taking a shower, her uneven breaths, the pounding of her heart, sense the temperature rise of her body. He imagined standing in the shower with her, touching her, the sweet scent of her damp clean skin. This was torture. He had told his staff to put him across the hall from her so he could keep an eye on her. But he could have left that to his agents and stayed in the B.O.S.P. safe house in the Châtelet area of Paris.

He kept a casket there with his homeland soil in it. He could have slept very soundly miles away. He should have been prudent, but he wanted to stay close to Takala. He couldn't trust her not to get in his way or do something stupid like let Culler know that he was watching her. He had to keep her under control, and he couldn't trust anyone else to do it.

Takala's strange resemblance to his sister plagued him. He had tossed that painful image of his sister away long ago, but Takala had dredged it up. And he was feeling again, experiencing the painful twitches of having loved his family, like needles being sewn through his heart. Takala, with her beautiful proud face, was a constant reminder of that bittersweet time in his life. He wanted no reminders of love. None. He just wanted Raithe.

He ground his jaws together and walked to his overnight bag. He pulled out a plastic pouch. The freeze-dried blood looked like the color of liver. He made a face at it, then poured cold water from a pitcher into the bag. He kneaded it with his hands, thinking of the sweet scent of Takala's blood.

This desire for her was becoming an obsession. He had to end it. Here and now. Perhaps that was another reason he'd taken this room: to prove he was above wanting her. He put the bag in the microwave, hit forty-five seconds. It beeped, and he took the bag out.

He raised the pouch to his lips, bit the bag, sucked it down in gulps. The metallic stale taste didn't come close to fresh blood, but it kept him alive. He retracted his fangs and tossed the empty container into the recycle bucket, then loosened his tie and fell back on the bed.

He could hear the shower stop. He envisioned her naked body wet, the pulsing of veins, the sweet taste of her mouth. He rolled on his side and stuffed the pillow over his head.

Chapter 13

Takala ran for her life. She held Lilly's hand as they dashed toward the Eiffel Tower, sprinting for the steps. The tower's lights gleamed out into the darkness like thousands of beckoning eyes, guiding their way.

"This way." Takala pulled Lilly toward the stairs, hearing pursuing footfalls getting closer and closer.

"No, this way." Lilly jerked her forward to an elevator.

"No, Mom."

"You never listen. We'll die! He'll catch us. I don't want you to die because of me."

"I won't." Takala felt the determination to keep her mother alive like an iron anvil expanding in her chest. "Come on, faster."

Takala forced her mother to the stairs, past signs for the restaurants inside the tower. Up, up they ran, so many flights. She couldn't breathe fast enough, couldn't catch her breath.

The footsteps behind them pounded louder still.

"Oh my God, he's going to get us," Lilly said.

"No, he's not." Takala reached a landing and pulled up short.

Striker blocked their way. He had the most evil leer she'd ever seen on any face, fangs exposed, eyes solid black. "You're here. Let me help." He extended his hand.

"Don't take it!" Lilly pulled Takala back.

Footsteps stopped on the stairwell behind them.

Takala wheeled and saw Striker. Two Strikers. This one had his fangs bared, blood dripping from the corners of his mouth. He said, "He's evil. Take *my* hand. *I'll* help you."

Lilly screamed, "Never!"

The Striker in front of her commanded, "Takala, come with me."

She felt a kind of tractor beam taking over her body, and she knew it was Striker's will. He forced her toward him. Her hand wasn't connected to her body; she couldn't vary the path. Any second she'd touch his fingers, and she knew something dreadful would happen. She trembled and shook as she tried to fight his power.

"Trust me," he demanded.

Lilly seized Takala's hand. "No, you can't have my daughter!"

"She's mine already." The Striker behind them grabbed Lilly and tossed her over the railing.

Takala still had a death lock on Lilly's hand; the weight of Lilly's body jerked her to the railing.

"Don't let go!" Lilly yelled up at Takala, thrashing against the metal tower railings.

Takala couldn't use her strength to pull Lilly up. What was wrong? All she could do was hold on. She felt Lilly's fingers slipping from her own. No, no, no!

Then Lilly was flying, screaming, her face contorted and bloated by the force of gravity sucking her down.

Takala screamed…

She felt someone shaking her, and Takala thrashed at them.

Suddenly her arms were trapped in a vise. She opened her eyes and stared into Striker's face.

Takala realized she was still screaming, and she closed her mouth, her heart hammering its way out of her chest, her body covered in perspiration. Striker held her so tightly she found it hard to breathe.

When she could speak, she said, "Let me go. *Now*."

He backed off and dropped his arms. He looked wounded by the glare she was shooting him. "I heard you scream," he said.

"I thought you needed permission to enter a room."

"That's Hollywood. I go wherever I want."

"Where's Lilly?" Takala scrambled out the opposite side of the bed from where Striker sat.

She realized she was wearing only her bra and panties when the cold air hit her skin. And to judge by the sudden fascinated expression on his face, he was enjoying the view. "Stop looking at me like that. Where's Lilly? I want to see her."

"What is the matter with you? Are you going to let a nightmare turn you into a raving lunatic?"

"I just need to see Lilly."

"I cannot let you do that."

"Don't tell me what I can and can't do." Takala was flinging clothes out of her carry-on. She found a pair of jeans and a sweater and slid into them; then she was pulling on her boots. His grin had vanished, but he was still devouring the sight of her as she said, "I need to know that she's okay."

"I give you my word she's all right."

"I have to see for myself." Takala picked up a brush and quickly ran it through her hair, feeling his gaze following her every move.

"Who are you? You are not the same woman I left at the door three hours ago."

"Who are you, underneath all that charm and the starched suits?" She paused, aware she might be going a little mad. But that dream. "I must see Lilly." Takala headed for the door.

Striker was there in seconds, blocking her way. "I won't have my one lead to Raithe compromised because of you."

She realized his irresistibly handsome face had more color in it; his lips were red instead of pink. He must have fed. Who did he have for dinner?

The thought irritated her as she said, "I won't tell her about you. I'll say I searched for her hotel and found her. I just need to make sure she's okay."

"She is fine. I have agents watching her every move."

"That's what you keep saying."

"I will not argue with you about this, but I *will* let you see her." He pulled out his cell phone.

One day he would see that she didn't need his permission. "How do I know this isn't a trick?"

"I could have made you believe it." He shot her a superior look.

That's what he thought. She wasn't about to tell him that his hypnotic suggestions had no sway over her. She only stared hard at him and said, "All the more reason not to trust you."

The purple of his eyes turned the color of coal. "Unfortunately, I am the only person you *can* trust."

She searched his eyes and saw a depthless dark void that could pull her down into it in seconds if she let it. She heard herself saying, "All right. Let me see her."

His eyes narrowed slightly in thought, then Lilly's likeness materialized on the one-inch screen. She was lying on her bed, watching television. Prevalent dark circles had formed under her eyes, and she looked weary.

"How does this work?" She motioned toward the phone.

"Crystal energy. All I have to do is think about her, and the image displays here." He pointed to the small screen. "I wouldn't lie to you, Takala."

"You would if I got in your way of getting Raithe. I think you'd lie to the devil to get Raithe."

"How can I gain your trust?" he said, that confident glibness gone from his voice.

"You have to earn it."

"I thought I had."

"It'll take more than a few confidences and that charming vampire charisma you have." Takala gulped, remembering how she'd opened up to him. He'd been kind and patient the way he had listened and offered her advice. Up until now, he'd only been nice, aside from glamouring her and the arrogant way he bossed her around. It might be his suave way of manipulating her, too.

She stared long and hard at the image on the screen. Lilly had sneezed, and she was wiping her nose with a tissue. "Is another agent's phone image the same?"

He nodded.

"I'd like to see one."

He flung open his phone and barked an order. Immediately a knock sounded at the door.

Takala answered it. Brawn paused at the door, eying them both as if unsure why he'd been summoned.

Takala said, "I need to see your image of Lilly."

Brawn quickly pulled out his phone and showed her. Lilly balling up the tissue she had used and tossing it into a trash can. Two points. She smiled to herself.

Takala stared at the image for a moment. Then she felt satisfied. She said, "Thanks."

"Sure." Brawn nodded and left.

Striker said, "The sun sets in twenty minutes. Laeyar will be stirring."

"We better hurry." Takala grabbed her coat, then remembered something. "Hey, I want my gun back."

"Look in your carry-on."

Takala scrounged through the few rolled-up shirts and jeans she'd packed at the bottom of the bag and found the Glock. She checked the clip. Empty.

"Is this some kind of joke?"

"I do not call keeping you safe a joke."

"Hey, I have a permit to carry a concealed weapon.

I know how to use one." She shook the gun and empty clip at him.

"Unless you have silver bullets, a gun is useless against the evil we are fighting. Your silver bracelets will keep you safer than that weapon."

Takala knew arguing with a know-it-all, arrogant vampire was useless. She'd find bullets somewhere. She popped the clip back in and stuffed the gun in the holster she'd made for her left boot. The many silver bracelets on her wrist rattled and caused him to glower at her.

"You're still carrying it?" he asked.

"Feel naked without it." She saw his gaze languidly comb her body as if he were trying envision her with no clothes. A tingling frizzed through her belly. She tried to ignore it while she stuffed her arms in her coat and flicked her hair out from beneath the collar. "You got a problem with it?"

"Not if you keep it concealed."

"Don't worry, I only flash it around in a crowd." She pursed her lips at him and stepped out the door, leaving him to glower at her.

"You are aware we're being followed?" Takala swiped lipstick across her bottom lip, then gazed to the right of her reflection in the passenger-side mirror. Yep, the two headlights were still there. The car had been following them since they left the hotel.

"Our backup," he said.

"You could have told me." She was actually glad they weren't alone. She hadn't looked forward to going into that tunnel with a bunch of hungry, angry vamps ready to pounce on the people who had set their food supply free. When Takala thought about the humans lucky enough to have gotten free, it started her wondering how many others died like that, and how many other human restaurants they had hidden in Paris alone.

"You're on a—"

"Need-to-know basis." She finished his sentence. "Hey, either I'm in or out. What's it gonna be?"

"Looks as if I have no choice but to let you in," he said.

"Okay. I'm going to ask a question, and I'd like a straight answer."

"Very well."

"How many feeding warrens do you think Laeyar may have in Paris?"

"Hard to tell. Depends on how large a family he has to support. It could be one or more."

"So he could be feeding an army."

"Yes."

Takala saw the victims again, and fear ground through her gut. "Do you know Laeyar?"

"We have a history."

Takala didn't like the sound of Striker's voice when he'd spoken. There were so many shadows and shades of darkness looming below the words. "Why was he feeding this serpent shifter?"

"Using him for his own gain, no doubt. I've had recent reports of brothel owners in Paris disappearing. One was even attacked in his bed, claiming it was a monstrous snake."

"So he was a hired killer?"

"Probably."

"You think he worked for Laeyar or Raithe?"

"I am hoping both."

"You think Laeyar will lead you to Raithe?"

"Nothing will be that easy when it comes to finding Raithe. I've hunted him for hundreds of years. He covers his tracks and evades me at every turn. I have no expectations that Laeyar is in Raithe's inner circle, for he allows very few into his confidence, and, if he does, he eventually kills them. So, to answer your question, no, but Laeyar might have information or know someone who is in contact with Raithe."

Takala lapsed into silence and listened to the road noise strumming loud in her ears. She hadn't broached this subject yet, and since Lilly was caught between them, she needed an answer. "Why are you so obsessed with finding Raithe? I know it's got to be more than a State Department warrant. This thing is soul deep with you, isn't it?"

Striker's mouth hardened, and his cheeks looked deeper than usual. He wouldn't look at her, his gaze glued to the road. "I have never told anyone other than my priest."

"Your what?"

"Father Sean O'Malley is a great friend."

"He hears your confession?" Takala couldn't imagine any of the priests she knew hearing a vampire's confession. They'd probably die of a heart attack if one walked into their parish.

"Actually, we go to lunch on Fridays in the District, and we talk. It is a form of confession."

"How did you meet?"

"Interesting happenstance, that. He was a vampire hunter, and I spared his life. He was so shaken by my act of mercy, that a vampire could actually show compassion, he became a priest. I got an invitation to his ordination, and we've been friends since. His church is half a block from the B.O.S.P. office."

A vampire and a priest, friends? "You astound me," she said, meaning it.

"We are not all bloodthirsty villains as the Hollywood producers would have you believe." He cocked a brow at her.

"Sometimes I wonder if *they* are vampires."

"Some are."

"Like who?"

"State secret." His lips parted in a slow, easy smile that held just enough guarded secrecy to maintain his enigmatic mystique.

"Does one of them have a last name that starts with a T?"

He nodded.

"Hah, I knew it." She realized he had skillfully managed to not tell her about Raithe, and she said, "So, Father O'Malley hears your confession. Do you have a lot to confess?"

"I try not to."

"But don't you have to drink human blood to live?"

"I drink freeze-dried blood that my lab provides. The base comes from slaughterhouses."

"Can't you drink from a human without killing them?"

His expression darkened. "I can, but I won't. Everything I've worked so hard to destroy inside me will be reborn. Once I taste fresh human blood…" His voice trailed off, and he seemed lost in a memory of doing just that.

"You won't be able to control yourself, is that what you're telling me?"

He nodded.

"You're stronger than that."

He turned to look at her now, the purple in his eyes artful and depthless and hiding a stoic ruthlessness that seemed to be buried within him. She wouldn't want to be the main course at his table.

"You don't know what I can become," he said, a warm touch of warning riding just below the surface of his voice. "I hope you never see it."

Takala felt a shiver chill her to the bone. She couldn't begin to imagine a vampire with his strength turning into a bloodthirsty killer. She wanted to believe he wasn't capable of giving in to his true nature, that he was just trying to scare her, but now she could see a possibility that he was just being honest. Still, she wasn't about to give up so easily on him, not as easily as he was willing to give up on himself.

"But you've gone years without drinking human blood."

"It is not easy. The cravings are still there." His gaze swept her, and it was avaricious and predatory and visceral, and she knew she was seeing a hint of what he could become.

She remembered how he had had to leave Laeyar's den after seeing the blood, how he'd mentioned her blood and kissed her hand. A tremor tore through her chest, and her breath caught in her throat, and the image of him in her dreams crashed back into her mind, his fangs extended, blood trickling from them, fighting his power to sway her. She leaned back in her seat, struggling to control her pounding heart.

"I frightened you." He seemed a little too pleased with himself.

"You didn't," she lied.

"Why is your heart thumping like you just ran a mile?"

"Would you please stop listening to my organs? It's creeping me out."

They said nothing else to each other, and Takala realized he'd managed to dodge her question about his revenge issues with Raithe. Later, she promised herself.

"So, do you date?" As soon as the words left her mouth she regretted them. It was something you asked a guy in high school, and it sounded so personal and prying.

"Not for a couple hundred years."

"Wow, a long time to be alone." She couldn't imagine living such an isolated life, not needing the touch and adoration of another soul, living so long that you became emotionally isolated from everyone. She felt her heart going out to him. There was something so solitary and depressing about it.

"When you dated, did you prefer humans or vampires?" She didn't know why his mating habits interested her, but they did.

"Female vampires. They do not easily become emotionally involved and expect nothing from you."

"You think human women are too clingy?"

"Let's just say they demand more than I can give them."

The coldness in his words made her shiver; then she felt the car slowing and glanced up to see they were pulling into a parking space near the subway entrance. She was so lost in Striker's private life, she hadn't realized they were this close.

A steady stream of people moved up and down the stairs, the rush-hour pedestrians in a hurry to make it home. When Takala thought of the dark tunnel and what could be waiting for them, she didn't know if that frightened her half as much as the vampire sitting next to her.

Chapter 14

Seconds later, Striker touched her arm and said, "Stay here." His gaze held hers for a few moments, as if he'd brook no opposition.

Why wasn't he trying to glamour her? Then he answered her question.

"So you will trust me, I'm not using my telepathy on you. I am asking you to do the wise thing and stay here." There was an open honesty and respect in his manner that surprised her.

She found herself nodding. "Okay," she said.

After a long assessing glance, he left.

She looked in the rearview mirror and couldn't see his reflection. She carefully glanced over her shoulder and found him.

He was meeting with four people, three guys and a woman. They were dressed casually, like the average Joe on the street, but their skin was pale and pasty in the streetlamp lights. Vampires. Agents she'd never seen before. She guessed he had hundreds stashed around France.

He'd left the key in the ignition, and she rolled down a back window and tried to hear what they were saying. She caught snippets.

"It could be dangerous," Striker said. "Lion, you guard Miss Rainwater."

A tall, thin guy with a bloodhound face and a crew cut nodded and glanced Takala's way.

She quickly straightened and looked ahead and felt a little betrayed and manipulated. So he hadn't believed she would keep her word at all. What a smooth operator. That bit about not using his powers on her was priceless.

"The rest of you, follow me."

They disappeared in a flash of spiraling shadows; then the sidewalk was empty save for Lion. He took up a stance, leaning next to a brick building, his gaze on the car. She saw he was dressed like a biker, with studs on his black leather jacket, holey-kneed jeans with frayed bottoms, and thick combat boots.

Takala fumed at Striker's underhanded tricks, and that was when chaos erupted.

She heard thumps and grunts. One quick glance behind her, and she saw Lion getting attacked by four vampires.

In a second, she was out the door.

That was when someone grabbed her collar. Then her neck was in a headlock. Takala wasn't going down without a fight. She stomped on a big foot, then elbowed the person, throwing them over her head and down onto the car.

She glimpsed the big hairy face of a vampire. He was huge, big as a tree trunk, with no neck. All muscle. And she could tell by the snarl on his fanged mouth that he wasn't used to having his ass kicked by a human female.

He leapt at her again, flying through the air, his vampire body seeming weightless. He crashed into Takala, and they both went down.

She pounded his face, going at him with both fists.

He rolled on top of her, pinning her arms.

She jerked up her legs, captured his neck between her ankles and pulled down with all her strength.

He came up and off her.

A square kick to the gut.

He careened back through the air, hitting the brick building.

Takala felt another attacker behind her, going for her arms.

Then another on her legs. She went down.

"Get the bitch! Watch out, she's strong as an ox."

Someone else piled on her. They flipped her like a fish out of water. Her face and stomach slammed against the pavement. Then three of the vampires grabbed her arms, legs and neck. Something wrapped around her wrists and ankles; then she moved so fast her head hurt.

She had the presence of mind to dig her nails into her palm and let the blood drip from her hand. But the velocity at which she moved was too much for her atoms. She felt as if her body was going to explode. Then she lost consciousness.

* * *

Striker knew something was wrong. The tunnel was empty. In the periphery of his mind, he had kept track of Takala's heartbeat. Now it was pounding and becoming hard to hear.

"Come with me." Striker reached the car in seconds. The door was open, the light still burning on the inside.

He ran to Lion and shook him. He roused and looked dazed. "What happened?" Striker asked.

"Laeyar has her. I tried to protect her. There were too many."

Striker felt his chest tightening, fear pulsing through his veins. Laeyar would kill her. "I want her found. Span out. Find her!"

At the deadly quiet in his voice, his agents disappeared. Striker started searching, too, his fear building by the second. She wouldn't last a minute with that honey-scented blood of hers.

Takala woke to the stench of moldy sewer and filth and something wet gliding along her palm. She opened her eyes and knocked whatever was licking her hand away.

She saw a female vampire's head fly back from the blow, her long black greasy hair billowing out around her body. She looked about thirteen and snarled at Takala, rubbing her mouth. She spoke something in French, then shot Takala the finger.

"Likewise." Takala felt the heavy manacles that shackled her wrists and the tiny wound she had made in her palm so Striker could track her. So that's what the teenage vamp had been licking. Takala closed the wounded palm tightly and glanced around her.

She was in some kind of basement, the dampness making her shiver. Plumbing pipes hissed overhead. Candles in empty glass jars burned around the dingy room. Caskets were stuffed up between the pipes, supported by metal fittings. Then she spotted Square Face, the brute who had attacked her near the car. He sat on an old empty keg, holding court, two female vampires hanging on either side of his wide shoulders. His bloodshot eyes had a bland, empty look, as if they'd never had much in them.

His female companions were twins, about thirty, brunettes covered in snarled dreadlocks. They wore glowing black lipstick and eyeliner, both stark against their pasty faces. Another male vamp, short and squatty and half the size of Square Face, reclined on a pipe. He had the number 666 tattooed on his forehead. All eyes were centered on Takala and the young vamp who crept toward her again.

Takala said, "I hope one of you speaks English, because I'm gonna hurt your little pet here if she tries that again."

Square Face snapped an order at the girl, and she hissed like a cat and backed away into the shadows. The nicer side of vampires. Takala found herself comparing Striker to these cretins. He seemed much more evolved and refined, yet in his own way just as deadly.

"You make threats when my family is hungry," Square Face said in broken English.

"That's not my problem." Takala added more bravado to her words than she felt.

He jammed a finger at her. "You raided their pantry, and you dare be flippant about it?"

"You were torturing and killing people. Should I have just stood back and let it continue?"

"You meddle with a vampire's food source and you quickly learn that you are on the dinner plate." He chuckled, a deadly, threatening sound.

His voice crawled along her skin like tiny spider legs. Panic clenched her gut.

He sniffed the air. "And, might I add, your blood smells sweet as candy, *mademoiselle*. It'll be my pleasure to rip you open and let them feed. What are you? Not totally human, I think—not with that strength." He raised his nose and breathed her in again.

Right now she was scared, but she couldn't say that. "I'm human with a little extra muscle thrown in. Nothing special." She turned the conversation. "You must be Laeyar." She tried to sound in awe, while fear chewed at her insides.

He seemed flattered and bowed. He couldn't manage a bow with all the tight flesh at his middle, so it was more of a deep head nod. "At your service, *mademoiselle*." He rubbed the full brown beard on his face.

"I've heard a lot about you."

"Pray, what have you heard?"

"That you're the man to see if I wish to get in contact with Raithe," Takala said.

Laeyar laughed. "I'm the only one he will see."

"Then you're truly special," she said, pandering to his ego, wondering if he was lying. If she were Raithe, she would want nothing to do with someone like him. But even cretins had their uses, she guessed. Still, it felt like he was lying. He seemed the type who liked to blow his own horn.

An unexpected cunning ember showed in his eyes, a hint of intelligence glowing there as if he had finally figured out the compliment. "What business do you have with him?"

"That's my concern."

"You tell me, or you don't ever see him." He looked stubbornly at her like a bull that wouldn't move.

He'd taken the bait. He'd demand more information. She said, "All right, I'll tell you. I wish to exchange Striker Dark's life for Lilly Smith." Takala had no intention of that, but she knew it might be a good lure.

When she mentioned Striker, Laeyar tried to hide the flicker of concern in his eyes. Then they turned almost calculating. "You're one of his agents. Why would you suddenly betray him?"

"First of all, I'm not one of his agents."

"You're with him." He shot her an accusatory glance.

"I was Lilly's bodyguard. Then we got separated because Raithe's men wanted her dead. Nightwalker is only helping me keep Lilly safe."

"You would betray Nightwalker when he gives you and this Lilly Smith protection. You are either a fool or very cunning. I just haven't figured out which." He turned back to 666 and asked, "Who is Lilly Smith?"

"A flesh peddler for Raithe."

Flesh peddler sounded horrid coming from the vampire's mouth, but Takala knew that could have been Lilly's cover.

Laeyar shifted his gaze to Takala. "What is she to you?"

"A good friend," Takala said, unwilling to let go of her secret. "I only want her to be safe."

Laeyar laughed, showing his wide tongue. "Then I pity you for having such misspent loyalty."

"What do you mean?"

He only laughed louder, a rolling belly laugh.

Takala wanted to kick him in the gut. She shifted her gaze to the girl. She didn't like the way she was slinking toward her like a rat, that insatiable glare in her eyes.

"It doesn't matter," Laeyar said. "I'm not introducing you to Raithe. Do you think me ignorant enough to take you right beneath Nightwalker's nose, only to let you go so you can see Raithe, or worse, report back to Nightwalker?"

"I wouldn't."

"I know, *mademoiselle,* because I'll never let it happen. Your death will be a message to Nightwalker. He'll know better than to intrude upon my hunting grounds again. Maybe I'll leave him a piece of you as a present."

"He'll find you and kill you."

Laeyar laughed, but it was forced. The other vamps gave a nervous little chuckle, too. "If I know him, he cares little for you outside his own agenda." He tsk-tsked his tongue at her. She saw it was oddly pointed and fat and coated with red scum. "Anyway, Nightwalker will not be so easily double-crossed. He'd never let himself be set up, unless you hold something over him. Do you?"

Quick, what could she say? "We're lovers," she lied.

Laeyar threw back his head and chuckled, the veins

in his tree-trunk neck bulging, mouth wide open, the tips of his yellow fangs bared.

An image of Laeyar driving his pointed teeth into her skin made the hairs on the back of her neck prickle.

When Laeyar had given her enough histrionics to make his point, he sobered and said, "Nightwalker doesn't keep mates these days." He turned sarcastic. "He's setting the example for all of us. Walking the straight and narrow—or could he have fallen into degradation with the rest of us?" This was a rhetorical question. Takala believed Laeyar liked to hear himself speak as he answered it. "No, I think not. You would be dead by now if you tempted him that much. If he went back to his old ways, he wouldn't have been able to stop from draining you dry. You see, *mademoiselle,* our nature is to kill, and when we deny ourselves this basic instinct for as long as Nightwalker has, we tend to get a little hungry." His large lips split in the grin of a cat that had cornered its prey.

Takala hoped to keep him talking and said, "How long have you known Nightwalker?"

"Since the eighteen hundreds."

"What was he like before he gave up the dark side?"

He raised a thick brow at her last two words. "Dark side? It is pure happiness."

"Okay, what was he like before he gave up his happiness?"

He had to close his eyes to dredge up the memories. "Nightwalker was, um, how you say, respected, when he was Raithe's first in command. But Nightwalker broke away, became a loner."

"What happened between them?"

"I know not, *mademoiselle*. This was before my time. I do know Raithe is older, more powerful. A god really. Nothing can stop him."

"If he can die, he can be stopped."

He shook a sausage-size finger at Takala. "No one has been able to kill him, not even Nightwalker. It cannot be done."

"I wouldn't be so sure. Nightwalker will not stop until he has him."

"Nightwalker is a fool. He should forget the bad blood between them." He laughed at his own pun. "He'll regret it if he continues to pursue Raithe. When he grows bored with Nightwalker's games, he will kill him."

"I can make it easy for him and give him Night-walker."

"You're a spinner of yarns, *mademoiselle*." He crossed his massive arms over his chest and glanced at her. "And not a very good one at that. I'm going to take great pleasure in eating you."

"What will Raithe say when he hears of my offer and that you denied him the pleasure of turning me down himself?"

"No one knows you're here. Even if Nightwalker comes looking for you, we'll be long gone. And there's no danger of him telling Raithe."

"You're wrong. I left word on the street and in the Petite la Belle that I'm looking for Raithe. I believe he was a friend of the snake shifter, your buddy."

A myriad of expressions passed over his face: uncertainty, indecision, anger, hunger, then finally fear.

She knew then that Laeyar had no connection to Raithe, had no idea how to locate him.

"Why would you feed a creature like that anyway? Keeping him for a pet?" Takala had a suspicion that the snake shifter was using his connection with Raithe to force Laeyar to feed him.

"He is good to have around," Laeyar said casually, pretending to pick at a hangnail.

"But eats a lot."

Laeyar lost his temper and glared at her. "That is my business, since I feed him. And you needn't worry about it now, anyway. I will not trouble Raithe with you, word on the street or not. You are our dinner." He heaved himself up off his keg throne and walked toward her, sniffing the air like a hungry wolf. "And I'll be the first to have you."

The young girl, the twins, and 666 were aroused by his words and gathered behind him, their fangs jutting, bloodlust in their eyes. They stared at her like she was dessert.

"Hurry, Laeyar, and leave some for us," 666 said.

Laeyar's fangs jutted out and over his fat lips, and he was on her in a blink.

Takala felt the saliva of his tongue, the tips of his fangs on her neck.

Chapter 15

Out of the corner of her eye, Takala saw a blur. Then Laeyar's head twisted to an impossible angle as his neck snapped. His body toppled to the floor, and she stared into Striker's severe face. She was never so glad to see anyone in her life. He didn't look at all happy to see her.

The vampires realized he was there and had killed their leader. They attacked him from every angle.

Striker moved so fast she only caught glimpses of his face and hands.

The young girl disappeared into the shadows, but 666 and the twins were bolder.

There was no contest. Even at three-to-one odds, Striker downed them with the methodical precision of a master predator. A whirlwind blur of savage force. Vampires fell like dominoes. She knew they would rise again, because Striker hadn't decapitated or staked them. He had only inconvenienced them.

When the carnage ended, he materialized in front of her, eyes dark and cloudy, deep in defensive mode.

"Are you all right?" His gaze took in every inch of her.

"Timed it kinda close, didn't you?" She teased him with a trembling grin.

"It took me a moment or two to find the trail of blood you left."

"I knew you'd pick up the scent," she said confidently. "Wait a minute. How long have you been here?"

"Awhile."

"And you almost let that cretin kill me."

"You were never in any danger. And I wanted to hear how far you would go in bargaining away my life."

"I only did it—"

"To help catch Raithe, I know. You were quite convincing at times." His purple eyes shimmered with amusement. He pulled on the manacles, and they burst with a loud clank.

"I tried to break those chains, but couldn't." She rubbed her wrists. "How much stronger are you than me?"

"No contest." He eyed her in that charming way he had that set the butterflies fluttering in her gut. Then he swept her up into his arms.

She couldn't get over the fact he'd picked her up like she weighed no more than a toothpick. She was no lightweight. She'd never had a guy do the Rhett Butler sweep before. Even as strong as Akando was, he couldn't pick her up. He'd tried once and hurt his back. He had spent hours in an emergency room, downing muscle relaxers.

She liked playing Scarlett to his Rhett Butler. It made her feel delicate and awkward, and to her chagrin, very, very feminine. It was like trying on a new dress that fit perfectly. And the butter-rum, clean-linen smell of him was driving her a little crazy. She found herself wrapping her arms around his neck and laying her head against his cheek.

She breathed him in and forced her mind off her unruly libido and back on the business at hand. "Laeyar didn't even know Raithe, but I guess you figured that out."

"Right away."

"Looks like we've reached a dead end."

A door closed above their heads. The sound echoed down the stairs.

"That must be the girl escaping." Takala glanced up the dark staircase that Striker approached. "Are we going to follow her?"

"No. The others will find her when they come around. She is a neophyte, not much of a problem. She will probably feed on dogs or rats."

Takala made a face and said, "You do have a heart when it comes to some vampires. Admit it."

"I just do not have the time or the manpower to track her down."

Takala wasn't buying that. He had a soft spot for the young girl. She glanced down at the limp pale bodies on the floor. "Are you just going to let them continue to kill?"

"No, I have already called the French director and

alerted him about their behavior. He'll see they are policed."

"The French have a supernatural bureau, too?"

He nodded and said, "The Département d'affaires Supernaturelles, French Department of Supernatural Affairs. It is as efficient as the B.O.S.P."

"Where are we?" Takala glanced up the stairwell as he carried her up it.

"The basement of an abandoned store."

He reached the top of the stairs, and they were inside. A streetlight shone through the broken boards that were supposed to be securing the building. She could see graffiti and holes covering the broken plaster walls. Grocery cases lay overturned and smashed. The windows were boarded up, but some of the boards, like the door, were jagged or missing. An air of empty gloominess fanned the abandoned building. Considering who took up residence in the basement, she hoped it would be torn down.

She should ask Striker to let her walk, but at the moment she felt secure in his arms. He could have carried her anywhere and she wouldn't have protested.

He easily maneuvered through the holes in the door and stepped out onto the sidewalk. The area seemed quiet, save for a few druggies on a corner.

She felt his blond ponytail thick beneath her forearm. What would it be like to run her fingers through his hair again? She remembered it being soft as silk, not coarse and lifeless as she thought it would be. She watched the streetlight shimmering through it, mesmerizing her. Then she recalled his lips on hers, and heat poured through her body, making her palms sweat and her heart speed up.

"Takala, be careful."

"What?"

"You are sexually aroused." He had spoken without an inflection in his voice, bluntly, a statement she couldn't refute.

Still she said, "I'm not." She pulled her arms from around his neck, feeling suddenly self-conscious.

"I hear your pulse running wild, smell the perspiration on your skin, the female pheromones dripping off you."

"It's only my metabolism, okay?" She knew he knew she had lied, but his awareness of her desire disconcerted her. It solidified her position on men. They just ruined her life. "Put me down," she said.

He ignored her request and said, "You do not know what danger you are in when you tempt me like that."

"Tempt you? I didn't—"

His kiss cut off her words. He devoured her lips. The coarse stubble of his chin tantalized her soft skin. She grew bold and brought her hands up, capturing his cheeks, eagerly smothering his lips. His forceful domination roused her, poured through her like molten steel, made her ache to have him. She thrust her tongue along his lips, demanding entrance.

He growled, a primitive sound, and opened for her. Takala drove her tongue into his moist depths.

Then she grew dizzy because she was moving at an unearthly speed. Suddenly the world stopped whirling without an axis. She realized he'd found a more private place for them: the side of the abandoned building.

He let her explore his mouth as he set her down and steadily waltzed her back against the side of the building. Then his tongue slid into her mouth, exploring the depths of her warmth. His forceful domination roused her, poured through her like hot lava. It wasn't like the tepid kisses from before. She was getting a taste of his unchecked desire. It made her ache all over to have him.

He slid a leg between her thighs, opening them, even as his hands went to her breasts and kneaded the high mounds.

Takala moaned and felt his erection rubbing the sensitive spot between her thighs.

"You taste extraordinary," he said against her mouth, his breath warm on her lips. The heat of her mouth still lingered in his.

"So do you," she whispered, rubbing her hands over his muscular chest, feeling his own heart throbbing, lost in the taste and feel of him.

He kissed her again, while his fingers moved up and over her breasts, then lingered at the base of her throat. She arched against him, moaning. He laid a finger on her jugular vein and left it there, feeling the pulse.

"You are too much of a temptation," he said, staring deep in her eyes.

She could see his fangs, extended. The all-consuming look in his eyes excited her like nothing she'd ever experienced before. His potent aura captured her, and she didn't want him to turn her loose. So this is what it felt like to experience a vampire's passion, one greater than her own. She found herself wanting to test the boundaries.

Suddenly a throat cleared.

Striker let out an impatient grumble, then immediately stepped back from her, his eyes consuming her.

Takala stared at him, wanting him, bombs still going off inside her body.

"Yes." Striker turned toward the vampire who looked like a bloodhound. Two other agents stood behind him.

Takala rarely blushed, but this was one of those "gotcha" moments that robbed her composure and caused the blood to rush to her cheeks. The interruption quickly put a distinct chill on her passion, and she couldn't believe how she'd been about to give herself over to him.

"Ah, yes, sir. Ah, s-sorry, sir...." The agent stumbled over his words. "You were gone so long we were worried."

"Thank you for your diligence." His words were as sharp as blades. "But as you can see, we are fine."

"Yes, sir." They turned and disappeared at the speed of light.

He broke the awkward moment between them. "That should never have happened."

His words struck her in the chest, and she found it hard to catch her breath for a moment. She stared back at him. His eyes were as black as coal and churning like class-five rapids.

"You kissed me," she threw back at him, hurting at this sudden rejection.

"I lost control."

The full brunt of what could have happened struck her, and she felt her insides quivering. She watched the flare of his nostrils, taking in her scent, and a shudder shook her body. Deep down she knew his strength was far greater than her own. No way she could have stopped him. Good grief, she hadn't wanted him to stop! That was the disturbing thing. She wanted to blame her passionate response on the glamouring, but he hadn't tried that vampire whammy on her.

At her silence, he said, "We shall have to keep a professional distance from now on."

"We can if you keep your lips to yourself." Takala threw out the last words like a snowball, turned and hurried off down the sidewalk.

She felt his gaze tracking her every movement and didn't care. She thought about parting company with him right then and there. But he was having Lilly watched, and the only way she could truly be certain of Lilly's safety was to stick to him like flypaper. So she trudged back to the car and got in.

He arrived in seconds, his presence like a looming predator. He started up the car.

Takala might have to stay close to him, but she didn't have to speak to him. With each passing second, pressure built in her throat, behind her eyes. Why she felt like crying, she didn't know. Maybe it was jet lag, or having her life threatened three times in two days, or Striker using Lilly as bait, or his saying their passion meant nothing. Professional distance. She'd show him what that was like. Her one goal was to keep Lilly safe, and that's what she intended to do.

Suddenly her phone vibrated, earning her a cutting glance from him.

She rolled her eyes at him. "Don't worry, this won't take long," she said.

He merely cocked an eyebrow at her.

She pulled out her phone, and Akando's number was blinking. Great! Just great! The more she watched the number flashing, the more she decided this wasn't so bad. She answered. "Hello."

"Takala, please don't hang up on me."

"Give me a reason not to."

She saw Striker's fingers tighten on the steering wheel and his brow wrinkle. Then he blinked, a sure sign he was annoyed. Served him right, kissing her and telling her it never should have happened.

"Because I love you, and I want you."

Striker's knuckles turned to tight-ridged bands across the back of his hands.

It didn't hurt to test the waters. "You're breaking up. What'd you say?" She knew Striker could hear every word spoken.

"I love you."

"Tell me again why you love me."

"You're the most bodacious, beautiful woman I know. Because you rock my world. Because I can't live without you. Tell me where you are."

"Why?"

"Because I want to see you. Make up with you."

Oh, he sounded sincere. She could almost forgive him, if she hadn't heard the voice of the woman he had slept with.

"I'll see you when I get back."

"No, tell me where you are."

Suddenly the phone was jerked out of her hand. Striker slammed it shut with one effortless motion.

"Hey!"

"I won't have this mission compromised by a civilian getting in the way." Striker handed her back the phone.

Was there a snippet of jealousy in those icy purple eyes, and in the tight set of his lips? "I had no intention of telling him where I am," she said.

"Fine. Don't." He sat in brooding silence for a moment, then said, "Are you considering letting him back into your life?"

"That's none of your business. You're on a need-to-know basis." She flung his own words back at him.

They said nothing else to each other.

Takala should have felt more empowered than she did. Was he truly jealous, or was he only worried about the mission as he had said? He seemed annoyed with her, that was certain, but was it because he felt a need to control her and her private life? Maybe his agents let him get away with that, but he'd learn soon enough that she didn't appreciate being bullied.

Chapter 16

They had been driving for what seemed like hours but had only been twenty minutes. They were heading away from the hotel, and she broke the mutual barrier of silence. "Hey, where are we going?"

"To a restaurant."

"I don't think that's wise, do you?" She was hungry. He could probably hear her stomach grinding away on empty bile acids. But she really didn't want to share a meal with him.

"You have to eat."

She couldn't argue that point. She was tired of his high-handed orders, so she added, "Okay, make it fast food."

He didn't respond, just kept his gaze on the road, tearing through the traffic like a bullet. Then the car slowed, threading into a street with lanes and lanes of traffic.

"It's twelve o'clock at night. Where are all the folks going?"

"Paris never sleeps."

Takala caught a glimpse of a lit street sign as they passed it: Champs-Elysées. Gaslights sparkled on the sidewalks and turned them to silver. Rows of chestnut trees towered over landscaped lawns and fountains. The gardens were in winter hibernation, but she could imagine what the flowers might look like in spring.

"Roll down your window, Takala. The Arc de Triomphe is coming up."

Takala touched the button. The cold air hit her in the face, but she didn't mind it for a famous glimpse of Paris. She could see a hulking stone monument spotlighted in front of them, getting larger and larger.

He said, "Napoleon began the stone arch in 1806, and it wasn't finished until 1836."

"How do you know?"

"I knew Napoleon."

"Was he a vamp—?

He nodded.

"Well, that explains a lot."

He pointed at the archway and said, "Look now."

Takala stuck her head out. All the pictures she'd seen of the famous stone arch did little justice to it. It was much larger, the car dwarfed as it sped underneath. It reminded her of the Natural Bridge in Virginia. She'd seen pictures of the Bridge her whole life, but when she had actually gone camping there with her sisters and grandmother, she'd been awed by its size.

"Awesome." Takala realized she was seeing her first tourist sight of Paris. When she pulled her head inside, she pushed the hair back from her face and said, "Thank you for taking me here."

"It's not that far out of our way," he said in an effortless dry tone.

Was she imagining things, or had a "moment" passed between them? Was he being nice, or just calculating? She told herself not to read too much into it, and she rolled up her window and kept her nose tight to the glass.

They had reached a place called the Tuileries Garden, or so the English sign proclaimed. It looked formal and beautiful. Moonlight glinted off the surface of the pond there, throwing thousands of blue diamonds over the surface.

"We will go to the Eiffel Tower, too."

"Not the Tower, thanks." The nightmare she'd had was bobbing on the surface of her memory, still clear. A warning rumbled through her as she realized that she'd almost fallen under Striker's spell, came a hair's width from taking his hand and letting him lead her down a path of danger. Maybe even death. What was wrong with her? She just wanted to believe there was more to him than the empty detachment that he portrayed to the world.

As if he could read her mind, their eyes met for a moment and held.

"Something wrong?" he asked.

"No." Takala gave the window her undivided attention.

They rode in silence for a while, until he said, "Look up ahead. You'll see the Louvre."

Takala spotted the hulking Romanesque building. It

filled two and half city blocks. One day she'd like to go inside. At least see the work of a few famous painters. Maybe get a gander at Leonardo da Vinci's *Mona Lisa* or see the Impressionists, Renoir, Degas and Monet. But at the moment, that seemed like an impossible daydream. The way things were going, she might not survive keeping Lilly alive.

Before long, they reached the Place de la Concorde. She asked about it and Striker supplied her with the details from his storehouse of knowledge. "This is the Square of Peace. Built in the seventeen hundreds. It holds eight huge statues, two fountains and the Obelisk of Luxor, a stone pillar from Egypt."

The pillar was the best-lit sculpture, and Takala caught a good view of it as Striker slowed the car to a crawl, much to the chagrin of the honking drivers behind them. He rolled down his window and waved them past.

Well, it wasn't like seeing the city on foot, but at least she'd been given a riding tour. "Thank you," she muttered.

"My pleasure."

They turned down a side street and paused before a restaurant, De la Vincennes Cuisine. It was shaped like a miniature castle, complete with turrets and crenellated walls. Flags of all nations spanned a portico. A red carpet led from the street to the door, where a doorman in red livery waited to invite guests inside. The second story rose above the wall. Dim candlelight flickered through narrow window slits. It looked like a restaurant you'd see in Disney World.

Striker pulled over and stopped at the awning.

"Hey, this isn't fast food."

"Did you really believe I'd let you eat in a fast-food restaurant?"

"This looks pricey," she said.

"But well worth it. You cannot leave France without sampling the food."

Takala wondered what Uncle Sam paid him to be the director of B.O.S.P. Had to be more than her meager income from her detective agency.

The doorman ran to open her door and said, *"Bon soir, mademoiselle."*

Striker hopped out of the car and instructed the valet to park it.

"I'm not dressed." Takala fussed with her hair. "I can't go in there looking like this."

"You will outshine all the women inside no matter what you are wearing." He held out his arm, looking so handsome in his suit, his dimpled chin, those wicked violet eyes gleaming like a satyr's.

Despite not wanting to, Takala felt herself warming to his compliment. She didn't think there was a woman alive who wouldn't. But he kept giving off mixed signals. Seducer one minute. Arrogant and domineering the next. On the way there a kind tour guide. Now an amiable dinner partner. Was this what he meant by professional distance? Maybe this was how he treated all women. Turn on the charm when necessary, lure them in, then, once hooked, use them like puppets. Well, he'd soon learn that she was made of stronger stuff than that.

She hesitated a moment longer, then took his arm. He stiffened, strain pulling at his arm muscles, moving up his neck and lips. An oppressive tension built between them. She could feel his body strung so tight his arm felt like granite. Her heart refused to stop thumping. Her awareness of him crashed like huge waves against her.

His forearm brushed her side, and her insides tightened into knots. Memories swarmed and she was back in his arms, kissing him, feeling his hands caressing her. She dreaded that he might read her vital signs and know that her libido was working overtime. When they reached the door, she was relieved. She quickly stepped away from him while the doorman opened the door. This was going to be one long night.

Striker saw Takala to a table. Then he said, "Excuse me for a moment."

She looked at him warily, as if she had done something to cause his desertion, so he added, "I'll be right back."

He walked to the restrooms, aware of the customers' eyes on him, mostly the females. He recognized a wolf shifter among them. He could spot them a mile off. They had wiry black, sometimes gray, hair. Their eyes were light blue, colorless, and they always had long noses. Their eyes met. Shifter to vampire. Striker nodded and kept moving.

Vampires did not metabolize human food, so they had no use for bathrooms. But he needed some distance from Takala. The restrooms were along a narrow hallway, and he stood near an ashtray, watching her across the restaurant. She was twining her hair around her finger while she read the wine list. He couldn't take his eyes off her. Her long legs crossed under the table, the way her jeans hugged her thighs, that beautiful face and expressive eyes. He remembered her hot body next to his own, the alluring smell of her, almost biting her. It made his soul quake. He had almost lost it. If Lion had not come when he did...

He felt himself growing antsy, and he stepped into the restroom. A waiter was just finishing up at a urinal. Striker headed to a back stall, the smell of urine and disinfectant assailing him. How could humans regularly use bathrooms? He only entered them in an emergency. And this was one.

He walked to the stall, already taking off his jacket. He closed the door, laid his coat on the top, and fished out the prepackaged dose of Meals Away, as the lab techs jokingly called it. He opened the package. The syringe was half the size of a normal syringe. And no needle necessary. It worked on air compression. He held the syringe between his teeth, took out his cufflink and rolled up his left sleeve. He set the vacuole over the middle of his inner arm and pressed the plunger. A burst of air penetrated his skin, carrying with it the serum that allowed him not to feed.

He'd already fed once today. He hoped that this injection would help curb his insatiable desire to taste Takala. He leaned back against the stall door, closed his eyes, felt the liquid enter his bloodstream. That strange euphoric feeling of satiety, of fullness, filled him. It came very close to the sensation of having fed, but it lacked the act and excitement of it, which he hadn't needed—until meeting Takala. He tasted spearmint in his mouth, and he knew he'd received the full dose.

His phone rang, and he put himself back to rights as he answered.

"Dark, that you?"

Striker smiled at the sound of his friend's voice. He spoke with a Scottish brogue, toned down by twenty years of living in the States. In the background, Striker heard people talking loudly, music playing, pool balls clacking. His friend must be in a bar.

"Yes, O'Malley, it is me."

"How the hell are yah doing? I was sitting here and knew I should be calling yah."

Striker didn't know how or why, but he and Father O'Malley had some kind of psychic connection. Perhaps it was divine providence, or the fact they had once tried to kill each other. Whatever caused it was beyond his knowledge. He'd stopped questioning it long ago.

"I'm glad you called." Striker meant that. "How have you been?"

"Forget about me. I want to be hearing about yah, laddie."

"Could not be better."

"You're forgetting who you're talking to. I know something's wrong. Been feeling it all day. Give it to me straight. You lose some men again?"

"Worse, it is a woman."

"Hmm, now yah really are in trouble. I thought yah were done with women, like me. Hasn't it been eons?"

"Yes, but I cannot get a handle on my desire for this one."

A long, flat pause, filled only by the bar noise. He heard O'Malley take a long swig on his beer.

"Have you nothing to say?" Striker asked. "No encouragement, no biblical platitudes?"

"You know what's right and wrong. You know you

can't get near the water, so it's better not to dip your oar in. I'm thinking God tests us, and this is your test. But God doesn't make it easy. If it was easy, all our paths to heaven would be paved in gold. It's his way to make things complicated. Yah could have feelings for this woman, and you're not knowing how to direct them."

Feelings? He couldn't remember ever caring about anyone other than his sister and parents. Surely this was just years of blood hunger resurfacing. True, she looked like Calliope and had opened up the painful wounds of her death. But care for Takala? "That is stretching it," he said, adding more than his normal uninterested tone to his words.

"Well, if yah don't care, then yah can conquer it. Yah've done it for a long time. Yah know the way. Keep to the yellow brick road, laddie."

"Thank you, Great Oz." He heard O'Malley chuckle, a deep belly-rolling sound. Then he said, "Take care of yourself."

"Yep, yah, too. And listen to what your heart is saying."

Striker closed the phone, sure his heart had been mute so long it had lost the ability to speak. He stopped to make sure his lapel and tie were in order and the vial was hanging where it should be, then walked back to the table.

Takala glanced up at him. He no longer saw the two different-colored eyes, only their expressiveness. They had a way of cutting into him, laying him wide open. Staying away from her was almost impossible. It was just like his desire to find Raithe: an insatiable need.

Chapter 17

Takala sat across from Striker, uncomfortable because his glances had grown infinitely patient and assessing, like a predator trying to decide his next move. He sat so immobile, a granite statue, looking deep into her eyes, as if he were reading her soul.

His eyes picked up the overhead lights and glistened like shards of cavernous quartz, reflections bouncing off them like endless mirrors.

She finished the last of her beef and potato gratin, looking everywhere except at his face. She was determined to forget their last encounter. But he was a sensual feast for her eyes. Handsomeness dripped off him like a waterfall that oozed all over the table and her. Her stomach turned over like she was on a roller-coaster ride. His scent of butter rum didn't help, nor did the fact that his black silk suit shined like a second skin and made his shoulders appear square and broad and utterly perfect male. And that golden hair, so soft, the ponytail trailing over his collar, those deep-set purple eyes hypnotizing the very air around them. Keep a professional distance from Agent Gorgeous here? Was that even possible?

She gulped her Merlot and fished around for a safe topic. "Tell me what started this hatred between you and Raithe," she said.

He ran a steady, unhurried finger around the rim of his glass. He hadn't touched his champagne. "I do not speak of it."

"But you'll tell me, right?" she asked, her tone softening to a question. "I told you all about my family, my miserable luck with men. All I know about you is that I look like your sister and you were probably a better gladiator than a physician." She tilted her head in a demure pose, a stiff smile on her face.

"How true." He grinned, and it lit up his face, softening sharp edges, mellowing the severity in his eyes. It made him more handsome—if that was possible. "I suppose you want the whole lurid story."

"Don't leave out a thing."

He fought with his hesitation for a moment, then said, "It goes back eons, actually." He paused and steepled his fingers.

Takala remembered the feathery softness of them on her neck, and a flush of excitement stirred again in her belly. She didn't want him to detect her attraction, so she forced her mind on something else. She picked up her glass, gulped her wine, and buttered a roll, waiting for him to open up.

After a while he said, "Raithe has always been power

hungry. He demands that his followers give him complete and utter loyalty."

"And you were one of them?"

He nodded, his brow furrowing. "I was taken in like the rest. Raithe is very charismatic when he wants to be."

"Another Jim Jones, uh?"

"Yes, but worse. He has some of the same pathology— the maniacal, obsessive, God Complex. But Raithe is more cunning and clever. He would never have allowed himself to die." Striker touched his fingertips together; then he tapped them as he frowned down at them, lost in a memory.

"So, what happened?" Takala slathered her bread with more butter, making sure all the surface was covered.

"There was an uprising among his followers. And he blamed me for it."

"Why you?"

"It all began with Morgan. She wanted me to make her a vampire."

"A human?"

"A banshee."

"Wow, never came across one."

"Be glad you have not. They are beautiful, but deadly if you cross them."

"I've seen a Wendigo, though. Let me tell you, they are nasty creatures." Wendigos were evil spirits who swept humans away and ate them. Patomani lore was full of stories of Guardians fighting Wendigos and bad children being abducted and eaten by them at night.

"Never encountered a Wendigo," he said. "We shall have to compare notes sometime." He gave her a casual stare, with the usual little bit of menace thrown in. His gaze slipped down to her neck, her breasts.

Takala felt him push her down another fast hill, her stomach weightless, somersaulting. She forced her thoughts back on his story and studied her bread. "I'm sorry I got offtrack. Where were we— Oh, yeah, the whole uprising thing. Where did this take place?"

"England, sixteenth century. Raithe was landed gentry, the Duke of Langolian. He lorded over most of the United Kingdom's vampire population at the time."

"What did humans think of having a vampire for an overlord?"

"The serfs, who worked in the castle, were not allowed to leave. They were completely under Raithe's control. Countess Bathory was one among his court."

"Isn't that the Hungarian countess who killed virgins for fun and bathed in their blood in an attempt to stay young?"

"That's what the historians would have you believe. But she was a vampire. Raithe turned her."

"Explains a lot. Guess you had a few countesses under your own spell, too?"

"A few." A self-satisfied expression broke over his face as he rubbed the stubble on his chin.

Did vampires grow whiskers? Did they have to shave? The same two days of golden growth had covered his face since she'd first seen him. It was just enough of a virile masculine appearance to make women drool. He probably didn't have to do anything to look sexy, part of his vampire allure.

She glanced around and saw that he'd caught the eye

of almost every woman in the restaurant—including herself, if she dared admit it.

Then he spoke and broke the moment. "Back in those days—" his smile disappeared "—we had to take extreme precautions when feeding. It wasn't like now. We didn't have supernatural organizations cleaning up our messes." Striker's eyes glazed over, and he wasn't looking at her any longer but lost in the past.

"That must have put a damper on things. I guess Bathory was one of the ones who got caught."

"She grew careless, greedy, took more than her quota."

"Quota?"

"Less humans to feed on, thus less vampires. Strict lines were drawn among hunting grounds. Of course, wealthy vampires like Raithe had larger areas."

"I see. That whole prey-versus-population thing." Takala ate a bite of bread, though she was no longer hungry and it sat in her mouth like a soggy mushroom.

"Anyway, Morgan was one of Raithe's many concubines. He exploited her dark magic for his own purposes, and when he grew bored with her, he just dropped her. She took a fancy to me, though, and began using me to make Raithe jealous."

"So you stayed in Raithe's family from Roman times to the sixteen hundreds?"

"Not all of that time. My visits were sporadic. I'd get bored with being ruled by him and leave the family for a couple hundred years at a stretch, but I always returned."

"The prodigal son."

"Something like that," he said, his voice distant, still stuck in the dark annals of his life.

"Until Morgan interfered." Just saying the woman's name set free the green-eyed monster inside her. She knew jealousy had no business taking up residence in her, but she had let it move in.

"Yes, she made Raithe so full of envy he and I almost came to blows. That night, Raithe told me the truth."

"The truth?"

"About my sister and parents. He killed them, drained them dry. Raithe had just turned me weeks before he murdered them, so I couldn't go back to my house and check on my family for fear of feeding on them." He fought to keep his face neutral, but a brief flash of unspoken pain broke through.

Emotion tugged at her heart. She empathized with his plight. Loving his family, but knowing it was too dangerous to get near them, later learning of their murder and feeling responsible for their deaths. She had always felt to blame for her mother's abandonment. She'd been too bad, or eaten too much, or cried more than she should. Guilt was no stranger. She knew it all too well. She wanted to touch him, comfort him, but his grim expression stopped her. Yet she couldn't help but feel the intimate disclosure bonded them together somehow.

After a moment, he said, "You know what really stabs me? Back then I believed anything Raithe told me, and he said they had died in a fire. I was so gullible."

"You couldn't help it. He was your maker. You were under his spell."

His brows snapped into an annoyed line, as if not wanting to hear justification for his behavior. Then he said, "That was no excuse. All lies. I should have known that he had killed them then set fire to their home. When he later blurted the truth in a fit of jealous rage, he mocked me for my ignorance. I wanted to kill him then."

"But you didn't."

"No, I had to choose the right moment. He was older than me and stronger, and he had a host of loyal subjects who would defend him to the death." Frustration smoldered in his eyes as he paused then said, "Waiting to end his life was another mistake I made. He found out where I slept and sent his henchmen to kill me."

"But you managed to escape?"

"Yes, I had a human mate who kept watch for me while I slept. She saved my life."

"Who was she?"

"A gentle lady."

"And you didn't harm her?"

He looked offended. "I never killed my mates."

"Did you make her a vampire?"

"Only because she wanted it," he said, his voice more open, relaxed.

"Is she still alive?"

"Raithe eventually lured her to her death during the Inquisition. She was burned at the stake. I could not save her."

"Did you love her?" Takala sucked in her breath and waited for his response.

His eyes turned the deep color of wood violets. "I wish I could say I did, but I was a selfish creature. I hate to think what I was back then…." His words trailed off, and he seemed to fight a war with his emotions.

For some reason his response pleased her. "So, what happened with Raithe?" she asked, tossing him back to the original story.

"Morgan had heard what transpired between us and of Raithe's treachery. She spread the word about why I left and what Raithe had done, and his subjects revolted. But not soon enough."

"Soon enough?" Takala hated to ask.

"I heard Raithe killed them all and put their heads on pikes around the castle wall."

"And you?"

"I vowed never to share his depravity or degradation again."

"But you can't let go of the need for revenge. So he still has left his mark on you."

His expression looked completely bared, open in a way she had never seen. She had a feeling she was glimpsing a side of him that he rarely let the world see.

"I cannot argue with you there." His lips strained in a taut smile.

Takala couldn't pass judgment on him for wanting revenge. If someone had killed her sisters, she wouldn't stop until she found justice. But Striker had gone one step further and made pursuing Raithe his whole existence. His need for revenge could destroy him and anyone else who happened to be unfortunate enough to step in his way, including herself and Lilly.

They lapsed into silence. The low hum of conversation and the soft melody of a piano floated between them.

He looked lost in thought, absently stroking the dimple in his chin.

What would it feel like to run her fingers down the dip in his chin? She found her hand moving toward his face, and she grabbed her glass instead. She chugged the last of the Merlot and said, "Have you considered that if you stop looking for Raithe, he's perverse enough to come looking for you?"

"I have tried that in the past. He's always one step ahead of me. Once I heard nothing of him for a whole century. I thought he'd been killed, but then I walked into a concentration camp in Germany after the war and found a vampire there who said Raithe had been getting his supply of blood from the victims, but he had moved on when they were shut down."

Was Raithe one of the assistants to Dr. Mengele? The thought repulsed her. The more she learned about Raithe, the more convinced she was that he had to be destroyed.

An idea struck her and she said, "You know what the problem was? You didn't have the right lure."

"Lure?"

"Me." She beamed a million dollar grin at him.

His expression turned to pale marble. "It's too dangerous."

"It's worth a try, isn't it? Maybe it's the one edge you need to finally get him."

He mulled that one over for a moment and said, "You might have something there."

"Okay, so my blood is extra yummy—you said so yourself. If we put a taste of it out on the street, it might entice him to find me."

"Culler will be all the temptation we need."

"Don't use Lilly as bait when you have me. He'll

just keep sending assassins to find her and kill her and never show up himself. My way is better. We'll be more in control. I'll be nothing but cooperative, where Lilly will not."

Indecision and vexation moved along his brow. "It will take more than just your blood alone."

"What do you mean?"

"You will be more of a temptation to him if he believes you are my mate." The shimmer in his eyes turned darker and calculating, the gaze of a predator.

The danger in them frightened her and thrilled her as she said, "So, how do we make him believe that?"

"We'll find a way." His gaze roved seductively down to her breasts, then up again and swept her lips, then her eyes.

The open, hungry look turned her insides to jelly. A shiver of wanting swelled inside her. Had she'd just sold her soul to the devil? Maybe she had.

Chapter 18

"How long will this take?" Takala glanced over at the agent Striker had called Doc. He was thin and reedy and had a pencil head with a mop of carrot-red hair. He wore jeans and a long-sleeved black T-shirt and carried a large briefcase. And he was definitely no doctor.

"Just about done." Doc tapped the swollen sides of the leeches.

Striker had left her in what he called the command center, which was just a suite at the end of the hall from her own room. It was decorated in generic red and blue paisleys and stripes and had a living area and small bar. Several doors led to, she guessed, bedrooms. Striker had made Brawn exit the room with him and left Takala alone with Katalinga and Doc for the bloodletting. Takala guessed Striker thought she'd be more comfortable with a woman present. But it hadn't worked. Something about being in a room with Doc was distressing no matter who was with her.

She would have preferred that Striker stayed, but she knew he couldn't handle the sights and smells of her blood. In fact, he'd just left her here and exited without saying a word. Katalinga had done all the explaining of what would happen to Takala under Doc's aid.

Takala noticed that Katalinga seemed fully recovered from her wound at the airport. The cleaners must have done the trick. She wore a double-knit blue pantsuit, striped red shirt, and blue suede boots, an outfit right out of the original *Avengers* set. She paced impatiently near the door, her catlike movements graceful, sleek and inaudible. Takala couldn't get Katalinga's shifter image out of her mind, and she could almost see her tail swaying as she walked.

Takala's gaze shifted back to Doc. "Using the leeches seems like we've stepped back in history four hundred years."

"Actually, leeches are used in medicine today to drain excess blood. You just don't hear about it."

"So this is the only accepted way to take my blood."

"The only way a vampire likes it. Needles give off a plastic metallic taste, and my little babies here—" he gazed down at the squirming worms on her arm as if mesmerized "—leave no aftertaste. It's definitely the preferred method for a true sampling."

"Oh." Takala refused to look at her arm.

Instead she watched Doc's T-shirt ripple as the leeches on his chest writhed against his skin. Not a much more pleasant sight. She was thankful he hadn't lifted his shirt when he'd pulled off the leeches. He'd just slid a hand underneath and come out with a handful of wriggling slimy black parasites. She couldn't figure out what type of creature Doc was, and at the moment she wasn't in the mood to ask him, but bloodsuckers seemed to play a major role in his existence. He gave new meaning to the term *leech*.

"Well, it looks as if we're almost done here." Doc bent and examined the leeches, probing the ones hooked to her arm one last time. "Did you know they have light-sensitive cells called eyes right here?" He pointed to the head of one. "And they have male and female reproductive organs."

"Hmm, how interesting!" Takala nodded, acting fascinated, but learning way more than she wanted or ever needed to know about leeches.

"My little darlings have done their part. They didn't hurt you, did they?" He smiled and wore the expression of a dog owner whose dog just bit you, his yellowish teeth glistening with thick saliva.

"They didn't," she said. They were just way up there on the gross-factor scale.

"It's the *hirudin* they secrete."

"What's that?" She wondered how much hirudin Doc drooled on his pillow at night.

"Chemical they secrete that keeps the blood from thickening so they can drink it easier. And it deadens the pain of the extraction. That's why they're so much better than needles. No waste, no pain, nothing to throw away later. Au naturel."

Takala wanted to tell him she didn't see anything

natural about having parasites attached to your body, but she kept that to herself.

Doc began pulling off his darlings and carefully putting them back under his shirt. He extracted the last of the engorged creatures from her forearm.

Katalinga paused near them, lifted her nose and inhaled deeply, a serene look on her face as if she couldn't get a large enough whiff of Takala's blood to satisfy her.

Takala noticed her blood must have hit Doc's bloodstream, for the whites of his eyes turned artery red. Then he tilted his head back and got this dreamy look on his face. "My, my, your blood is special. I feel as if I can do anything." There was that slimy smile again.

"Lucky you. How about just finishing up here," Katalinga said, motioning with her head toward the door from where they all knew Striker was impatiently waiting to enter.

Doc gave Takala an understanding look, sobered quickly and regained his composure. He blew on the eight red spots on her arm, his breath hot on her skin and smelling a lot like a swamp in the middle of summer. The wounds disappeared right before her eyes.

"Perfect," he said.

"So, how will my blood get on the street?" Takala asked.

"The leeches will distribute it."

"And you'll dispense them?"

Katalinga said, "Doc will get your blood to the right places. He's in big demand in the vampire community."

"Abso-freakin'-lutely. Command my own price." He made a sour face at Katalinga and added, "When I'm not doing jobs for B.O.S.P."

What did Striker hold over Doc's head to force him to work for B.O.S.P? He spoke with a definite American accent, not French. Did he patronize only vampires and go wherever he was needed or forced to work?

"You're paid well enough." Katalinga cut her cat eyes at him.

"I will be this time. One taste and her blood will be some of the most expensive I've ever sold. Definitely a bidding war."

"Just get the right bidders," Katalinga said.

Takala asked, "What if Raithe isn't among the bidders?"

"He has spies everywhere," Doc said. "Trust me, when the buzz about the quality of your blood gets around, he'll send an emissary."

"How will they know who to contact?" Takala asked.

"Don't worry, this isn't the first bidding war I've had." Something ugly blazed in Doc's eyes. "It'll all be set up properly. I'll sell you to the highest bidder in no time flat."

"Wow, I've never been a commodity before."

"Consider it a mark of distinction," Doc said with a greasy grin.

Takala didn't feel very distinguished as she watched the head of a leech emerge above Doc's collar, then slither back down. She hoped she would never have to work with him again. She gulped and averted her gaze; then there was a loud, succinct knock.

Katalinga opened the door and said, "We're done."

Brawn eyed Katalinga and looked at her as if the twenty minutes they had been apart made him nervous.

Takala wondered if Katalinga knew Brawn was in love with her. How come she could read other guys' feelings, just not in her own boyfriends? Something was definitely wrong with her.

"Where's Dark?" Katalinga asked, a slight, barely perceptible purr in her voice that hadn't been there a moment ago. It sounded huskier, a tad sexier. Maybe she wasn't as oblivious to Brawn's fondness for her as she seemed.

So, there might be romance ahead for these two. She hoped it ended better than her own relationships.

"Said he had to leave the building," Brawn said. "He'll be back here any minute. Left orders for me to take Doc wherever he needed to go."

"Who's watching Lilly Smith?" Takala asked.

Brawn said, "Don't worry, she can't move a muscle without us knowing. Want a peek?"

"Sure."

Brawn pulled out his phone and leaned over toward Takala.

In the screen, Takala viewed Lilly watching television. The screen flicked shadows over her face. She had that zombie, dead-eyed look of someone who had overdosed on the tube.

"She hasn't budged," Brawn said.

Hiding out didn't seem to bother her. Takala guessed she was used to it in her line of work. She hoped Lilly stayed there. At least she was safe. "Thanks," she said.

Brawn snapped his phone shut.

Doc gathered up his black bag and took Takala's hand. "Been a pleasure."

She stared at his squirming chest and hoped they never met again. What she said was, "Same here."

Doc grinned and watched her as Brawn escorted him out the door, asking him where he needed to go.

Katalinga was about to walk Takala back to her room, but Striker materialized. His lean, handsome face grim, his purple eyes ominously focused on her. She felt the tension emanating from him, an intense impatience.

What did he have in mind? His voice kept repeating in her head. "We'll find a way." To make Raithe believe they were mates. She tried very hard not to give away her nervousness and excitement, but her heart fluttered like it had wings and her palms grew clammy.

His eyes raked over her body as if he'd like to be the first bidder for her blood. "I'll walk you back to your room," he said, his mesmerizing voice filled with that self-assured, confident timbre that could charm and allure but also strike terror into anyone he chose, a silver-tongued devil. Still, truth be known, she'd missed him the half an hour they'd been apart.

Katalinga nodded, an amused twinkle in her eyes. Then she turned on her heels and walked back into the command center.

"Did Doc treat you well?" Striker asked with genuine concern in his voice…and something warmer, something much more than casual interest.

"He did, thanks." She felt her insides shift around in the wrong spots, felt her body grow feverish, responding to his dark smoldering glances, his nearness so charged it was as if he were already touching her.

She walked beside him and forced herself to breathe. *Calm down, or he'll know how he stirs you up.* She kept her gaze on the blue and red paisley rug and wallpaper as she made her way to the stairwell, but her mind wouldn't budge from him.

They hadn't spoken aloud in the five minutes it took to descend four flights of stairs, but their bodies were doing a heck of a lot of communicating on their own.

Their brooding silence drenched them both in tension, strung them as tight as barbwire. She felt something loud that stirred between them, a hunger, some charged impulses that radiated like connected electrical wires. Her nerves were frayed, excited, tempted.

She paused at her door, a hand on the knob. "Good night," she said.

She made the mistake of looking at him.

He stood a foot from her, his eyes large and liquid, caressing her with an intensity that unnerved her to the core, but also teased and tempted and demanded exploration.

They both stepped toward each other at the same time, but he did not reach out to hold her. So much concentration and resolve filled his expression, he could have been moving a mountain. Takala was determined not to make the first move, though her arms hurt from wanting to reach up and wrap them around his neck.

"Is—um—something wrong?" she asked, her voice tight.

"No, everything is as it should be."

"Good. Doc will get my blood out on the street and

maybe we'll be hearing from Raithe soon and we can be done with this whole thing."

"One can only hope."

The enthralling lilt of his voice hadn't changed, but his words stung her into silence. She half expected him to disagree with her.

Another moment of his gaze eating her alive, standing so still his feet looked rooted to the ground.

When Takala couldn't take the uncomfortable uneasiness any longer, she said, "Well, good night." She forced herself to turn and run for the cover of her room.

She slammed the door and leaned against it. Big gasps of air gushed through her open mouth. Her body broke out in a sweat as if she'd finished a marathon. A muscle in her right eye quivered from tension. She heard his door close; then her chest deflated and she banged the back of her head against the door. Get a grip. Keep her professional distance; that's what she had to do. And they hadn't addressed the issue of how they would make Raithe believe she was Striker's mate. That scared her more than anything. Would she have to let him bite her? Drink her blood? She knew it was going to be an arduous night, and she headed for the shower.

Striker walked to his window, the scent of Takala still filling his senses, pumping through his veins. He had felt her lust and his own, and it had taken all his determination and strength of mind to not take her and make her his. But he knew how dangerous that would be. It would take only one weak moment, one little slip.

Warmth was one of his weaknesses, and Takala's

body ran hotter than a normal human's because of her metabolism. Yes, her heat drew him. When he had lived like Raithe, out of control, he had preferred female vampires for sexual pleasure, something he had admitted to Takala, but he had not told her the whole story. Early on, he had learned the most positive thing about women of his own kind: they weren't warm-blooded. They didn't make him aware of the changes he had suffered when he had turned vampire, like having no internal body temperature and not being able to hold warmth in his body. He had all but forgotten what it felt like to press a warm human female mouth to his, the moist heat of it. And kissing Takala Rainwater, feeling the unusually intense hotness of her lips had inflamed all the dormant yearning in his own body.

He cursed his weakness. Through the "dark ages"— yes, that was how he termed the unbridled centuries of his life—human females had been his chosen prey. During those years he hadn't had a conscience and had rarely denied himself anything, including a meal. But if he was being truthful, he had never confused lust with hunger. He had kept them separated until much later when he could no longer distinguish bloodlust from physical lust, and he realized how destructive living a life of dispensation and immoderation could be. That was when he'd known he would destroy himself if he didn't change. And he'd climbed onto the narrow and arduous road of making reparations for all the evil he'd done in his life. He hadn't strayed since, until Takala appeared.

He'd have to mark her, and soon, so Raithe would be fooled into believing she was his mate, but he had to build up his self-control, make certain that he would not hurt her in the process.

He leaned his forehead against the glass, needing to feel the cool smoothness against his brow, anything to tease his senses into letting go of Takala's hold on him. But he knew it would take a natural disaster, or something close to it, to get his mind centered again.

He scanned the lights of the city. They glowed back at him, masses of accusatory eyes. The window had a safety bar holding it shut; he pulled it off, then flung open the sash. Cold air chafed his cheeks and stirred the strands of hair around his face as he stuck his head and shoulders out the window. A huge moon glowed bluish gray and shifted behind scudding clouds.

A stray breeze funneled down the twelve-story building and blew past him, urging him into the thrust and ancient fist of nature, the earth's bewitching call. When he'd first become a vampire, the wind was what attracted him so readily to flying. It was magical and freeing, and there was something alluring and inviting about the airstreams that swept to the four corners of the earth. He could travel anywhere, be there in minutes. The power of that was heady.

He leaned out more, the wind tearing at his suit, thrashing against his body, but it didn't dispel his awareness of Takala. His nerves still pinged from being near her, hearing her, and it only heightened his awareness of every living creature within Paris: hearts beating, scents of mammalian salty warmth, perfumes, body odor. People's voices, speaking, crying, screaming, murmuring in sexual throes. He could hear the constant drone of traffic drowning out the night cries of gulls along the Seine. A mishmash of cooking smells, car exhaust and the moldy driftwood scent of the Seine's brackish water bombarded him, the wind intensifying the odors of Paris's humanity.

He remembered the city in the eighteen hundreds. The odors were different then, more primitive. But the sounds and smells of humans, his prey, had remained the same. Lifetimes went, but the desire for blood would always be a part of him. He'd all but conquered this craving because he hadn't been lured from his steadfastness. But he had a massive temptation now, and she was across the hall taking a shower, naked.

He rarely if ever gave in to his desire to fly. But tonight the urge raged in him; the wind and the darkness called him. He needed to be miles from Takala. He could hear her shower running, distinguish her distinctively strong heartbeat, louder than a normal human's. He could detect it from thousands of heartbeats, just like he could smell her blood and know instantly it was hers.

Striker leaned over and let the wind take him. He tumbled head down for a moment; the world flew past him, and then he was light and free and soaring, one with the city and the night. But he knew his pleasure was fleeting, because his craving for Takala was as strong as ever.

He glanced at her room window. The curtains were drawn, but he could see a shaft of light beaming through the opening where they met. He frowned as he turned and forced himself to head in the opposite direction.

Takala couldn't sleep. She felt wired, as if something inside her were about to detonate. The four walls of her hotel room grew smaller by the second. She paced past the end of her bed and knew if she didn't get out of there she'd go stir crazy and do something stupid like knock on Striker's door. No, she wouldn't do that. But she could take a walk.

Takala dressed in black boots, jeans, and a black sweater that had a pink collar and cuffs. She put on her silver bracelets and a silver necklace that consisted of seven silver waterfalls, defense against vampires who got overly friendly. She made sure her revolver rode securely inside her boot, grabbed her leather jacket, and left.

She paused at Striker's door only for a second, then forced her legs into action. She knew Striker's agents were probably watching her. So what? She wasn't breaking any rules. She promptly turned, found the stairs and ran down them, reaching the first floor in moments.

White and peach marble columns and tiles glistened throughout the lobby. Huge palms grew out of the center of strategically placed round seats. Gold filigree and plaster seemed to cling to everything: the walls, the ceiling, around doorways. Art deco at its finest. The lobby was deserted, only a clerk doing a Sudoku puzzle at the desk. He didn't even look up as she passed him and stepped through the revolving door.

Icy air whipped around her as she walked out into the night. Streetlamps burned along the sidewalks. Tall buildings around her cast looming dark shadows over everything, making her feel small, closed in. She quickened her pace, walking past maids and hotel workers hurrying in for the next shift change.

One lap around the block would do. She'd seen a

little all-night coffee shop on the corner, Café de la Nuit. Maybe she'd get some hot chocolate and a snack. The carbs might settle her down, make her sleepy.

That's when someone grabbed her from behind.

Chapter 19

Takala dipped low, both fists punching.

Her attacker caught her hands mid-swing.

She cringed because it was like hitting iron, every joint and bone in her hands aching from the contact.

Her assailant jerked her around like she was a dog on a leash, and she stared into Striker's face. His furious scowl could have peeled off wallpaper.

"What are you doing out here?" He released her hands. His anger rode the air like a thundercloud. His eyes shot fire at her.

It was the first time she'd seen him drop his guard and show blatant hostility. She rubbed her fingers and retreated a step. "I could ask you the same thing," she tossed back at him.

"Answer me. Why were you out here?" He was all but showing fangs now.

"I couldn't sleep."

"Do you know how dangerous it is for you to be out here? Your blood is probably on the tongues of shifters and vampires all over the city."

"I'm not afraid of vampires, okay?"

"Your blood has never been used as bait."

"Like I told you, I can take care of myself. And if I want to walk, I'll walk."

One moment she was standing, the next her body was weightless and she was in his arms, and the world whirled by so fast her temples ached and she felt as if her body might burst.

Then suddenly the world stopped scrambling and the force of gravity weighed her down again.

She opened her eyes. They were high above the city. Lights gleamed in every direction and bounced off metal and glass. They stood near a railing at the very top of a building. She stared down at the tourist boats floating along the Seine, and her blood ran cold.

"Oh, no! We're on the Eiffel Tower?" He hadn't set her down, and her arms tightened around his neck.

"I wanted you to face your fears." The anger had left him, and his voice was almost compassionate.

His face was inches from hers, his breath as velvety as silk, caressing her face. Desire stirred in her belly. "Not fears, really. Just a nightmare I can't get out of my head. But you know that already."

"I have respected your privacy, Takala. I haven't invaded your mind after you asked me not to. What about it terrified you so much?"

"To be honest, you did." She recalled the nightmare, Lilly warning her not to trust him, taking his hand, the push, and then she was falling.

"Are you afraid now?"

Those four words held so much meaning. She knew what he was asking. Something dangerous gnawed below them, something different in the cadence of his voice and how he asked it. She sensed a fluid ruthless edge about him that turned her insides to gelatin. And she knew she didn't have a chance against what was happening between them.

"Yes," she said, surprised that she had so easily admitted fear. She had always been the strong one among her sisters, never showing alarm, forging ahead in blind fearlessness, using her brawn to see her through or get her into trouble. She could never admit she was afraid, even when she was. But this was different, an omission, a resolve to give in to whatever he had in mind. She had fought it long enough.

He tightened his grip around her, and she was glad his strong arms held her tight. She knew it was a false feeling of security, but somehow, right now, at this very moment in his arms, she strangely had never felt safer or closer to a man in her life. It was as if she understood him, expected nothing from him, unlike the others, especially Akando. This was visceral, pure desire that transcended both of them. She knew she could no more stop it than she could stop the moon from rising. He wasn't glamouring her; this was just soul-deep physical attraction.

"Let's go inside." He set her gently down, his face lingering overlong near her cheek and neck, so close the roughness of his five o'clock shadow brushed her cheek.

Her skin felt ultra sensitive from his nearness, and

a shudder slid down her neck, her chest. She felt her nipples instantly harden.

He stepped toward the door. Abruptly she felt the loss of his closeness and had to stop her hands from reaching for him as she watched him pivot, delve into his pocket and pull out an ID card. One swipe and he let her inside.

The glow from Paris's lights shined in through the windows and carved out long shadows over the room. She could make out desks, computers, boxy equipment with telemetry displays and dials that looked like the cockpit of an airplane. A lounge area was near the door with a couch and a table that held a coffeepot, Styrofoam cups, sugar and cream packets. They were alone in this office, and it was like they were on the top of the world, the only two people alive.

"What is this place?"

"Not in your dream?"

"No."

"A weather station," he said. "A lab for experimentation is right below us. During World War II these offices were used as an observation tower."

"I had no idea there was a weather station or lab here. And the restaurants?"

"Below us."

"So you have your own passkey to this place."

"You could say that. We have friends in France." He stood right behind her, gently drawing his fingertips through her hair.

Tingles rippled down her neck, and she leaned into him. He clasped his arm around her waist, and they swayed there for a moment. She felt him lay his cheek against her hair and breathe her in. And she was lost in the feel of him. The room, the tower, him: it all seemed so surreal.

She turned in his arms and faced him, the angular planes of his handsome face shadowed, his eyes deep black hollows.

"Are you still afraid?" His voice was soft, hesitant.

Darkness quilted the room, covered them, held back the world. There was no Lilly, or Akando, or Raithe, just the two of them. The only thing she could feel or think about was his desire pulling her into him, drawing her with an unstoppable force.

"No...yes," she admitted.

"I would never hurt you," he said in a soul-stealing drawl.

She pulled back enough to look into his shadowy face. "Don't make promises you don't intend to keep," she said, remembering all her failed attempts at romance. The irony struck her. Trusting a vampire to keep his word. Why not? It was no different than trusting Akando. They both had testosterone issues.

"My word is my honor."

"Then I'm not afraid." She splayed her fingers against his chest. She felt his heart pounding through his shirt and wool jacket, a racing supernatural beat, the vibrations as strong as a jackhammer's. "I can feel your heart," she whispered, her lips brushing the stubble on his cheek.

"What is it saying?" His fingers glided down her hair, then lower along the curve of her back. Now cupping her bottom, easing her hips closer to his erection.

She slid her hand inside his jacket, the elegant

expensive satin lining brushing the back of her hand. She found his heart and let her palm rest there, sandwiched between his shirt and jacket. She felt the pounding intensify.

"Hmm, it's saying it belongs to me…tonight," she added, her lips barely touching his, feathering over them in a teasing sensual way. It was just the two of them, bound by the darkness and shadows.

"Then it is yours to command." He covered that last hairsbreadth separating their mouths and kissed her.

His lips were soft, not hard and unresponsive as when he had glamoured her on the plane and that unexpected ravishing in the strip joint and outside Laeyar's den. She held his full desire, and she felt the fire of it sizzle down to her toes.

His tongue slid into her mouth, slowly exploring the dark recesses, twining and teasing her own tongue. She grew vaguely aware of being waltzed over to the couch, while he pulled off her jacket, her sweater, and popped off her bra with one expert twist of his fingers.

She slid her hands up inside his coat, felt him tense and inhale. Then she pushed his jacket over his shoulders. It hit the floor with a plop. She worked his tie loose and tossed it over her shoulder, then the buttons on his shirt.

Her torso was bare, and her jeans down around her ankles by the time he eased her onto the couch. He pulled off her boots. The one with her gun hidden inside hit the floor with a loud thump. Then he grasped her calves, his fingers trailing down her leg.

His hands left a hot path of prickles that shot up to her groin.

Almost agonizingly slowly he pulled off the rest of her clothes. He paused and drew back, looking at her body as if he'd found gold in a stream.

"You are so beautiful," he drawled. "Do you know how long I've wanted to touch you like this? I've tried to hold back…."

"Me, too. Maybe it's time to just let go." She grinned at him, wrapped her legs around his thighs, her hands around his waist, and drew him closer. The darkness made her feel bolder, more confident than she'd ever felt with a man, and she knew she didn't have to hold back with him. He could take what she offered and give it back tenfold.

He let her control the moment, and she pushed him down to his knees between her legs. Then she was ripping off the last of his shirt buttons.

Ping, ping, ping.

They hit the linoleum floor. His shirt's white linen was starched to within an inch of turning into cardboard, and it felt like wax paper. Now she knew why his clothes never looked rumpled. She crumpled it into a ball before she threw it behind him.

She touched the vial hanging on a chain around his neck. "What's this?"

"The soil of my birth," he said. "It's my lifeline during the day." His hands moved down her neck, to the soft area at the base of her throat. Then he bent and kissed her there, letting his lips linger.

She felt his fangs surface, the tips barely raking her skin.

A shiver racked her, and the necklace was forgotten. She explored the hard contours of his chest, learning every inch of him in breathless discovery. Golden-brown hair splattered across the center of his chest, then trickled down to below the waist of his pants. There wasn't an ounce of extra flesh on him. He was all corded male muscle, six-pack rippling along his abdomen, nipples taut and puckered. Somehow she knew he'd have a perfect physique.

His head lulled back as he luxuriated in her touch, letting her explore his body.

She breathed in the scent of butter rum and starch and his own clean musk as she dipped down and suckled a nipple. He groaned as his fingers dove into her thick hair. Then he caressed the back of her head, her hair, tickling and tantalizing her scalp.

She moved her exploration lower, stroking his erection through his pants, engorged and hard and ready for her.

When her fingers went for the zipper, he groaned as if he were wounded and then helped her. In minutes his pants were off.

He pulled her faceup so he could capture her lips. His body trembled with need, every muscle alive by what was opening up inside him. His lips were no longer relaxed, but urgent, his tongue thrusting into her mouth.

She ran her tongue along the tips of his fangs.

He kneaded her breasts, teased her nipples until they were hard and aching.

She arched against his palms; then he slid a hand down between her thighs and parted her, found the center of her desire. Heat built and tightened in her, and her hips writhed against his hand. She drove her back into the couch and her hips rose off the cushion as he brought her to a climax. He kissed her at that moment, absorbing her scream and passion as if that might fuse them together in that one moment.

Then he plunged into her.

She felt him filling her, thrusting, touching her womb.

He continued his skilled onslaught and Takala came again, and he was kissing a line down her flat belly, parting her thighs and using his mouth to drive her onward into another burning tumult.

Takala had never felt passion this intense, such stormy heat. It all but consumed her, drummed her temples, melted her flesh, pressed her heart, until she was panting and digging her nails into his back and her whole body was one liquid flame.

They cried out together as they both came.

Then he was guiding her back into a dark oblivion again, and she rode the storm with him.

Chapter 20

Takala had never felt so sated as she lay curled up next to Striker's bare chest. He held her close, one arm thrown over her shoulder. A delicious, hypersensitive tenderness throbbed between her legs.

She rubbed her palm over his chest and noticed that his body was still rigid, strung as tightly as cable wire. "You gave me pleasure," she said coyly, feeling just a little uncomfortable now by his unmoving silence and tenseness and his preoccupied expression. "But I feel like something is missing for you."

She could feel an uncomfortable gulf dividing them the moment she'd spoken, slipping away by the second, the world rushing back in to claim them.

"I'm fighting my desire to taste you."

She had forgotten that the culmination of sexual desire for him would be the *bite*. He'd held back so he wouldn't hurt her. She realized just how much of his willpower it must be costing him to hold her this close and not feed, and something that was running out of control inside her said, "Do it. Do it now."

"No, Takala. I gave you my word. I won't hurt you like that, ever." His voice was rough and edged with iron.

"But don't you have to so Raithe will believe we're lovers?"

"This is enough. He will smell me on you. But I must thank you—" he ran a finger along her chin "—for giving me more pleasure than I have felt in ages, but I cannot let my desire for you go any further."

Further. Something about that one word sounded cold and final, and it hurt like he'd stabbed her. She pulled away from him and sat up, feeling the loss of his nearness. She shivered, aware of the chill in the air now as she said, "I guess we've fooled Raithe. We should get back."

She stood and began searching the shadows for her clothes.

"Yes." He seemed a little more relaxed now that she wasn't near him.

She found her jeans and boots and realized what discomfited her the most was this empty expectation between them. He meant to sever the relationship. That was obvious. This was only a means to an end for him.

When had it become something deeper for her? She had promised herself not to get involved again. The old Takala was surfacing. *Just let it go.* He'd set the boundary, and she had to respect that, expect nothing in return from him, not his love or approval or admiration, a call for a second date. It was what it was. Two people sharing intimacy, lost in a few moments of bliss, accomplishing something that needed to be done, making her more desirable to Raithe. *Just accept it and get on with your life.*

She turned as she snatched up her bra and forced out the words, "Thank you for not biting me. I lost my head there for a moment, and I'm glad you kept yours. I can't imagine what it cost you, and I just want you to know I'm grateful."

He had picked up his shirt and was shaking it out, but now he paused. The dim haze of lights filtering in the window behind him outlined his tall silhouette. His chest and shoulders looked massive in the shadows, all muscular ridges. She longed to cross the four feet separating them and touch him and kiss him, but she forced her resolve and her feet to stay put while she quickly dressed.

There was a somberness about him, a severity in the straightness of his shoulders and back, in the tense set of his jaw that made her uncomfortable as he said, "Do not thank me. You have no idea what was going through my mind."

"Well, I'm glad this is over." She forced the words past the lump in her throat. "We won't repeat this, ever."

He cocked his head at her kind of strangely and said, "Wait a minute. Is that not my line?"

Yes, it was, yet something about her saying it first empowered her. Maybe he had been right about her. She had been searching for self-esteem and love from the men in her life, instead of from within her own self. Realizing it hurt, but it also felt freeing to admit it.

"Doesn't matter who says it, does it?" She didn't wait for his answer. She suddenly felt the need to get out of the room, get her mind in the right place. She said, "I need to find a restroom." She had to do something with her hands, and she made sure the Glock was back inside her boot.

"Turn left past the door. It's on your right." His voice had taken on its hard agent-mode tone again.

"Thanks." She forced herself to stand and strode to the door, her nub of pleasure still swollen and throbbing inside her bikini panties from their lovemaking.

Her decision to keep her distance was already being tested by the sensations he'd left on her body. She bit her lower lip and felt the puffy tenderness from kissing him. She could still feel his mouth against hers, his arms around her, his erection filling her.

Abruptly, emptiness moved inside her. It was just her emotions adjusting to this new confident Takala, she convinced herself.

She frowned and hurried out to find the restroom. For a little while she'd forgotten that they were at cross-purposes. She wanted Lilly safe, and he just wanted Raithe and was willing to use Lilly as bait. She couldn't let that happen.

Striker put on his shoes as he watched Takala step through the door, chin raised, coltish long legs adding to her confident feline prowl.

He still tasted her essence on his lips. It would be so easy to glamour her and force her back to him, take what he wanted. He couldn't believe that he had held back his desire, found a spark of human caring that allowed him to give her pleasure but not find fulfillment. He had denied every predatory instinct within him. Had O'Malley been right? Could he actually feel again, after the long dry years of emptiness?

It had bothered him just a bit that she had so easily dismissed their encounter and spoken so coldly about it. Perhaps that had been a good thing; still, it annoyed him and didn't stop the possessive emotions he felt when he held her in his arms.

Striker slid on his jacket, smoothed out the wrinkles in his shirt, then adjusted his tie. He decided he did not want his life complicated with emotions. Better to not feel at all and not deal with the temptations.

Raithe was his priority anyway, and for about the last hour he'd been aware of his nemesis. Just like he could discern Takala among thousands, he could feel Raithe's presence, his preeminence and potent darkness. It was like a ripple from a comet hitting the earth, the aftershocks rocking every primal instinct inside him. It was an acuity older vampires obtained, strictly primitive, a connection to the powers of darkness. It only worked if a vampire dropped his guard and put out the extrasensory vibrations. Striker knew that Raithe was teasing him, letting him know he was close. Perhaps that was what had distracted him and kept him from biting Takala. Whatever it had been, he was certain it wasn't emotional attachment.

Striker didn't have time to ponder this before his phone vibrated. He reached in and answered it. Brawn's image appeared on the screen; he was nervously thumping a pencil on the desk.

"Two things, boss. Doc has already sold Takala, and our target is on the move."

"Get a team together to guard Takala. And who is on Culler?"

"Que, Bull, Hammer and Lorenda, but the sun will be up soon and we'll lose everyone but Que."

They were some of Striker's best European agents, but they were vampires and had to sleep during the day. Que was older and able to brave the day. "Okay, call Mimi and have her get a day team together. I'll be there momentarily."

Striker strode to the bathroom and pulled Takala away from the mirror, snatching the lipstick out of her hand.

"Hey, what's up?" She looked at him, her eyes bright, on the alert and wary.

He disliked that she did not fully trust him. "We have to go," he said.

"What's happened?"

"I'll brief you on the way."

He grabbed Takala and held her close. He closed his eyes, let her scent fill him; then they were moving faster than the speed of light and he found himself not wanting to let her go.

Chapter 21

Takala and Striker arrived at the hotel so fast he hadn't told her what happened. She didn't like this cloak-and-dagger stuff, and she started to tell him so when Brawn met them in the stairwell.

Brawn looked tired to Takala, dark circles around his eyes. He was multitasking, sipping coffee and watching Lilly's image on his phone as he said, "The team's assembled."

"Good job." Striker held the door for Takala to walk through. She stepped into the hallway as he continued to grill Brawn. "Do you know who bought her?"

"Bought?" Takala perked up. "Already? Doc is quick."

"I am not surprised, given the quality of your blood." Striker didn't even turn to look at her as he spoke.

"So, who owns me?" she asked, irritated at his sudden dismissal. The hunt the most important thing to him.

Brawn said, "Bloke named Psycho. Checked his priors. Nothing, but that doesn't mean he's not one of Raithe's toadies."

"You have Culler covered?"

"Yes, all sides. Eight agents. She's in a taxi, heading west on the Avenue de New York."

"Destination?"

"She told the driver 180 Quai de Bercy."

"The docks." Striker's eyes gleamed, the wheels of his mind churning behind the purple depths, considering something only he could see.

Lilly was on the move? Takala felt the pit of her stomach drop to her knees.

Striker asked, "Did she make a call before she left?"

"No, but a telegram arrived."

"I want in on tracking Lilly," Takala said.

"It's too dangerous." Striker turned a cold stare on her, wearing the dark mask of a father speaking to a recalcitrant daughter. "You'll stay here."

"I'm not leaving Lilly out there alone. She's my biological mother." Takala's voice cracked on her last words. She hated hearing it out loud, hated that Lilly was a disappointment. Still, they shared the same blood. She couldn't let Striker send Lilly to her death so he could locate Raithe.

"Nonetheless, you're safer here."

Takala knew arguing with him was futile, so she calmed her voice and said, "Okay, Lilly's off the table. What about my buyer? I'll have to put in an appearance."

"I hope it will not come to that. I hope Culler will

lead us to Raithe. Selling your blood was just a backup plan."

"Wait one minute. You can't stone me totally like this."

His pupils swirled, expanding. Takala knew he was trying that telepathic crap on her again. She stood there, looking blankly into his eyes, while his power bombarded her psyche. But she channeled all her anger and forced it back.

"You will do as I say and forget everything you just heard."

"Forget," she repeated for his benefit.

At that moment, the elevator pinged and two men stepped off. One was broad-faced with a Neanderthal brow. Full thick lips and a black beard hid his teakwood-colored skin. His eyes glowed blue, as if they were lit within. Primate two-skin of some sort. The other was short, shaved head with just a tuft of hair in the center. He wore a long black overcoat, mirror sunglasses. A metal hook prosthesis protruded where his right hand should have been. He walked with a limp, and there were scars running across his cheeks, chin and neck.

He reached her first and extended the hook. "Hi, I'm Nine Lives," he said in a pronounced Southern accent.

If Takala had to guess, he sounded Georgian. "This walking lump of flesh here is Saturn."

Saturn grunted.

"Glad to meet you," Takala said in a dreamy voice. Then she shook Nine Lives's cold metal appendage.

Striker rounded on them, stepping between her and Nine Lives. "You are late."

"Sorry, sir," Nine Lives said, his smile dying. "We

were called at the last minute. This pretty little lady our problem?" Nine Lives gave Takala's body a once-over, his glasses moving up, then down.

Takala hated meeting people who wore sunglasses. You couldn't see their eyes, and if you couldn't see a person's eyes, then you couldn't make a judgment call on their personality. It was like they had something to hide, probably a dark side.

"That's right. Keep her safe. Don't leave her for a second." Striker shot them a warning glance not to blow this one. Something in the way he held their gazes a moment too long suggested he was worried about more than just her safety.

"Will do, boss man." Nine Lives saluted with his metal hook.

Striker looked at Takala and pointed to her door. "Now go to your room."

She turned on her heels and walked into her room, closing the door. She pressed her ear to the crack. Nothing but mumbling that she couldn't make out.

What had Brawn said? Lilly was in a cab going to the Quai de Bercy. Well, there was more than one way to find a rat and shake it. Let him put his guards out there.

Takala gave Striker enough time to leave, then she quickly rummaged through her suitcase and dressed all in black, including a pair of tennis shoes and a head scarf. She grabbed a pair of sunglasses, a flashlight, and an extra clip for her gun, which she stuck in the back of her jeans. She slipped on her leather jacket.

She listened again for voices and heard nothing. Striker was gone.

Takala walked over, picked up a ceramic lamp from the nightstand and hurled it against the wall. A loud crash and shards flew. She hid behind the door.

It opened and Nine Lives barreled through. "What the hel—"

Takala caught him from behind and grabbed his neck. He fought and gasped, but she had him in a headlock and was a lot stronger than he was. He began saying a spell in Latin. A witch with nine lives. Nice.

She squeezed harder, not wanting to break his larynx, only shut him up. Finally he passed out, limp in her arms. She dragged him behind the door.

Suddenly Saturn stomped through, holding a soda and a pack of vending-machine nabs, the Jolly Hungry Giant. He saw Nine Lives at her feet and his eyes grew to saucers. He dropped his goodies, but it was too late.

Takala aimed for his face.

With surprising speed, he leaped aside. He caught her fist in his huge boxy fingers and squeezed.

She fell to her knees, the pain soaring up her arm as he crushed her hand. She had a clear line to his crotch, and she head-butted his family jewels.

He screamed and bent over.

She drove her left fist into the side of his temple.

He staggered, picked her up by the scruff of her neck, wobbling. His eyes were unfocused, his gaze all over the place, then he grumbled and tossed her across the room.

She hit the television.

It crash-landed next to her.

She threw herself at his spine and watched him fall to

the ground with a loud thud. She stood and rubbed her fingers and arm and knew she'd be sore all over later.

She ran out of the room, stepping over the two agents and headed down the stairs to hail a taxi.

Takala saw a cab sitting outside the hotel. It crept forward and stopped in front of her.

She opened the door and looked at the back of the driver's head. He wore a snap-brimmed cap. A thick lock of black collar-length hair stuck out below the cap. She could only see his eyes in the rearview mirror. He spouted something in French.

"You speak English?"

"Yes, madam," he said very slowly, enunciating each word.

"Where would you like to go?"

"The Quai de Bercy, number 180."

He nodded.

"Big tip in it if you get me there pronto."

"Yes, madam."

Takala hopped into the backseat.

The driver sped down the street. She noticed that the streets were starting to come alive with trucks making early deliveries. It was still dark, but the sun would rise soon. She asked, "What time is it?"

"Four in the morning." The driver cut his eyes at her in the mirror.

Something about his shifty eyes she didn't like; then the locks on the doors snapped into place with a grating click.

Takala's hand went instinctively for her gun. She clasped the hilt as she said, "What's going on?"

"Nothing but car locks." He shrugged, his eyes darting nervously to the rearview mirror. "When I reach a certain speed, they engage."

She noticed tail lights behind her now, reflecting off the rearview mirror, right in her eyes. Was she being followed? The car had appeared out of nowhere; now it was on the taxi's bumper, taking an aggressive position.

Takala eased the Glock up and jammed the barrel in the back of the driver's neck. He didn't flinch. "I don't know what game you're playing, buster, but it ends now."

He grinned, a set of sharp fangs gleaming in the mirror. "I beg to differ, madam. It has just begun."

Takala heard the rear windshield break. Her neck stung. Oh, no! She reached behind and pulled out a small dart. Someone in the car following them had shot her. Raithe's goons, no doubt. "What did you just put in my bloodstream?" She held the dart. It turned blurry and shifted. Suddenly five of them appeared. Then darkness took her.

Chapter 22

Striker was already hidden across from the warehouse at 180 Quai de Bercy. It was one of many large turn-of-the-twentieth-century brick warehouses, the brick cracked and weathered, almost black in places.

No lights shone in the dirty windows. Two exits, a set of huge bay doors at the front and back. The warehouse faced a dock that ran along the Seine. In the front lay quayside railroad tracks, long in disrepair, rotting in the tarmac that didn't cover them.

A strong smell of decaying fish and creosote hung about all the warehouses in the area. It made Striker grimace. He was hiding in the shadows, his back pressed against a grain terminal, its huge silos behind him. His agents were in place, all angles covered, but he had given orders that no one should enter when Culler arrived. He would go in first. He wouldn't have another repeat of the destructive killings Culler had given him last time.

That was when his phone vibrated. He opened it and saw Katalinga's face. "We have her, boss. Just like you said. She's a handful."

"Tie her down, keep her drugged. I do not care, just keep her safe."

"Yes, sir."

Striker closed the phone and smiled to himself. He had felt her white magic warring with his dark powers and knew his mind control wasn't working on her. It was a good thing he'd had another set of agents keeping tabs on her. He couldn't afford to let her interfere, nor did he want her harmed. She was the only innocent in all of this.

Striker felt Raithe's soul, stronger now. He was close. He could hardly believe what he was sensing. So many years of tracking, so many cat-and-mouse games. Now Raithe just appears. Much too easy. This was a trap. Maybe Raithe decided to stop becoming the hunted and become the hunter. He'd wait Raithe out, certain he'd find out soon enough what his game was.

Katalinga glowered over at Tongue and Vaughn. She didn't mind Tongue, a little overbearing sometimes but okay. It was new recruits who irritated her. They never followed directions. She wished Brawn was with her. They made a great team, when he wasn't flirting with her. Secretly, Katalinga liked it, but she'd never admit it to herself or to him.

Katalinga had seniority, and she was the OIC on this mission. She used her most authoritative voice. "Tell Blake to stop, and we'll pick up Takala. I want her with us."

"Right," Tongue said, her wide lips gleaming. She

pulled out her phone and thought of Blake, the driver of the car ahead of them. The phone did its magic and Blake answered. "Hey, pull over, we're picking up the mark."

"Right."

Blake found a fire zone and pulled the taxi over. The street was empty and still dark. A good place for the switch.

Katalinga pulled in behind the taxi.

Vaughn said, "Do we get out now?"

"Yes, stupid." Tongue glanced at him. "Just follow my lead and don't say a word."

Katalinga shook her head. She almost felt sorry for Vaughn.

She watched as Vaughn gathered Takala in his arms. Apparently, fallen angels were still powerful.

Suddenly the sound of wings became a roar. The sky filled with black, blurs of flapping dark wings. Bats. Thousands of them. Not small bats, but large hummers, the size of hawks, the kind you saw in South American caves.

They swooped down, moving in unison, as of one mind. They snatched Takala's body from Vaughn, a black cloud of them lifting her in tandem while the others bit him, beating him in the face until he fell, screaming, covering his eyes.

Tongue tried to leap for Takala, but the creatures overpowered her, too, swarming around her like bees, biting and screeching.

"What the hell!" Katalinga was out the car in breakneck speed, but the cloud of bats filled the sky in black ink, disappearing over the city with Takala.

"No, no, no! Tell me this didn't just happen," Katalinga yelled.

"What the hell was that?" Blake said, walking back to them.

"Our execution if Dark finds out about it," Katalinga said.

"Who the hell was controlling the bats?" Vaughn said.

"Gotta be a sorcerer," Tongue said, holding a nasty bite on her hand.

"Not necessarily," Katalinga said. "Could be a demon or a vampire." She brought up the truth that they had been dancing around. "And there's only two I know powerful enough do that. The director and—"

"Don't say his name." Blake's thick black brows darkened into a line beneath his cap.

"Who's gonna tell Dark?" Vaughn said, shaking his head as he stood.

Katalinga and Tongue looked at each other, then pointed to Vaughn.

"You can," they both said at the same time.

Three things hit Striker all at once. His phone rang, a taxi pulled up in front of 180, and the sky filled with the pulsing of thousands of wings.

He went for his phone first, his eyes on the sky above him. A black cloud had blocked out the moon and clouds, darkening the sky in impenetrable black. The torrent of thousands of wings beat the air into a whirlwind. He felt the minds of the bats locked by a force: Raithe's.

"Yes," he said, looking at Vaughn's pale face.

"We lost her, sir. Bats got her."

Striker couldn't believe what he was hearing. Before he could get angry or reply, he watched the bats descending in a spiral toward the warehouse, a dark form hidden in the middle of the throng.

Striker slammed the phone closed and was about to command the creatures of the night to bring Takala to him, but they swooped down and dropped her through a ventilation window that ran a fourth of the length of the roof. Her body fell through the glass.

His heart leaped into his throat as he heard the shatter of glass. Then the bats disappeared into the night.

At that moment, Culler leaped out of the taxi and darted into the warehouse. Like clockwork. All timed to perfection.

Striker used his phone and barked an order for his agents to not come into the warehouse until he gave the signal. Then in seconds he crossed the street and stood to the side of the open doorway.

Instantly, he could smell Takala's blood, pungent in the air. He heard her heartbeat steadily thumping. Still alive. He felt the band around his chest tighten as he frantically searched for her.

His gaze scanned the hundreds of shipping crates, some stacked almost to the ceiling. Long, narrow walkways separated the rows of crates. Overhead, a rusting steel walk circled the warehouse and formed a path down the center. A swing-arm crane stood above it with a hook and cable attached to it for moving the heavy crates.

He spotted the hole in the roof, the glass jutting out in jagged angles. He didn't see Takala. But he felt Raithe's evil closing in around him.

Someone lit a lantern at the end of the warehouse. He moved inside closer to the light. When he saw Culler holding a lantern and standing at the end of an aisle, he paused. Out of the shadows, six vampires appeared on top of the crates near her.

Culler grinned, a "gotcha" smile.

"So nice of you to join us." Raithe's voice cut through Striker as he stepped out from the shadows into the sphere of the light. He held Takala up by the back of her jacket with one hand, dangling her like a puppet. Chains bound her feet and hands. The metal pulsed and glowed gray with some type of magic.

After all this time, Striker thought he would experience something more at seeing Raithe again—hatred, anger, loathing—but his only feeling was for Takala. He wanted to snatch her away from Raithe and fly her to safety, but Raithe held the back of her neck in a way that with one jerk he could snap it. Frustration ate at Striker. If he moved a hair, Raithe would kill her.

His archenemy appeared remarkably unaltered, same cruel gold eyes, high forehead, patrician nose, thick black hair, though he'd shaved it short; the face of the demons that ran within Striker. He looked the same, though black eyeliner outlined his eyes and his ears and nose were pierced. He wore black silk pants, boots, and a red velvet shirt that opened down to his navel, exposing a heavy gold dragon necklace. He had always preferred the soft texture of velvet against his skin and wore his clothes so it exposed some part of his body, vainly believing he was beautiful. He appeared no older than forty, much younger than his true age of two thousand years.

He bared his fangs and brought Takala's face close

to his. She bled from a cut on her forehead. He licked the wound, deliberately slathering her blood over his lips and mouth. In that moment, Striker saw himself, glimpsed a darker side of what being a vampire looked like. He hated himself at that moment, because his fangs had extended and he was fighting an ever-present desire to taste her blood. And so were all the other vampires present, bloodlust glistening in their eyes.

"I sense your concern. She *is* fine," Raithe said in a singsong voice. "Umm, very nice indeed. Potent." He ran his tongue around his lips. "You found a tasty morsel here. I can smell you all over her. Was she a good lay? Maybe I'll find out before I kill her."

"Up to your old tricks, I see." Striker kept his voice composed, though dread stirred within him. His safety didn't matter, but seeing Raithe anywhere near Takala turned his blood to molten fire. He knew he couldn't let his anger get in the way. He must stay focused to fight Raithe and get Takala out of here alive.

"You know me, never run out of them, Domidicus— wait, it's Striker now, is it not?" He didn't wait for Striker's reply and said, "Goes quite nicely with that new highly principled persona of yours." Raithe laughed, a discordant sound that carried through the warehouse.

"You have me. Why not settle this between the two of us?"

"Because—" Raithe's expression turned ugly and vicious "—I owe you years of pain and aggravation, my old friend. At first, this vendetta of yours amused me, but recently you have cost me greatly. Quite frankly, I'm hurt. Is that any way to thank your maker? I care for you, treat you as a son and then you hunt me, ruin my business affairs, then send an undercover chit to infiltrate my family. You have no loyalty, Domidicus."

"I could say the same of you."

Raithe's lips lifted in a sideways grin. "You'll never get over your family, will you?" He shrugged. "They were humans. What good were they to you? You would have killed them eventually, if I had not. Your sister's blood was quite tasty, I should add." He gave Striker a bored smile.

Striker wanted to yank Raithe's heart out right then, but he would not let Raithe know he had any effect on him. He had seen Raithe disarm his opponents mentally, pick them apart until nothing was left. He had to stay focused.

Takala's eyes fluttered open.

"Ah, Sleeping Beauty wakes." Raithe still held her up by her collar with one hand. If he chose to, he could snap her in half like a fortune cookie. Striker tensed as Raithe said, "How are you, my dear?"

"Where am I?"

"You have had a busy, busy night."

"It would have been nice if I'd been awake to enjoy it." Takala's eyes cleared and focused on Striker now, then back to Raithe. She made a face and said, "I'm guessing you're Raithe?"

"Tasty and clever, too—at your service." He smiled, his fangs glistening red from her blood.

"You drugged me."

"No, that was Domidicus. He can be more cunning than I." Raithe winked at her. "But alas, it made capturing you child's play."

She turned her gaze on Striker. "That true?"

Striker nodded, hating that look of betrayal in her eyes.

"Where is Lilly?" Takala had spoken to Striker, as if she had already passed judgment on him for his duplicity. "You better not hurt her." She glowered at Raithe. "You, either."

She struggled now, to no avail. The enchanted chains held her tight.

Raithe, sounding like the perfect host, said, "Please put her mind at rest, Lilly."

Culler stepped into Takala's limited line of vision. "I'm right here. Thank you for being so concerned."

Takala's beautiful face fell when she looked at Culler. Her eyes glistened with tears. "How could you set up agents and have them killed and lure Striker to his death? What's wrong with you?"

"Nothing, but there is definitely something wrong with you. Why did you become Striker's plaything? He's only using you to get to Raithe and me." Culler pointed to Raithe and herself with a flourish of her hand.

"I know that." Takala stared at him with such knowing coldness it left a chill in his chest. "I know this is all about revenge."

Culler looked speechless, as if she hadn't expected that response.

Striker hated looking into her beautiful eyes, seeing the hard wall that she had erected. He wanted to tell her how he felt, but Raithe would certainly use it against him. He couldn't tell if she seriously believed what she was saying or was just trying to be convincing to fool Raithe. Either way, he went along with it. "I'm glad you realized the truth."

"See, what'd I tell you." Culler threw up her hands in victory.

Takala's lips hardened into a tight line. "Great. Now that we have that straight, I'm sick of being in the middle of this." She glowered at Raithe, then Striker.

"It'll be your last irritation before you die," Culler said.

"You're truly wicked." Takala's words were bullets aimed straight at Culler. "I didn't want to believe it. Tried not to. But you're evil personified."

"I'm sorry if I don't live up to your standards. Who the heck are you to judge me, anyway?"

"I'm your daughter, that's who."

Culler only grinned. "Hear that, Raithe? I'm her mother. I don't feel like a mother."

"Well, the truth comes out now, doesn't it?" Raithe's lips lifted in a sideways twisted grin.

A dam of emotion seemed to break inside Takala, and she blurted, "Where were you all my life? Why didn't you come to see us? Did you care so little?"

"I'm not the motherly type."

Culler looked to Raithe for support. "Tell her."

"She's not." Raithe shrugged and dropped Takala.

The chains around her ankles were so tight, she couldn't keep her balance and she tumbled sideways.

Striker wanted to catch her, but Raithe snatched a handful of her hair as she went down.

Her head snapped back.

Raithe held her off the ground by her hair, one hand gripping her throat. He glared at Striker, daring him to make a move so he could snap Takala's neck.

Takala's brow wrinkled in pain. She swallowed hard,

cutting her eyes at Culler, and rasped out, "That's an understatement."

"Be nice." Raithe dug his fingertips into her wind-pipe.

Takala coughed and stiffened, gritting her teeth, fighting the crushing power.

Then Culler kicked Takala hard in the gut.

Striker had never felt so powerless in his life. It took all of his willpower to stay rooted to the floor. He wanted to carry Takala off to safety, console her in his arms, but he knew one wrong move and Raithe would destroy her. He could only watch helplessly as Takala's eyes glazed over with tears, more, he suspected, from the emotional agony of betrayal from her own mother, than any physical ache.

Tears rained down Takala's cheeks as she managed to rasp at Culler, "Striker was right about you. You're a cold-blooded waste of humanity."

Striker kept his gaze on Raithe's hand, waiting for him to make a mistake and free Takala's throat. All Striker needed was a split second. One quick distraction.

"Still, you're worried about me." Culler jabbed a finger at her chest. "I feel it, the goodness in you. You'd help me, still, wouldn't you?"

Takala said nothing, only glowered at her mother.

Striker hated to see her going through this. He had wanted to spare her the heartache, but he couldn't. When the truth was barbed, it hurt like hell.

Takala said, "I'm glad Fala and Nina know nothing of this."

"Oh, you mean your sisters. They'd probably take it better than you."

A woman's garbled yell cut through the air, echoing through the warehouse. It came from the shadows.

"Shut her up," Raithe bellowed, and a woman's flustered voice said, "Yes, master."

"Who are you hiding?" Takala asked.

"No one," Raithe said, wide-eyed with innocence.

Striker tuned in to the heartbeat of the woman who had tried to scream, and he couldn't believe what he was hearing. Two heartbeats the same. Culler's and the one coming from the shadows. Identical. "You are lying," Striker said.

Takala looked confused.

"Ollie ollie oxen free. He's found us out." Raithe feigned fear as he looked at Culler. "What shall we do?"

"Ah, phooey, no more fun." Culler's lips stretched in a cheerless, devious smile.

"What else can we do?" Raithe sighed loudly for effect. "Let them see the real you."

"Must I?"

"Yes."

Suddenly Culler began shifting, balding, until there was no hair on her body at all. The skin not covered by her clothes turned multicolored and mottled. Her soft tissue flowed translucent, green veins pulsing within a mass of yellow undulating flesh.

Takala looked at the transformation and said, "You're not Lilly Smith. You're a chameleon demon."

"That's right." Her voice rasped. "A trap, you see, to lure Striker here. You were just an unexpected added bonus. But Raithe will turn you into his plaything."

"So, Lilly is innocent."

Raithe motioned to the shadows. "This is so touching, I'm going to cry. Bring her out."

A female vampire that looked like Barbie, with blond hair and wearing blue-and-pink-striped sweats, pulled a bound and gagged Culler, aka Lilly Smith, aka Skye Rainwater, from behind a line of crates. Two glowing crystals were strapped to Lilly's shoulders with duct tape, checking her power. She was bound and gagged. When she saw her daughter, her brilliant blue eyes filled with tears.

"How touching," Raithe said.

Takala blinked back tears, her eyes widening in disbelief. "Mother," she cried out, her expression filling with torment, sorrow, then anger.

Striker felt only relief. At least Culler hadn't turned. He glanced up and saw the first rays of the sun washing the sky with yellows and blues and purples. The younger vampires would have to flee and sleep. Striker might have a chance of rescuing Takala.

He and the real Skye Rainwater shared a knowing glance, that fighting spark Striker knew all too well evidenced in her eyes. Suddenly she rammed the female vampire holding her, and they toppled into a wall of crates.

Striker had been easing his hand inside his pocket, and he flipped his phone open so his agents would get the message: COME NOW. Then he sped toward Takala.

All the vampires, including Raithe, converged on him.

For a moment, he was caught in a defensive storm,

breaking necks, tossing bodies, taking the blows Raithe delivered. Some of the vampires fled the sun.

Then there was only the two of them. Striker's shirt ripped, and so did the chain holding the vial with it.

Raithe snatched it midair, grinning like the devil he was.

Striker fought Raithe, but he could feel his power waning. Where did Raithe keep his soil? Surely on his person.

Striker did not feed on fresh human blood, which already gave Raithe an edge. The injections and reconstituted animal blood kept Striker at three-fourths his strength, and without the soil he was no match for Raithe's power.

As if Raithe realized that, too, he hit Striker in the chest. The blow hurled him through the air.

Striker crashed into a stack of crates.

Hundreds of pounds of wood tumbled down on him, bags of rice ripping open and raining into his nose, mouth, body.

Striker felt the world whirling. He spit out dried rice and heard Takala scream before Raithe began tossing aside broken crates, digging Striker out from under the debris.

"Weakling," Raithe growled, glaring down at Striker. "You should not have given up human feedings." He tried to kick Striker in the face, but Striker caught his foot and jerked.

Raithe went down backward, crashing through the broken wood.

Striker rose, unsteady on his feet.

But he was slower than Raithe. He was already

floating above Striker's head, his mouth still smeared with Takala's blood, his face contorted into a half-crazed killing mask. Striker didn't see the long, jagged piece of wood until Raithe drove it into his abdomen, shoving him against a crate, impaling him there.

"Now you die, Domidicus." Raithe's voice rumbled with triumph.

Pain shot through Striker, but he kept his gaze on Takala. He hadn't wanted it to end like this. He knew now that his need for revenge wasn't half as powerful as what he felt for Takala. If he could have kept her safe, he would gladly have given up hunting Raithe. He had failed miserably.

Chapter 23

Takala fought the chains on her hands and feet, watching the blood spew from Striker's gut, his white shirt and suit covered in thick dark streams, a three-foot stake sticking out of his abdomen. His golden hair had come lose from the ponytail, and it fell around his face and shoulders. His form blurred and undulated, and his skin no longer held a faint glow. He didn't look so perfect now. In fact, he looked like a dying man. Takala felt a sick ache in her chest, and she couldn't swallow.

She searched the warehouse for signs of Lilly. She hadn't moved; the female vampire who had held her was fending off one of Striker's agents. Lilly was still bound, the crystals checking her power. Lilly squirmed, trying desperately to get loose. As if she sensed Takala, she glanced up and their eyes met.

In that instant, Takala was certain this was her real mother. Something behind her bright blue eyes was in Meikoda's and Fala's and Nina's eyes, something Takala knew that bound them through the power of their blood. How could she have been fooled by a chameleon demon?

She saw Striker's agents entering the warehouse, fighting, using some kind of red laser weapon. But they were too late, and a second line of Raithe's vampires, older and stronger ones, slunk out of the shadows like hiding roaches. They attacked the agents in droves, battled in a realm that she couldn't follow.

She caught glimpses of stop-action moments, like a strobe light going off, where Raithe easily dodged the weapons, then grabbed them and broke their necks. His strength seemed godlike in intensity, unstoppable.

"Time to be rid of you." Takala heard the chameleon demon hiss behind her; then it jumped her. Hands clasped around Takala's neck.

Takala bucked her off, and her foot hit the lantern. Kerosene spilled out in a long line. The fire followed it in a whoosh.

"Bitch, get off of her." Katalinga had spoken, and Takala saw her pick up the chameleon demon and hurl her into a blazing wall of fire.

Katalinga bent to free Takala, but she said, "Help my mother, please. Get her out of here."

"Suit yourself." Katalinga didn't waver and fought her way to Lilly.

In that moment, Takala admired Katalinga as she fought the chains. They were stronger than she was. She gritted her teeth and kept jerking on them.

Brawn appeared beside her and said a spell. A fireball

appeared in his hands. "Hold up your wrists and close your eyes."

"Hope you can aim that thing." Takala followed his orders.

"Let's find out." He threw it at the chains.

She felt the fireball spit and burn past her skin and roll to the floor, consumed by the growing flames.

The chains gave way.

Takala held up her feet, and Brawn hit the chains again with another fireball, freeing her totally.

"Thanks."

One moment Brawn was standing; the next, the chameleon demon jumped from the flames, hit his back and they were down and rolling in the fire.

Takala dove for the demon, pulled her off Brawn and slung her as hard as she could against a wall of burning crates. They crashed down on her, and the demon screeched as the flames consumed her.

Brawn didn't have time to thank Takala, for one of Raithe's vampires attacked him.

Takala couldn't see Lilly or Katalinga. As she ran to help Striker, she prayed Katalinga had gotten her mother out.

Flames burned all around him, smoke billowing. Takala held her breath and leaped through the fire. Heat singed her as she rolled near him.

He looked bad, pale as the broken crates, agony and the prospect of death shredding his cool demeanor, etching his handsome face in a tableau of pain.

She squatted near him. "Oh, my God! Look at you."

"Go," he gasped over the roar of the fire, his eyes

bleak with unspoken longings and regrets. "Leave me. Save yourself."

His expression tore at her heart. "We're in this together, buster." Takala coughed, braced her foot against his shoulder and grasped the stake. "This is gonna hurt." She jerked the stake from his abdomen.

He gasped, holding his middle, his head lolling back, the whites of his eyes rolling.

"Stay with me!" She jammed her wrist against his lips and held his chin. The smoke burned and stung her eyes, and she had to cough and breathe. "Bite me," she yelled at him.

"No."

"You need the strength, damn it. Bite me! I'm not letting you die."

Striker hesitated, his eyes glazed with fading anguish. He said something that sounded like "Only to save you," but she couldn't be certain.

His fangs snapped out, and he bit down on her wrist. Takala felt the points go deep, felt the jolt of pain. Then he gorged on her blood.

He drank until she felt light-headed and spots filled her vision, and she kept blinking away the stinging smoke to see.

Finally he stopped.

Takala watched the wound in his abdomen healing right before her eyes.

At that moment, Raithe appeared out of the flames like a demon from hell. He grabbed her. She punched at him, but she was weak, useless.

"There's my prize," he said, his laughter ringing in her ears.

He carried her straight up, moving at vampire rocket speed, making her dizzy. Already light-headed, she struggled to hang on to consciousness. Takala tried to fight him again, but he held her arms trapped at her sides. His grip felt like iron bands, tight enough her ribs would break at any second.

"No, Raithe," Striker yelled as he hit Raithe, the vibration rocking through Takala.

Raithe bellowed and buckled. He lost his grip on her as he was torn away.

The second before she fell, everything shifted into slow motion as if the world had stopped spinning. She glimpsed the crane and hook Striker had driven through Raithe's body and heart. Striker pried something from Raithe's fist before he jettisoned Raithe into a solid wall of flames. Raithe screamed, hanging there helpless, cursing Striker, his body turning to blue-black flames, sparking and fizzing like a firecracker.

Takala felt herself falling now, slowly, heading straight into the roaring inferno below her. Heat and smoke blasted her, searing her skin, hair, face. She was melting.

Suddenly strong arms broke her fall.

Striker's strength engulfed her, buoyed her. She closed her eyes, coughed, and that was the last thing she knew before blessed darkness and peace floated her away.

Someone's cool hand moved over Takala's brow. Striker. She opened an expectant eye, and it wasn't the face she expected to see. She gazed into Lilly's eyes—Skye Rainwater's face. Now that Takala could see her mother up close, it was impossible to miss the newly formed red scars that gouged her neck, hands and cheeks. Raithe's handiwork, no doubt. Anger washed over Takala until she remembered seeing Raithe being burned alive.

"Oh, Takala, you've grown up so beautiful." Skye stroked Takala's brow.

"Where is Striker?" Takala glanced around. She saw that she was lying on an emergency cot. The warehouse was half a block away, charred and smoking, the blaze gone. Cleaners combed the warehouse, zapping the building with their powerful handsets that restored order to the universe and put some of the atoms back where they were supposed to be and snatched some entirely away. The owners of the warehouse would find out there'd been a fire, but they wouldn't know who had caused it, or who had put it out.

A tall cleaner with large eyes stood at attention behind Lilly. He looked anxiously down at Takala. "You seem to be okay now. I was given strict instructions to secure your safety."

"Where is your boss?" Takala asked. She didn't mean to sound demanding, but she wanted to see Striker.

"Had to leave," Skye said.

"Left without saying goodbye?" Her chest tightened, right in the region over her heart. She had to remind herself that she didn't expect anything from him. They would probably never see each other again. Everything they had been through meant nothing to him. It hurt that he had no feelings whatsoever, not even enough to say goodbye or thank you for saving his life. Twice they had saved each other's lives. That counted for something in her book. Maybe not in his.

Skye had an intuitive look on her face, a mother's look. "He couldn't stay, Takala. You have to know that. After drinking your blood, he just couldn't be near you. You have to know how much of a temptation that would be for him. He asked me to explain that and say goodbye."

Takala wanted to ask if that was all he said, but she refused to go there. No, he didn't want to be near her, and she didn't need him around to feel good about herself. She didn't need anyone's approval or affection. Oddly, she didn't even need Skye Rainwater in her life, and if her mother wanted it that way, Takala could live with it. Striker's honesty and insight had given her an invincible inner confidence. So why did her chest feel like it was caving inward, making it hard to breathe? It was just the way he'd used her and left, a nasty, unfilled ending. That's all it was, she told herself.

A long, pregnant beat passed between them. Takala biting her lower lip and looking everywhere but at her mother. Skye leaning back and no longer touching her daughter.

"I'm so sorry, Takala."

She looked at Skye. "We don't need to do this now."

"Yes, we do. I owe you an explanation. When I heard your voice in the warehouse, I knew it was you. I just knew." Tears filled her eyes, wetting her long black lashes, making her eyes look like a blue sea. "I didn't think after all these years I'd recognize you, but I did. A mother never forgets."

"She just leaves." Takala strained to keep her voice even, not accusing.

"You don't understand."

"Help me to." Takala spoke past a growing lump in her throat.

"I turned my back on becoming the Guardian to be with your father. I gave up everything, my mother, the family, the tribe. We ran away and only had each other. He was my whole existence. And when he died, I just lost it. I loved your father more than life itself. I see so much of him in you. Same proud chin. His eyes were green like one of yours." She ran the back of her hand along Takala's cheek as if she were caressing a memory. "I know this sounds horrible, but I couldn't look at you after he died, none of you. It was just a reminder of the pain."

Takala vaguely remembered now. Fala, five or six, handing her a peanut butter and jelly sandwich, telling her not to eat so much. Skye lying on the couch, catatonic with grief, staring at the television set, an empty bottle of gin on the floor.

"When Fala didn't go to school, social services threatened to take you away. That's when I knew I had to do something. I knew I couldn't care for you girls, and I wasn't about to let the authorities have you, so I left you with my mother. I knew you'd have a much better life with her than me. I dried myself out and went to work for the State Department. When they found out about my power, I learned about B.O.S.P. I asked to be out in the field, as far away from Virginia as possible."

"But you kept a house in Fredericksburg."

"Something about the land of our people drew me."

"That's just how I feel. When I'm away from the reservation for too long, I get depressed and antsy."

"That's why I couldn't live anywhere else but Virginia. I suppose you've seen my house."

Takala nodded. "That's how I came across the chameleon demon."

"Raithe thought of everything, didn't he?" Skye shook her head in disgust. "Makes me mad that she was in my house."

"You still live there?"

"Oh, yes, when I'm not undercover. I rented it to a real nice couple when I was given this assignment with Raithe. I hope they are okay."

"I'm sure Striker will find out." At the mention of his name, Takala felt leather bands slap around her chest.

"Oh, yes, he's thorough, and the people under him are great."

Silence crept between them, the sound of cleaners giving each other orders, the morning sounds of Paris humming in the background.

Finally Lilly said, "You know, I can't count the number of times I started to go to the reservation, just to see you girls from afar, but I knew it would kill me to see you and get close. I felt certain you wouldn't want to see me anyway."

"I don't judge you, Mom." The word sounded foreign on Takala's tongue. "Can't speak for Fala and Nina, but I don't judge you. I just wanted an explanation. That's why I had to find you. I guess I've gotten it." She summoned all her inner courage and finished with, "The big question is, what do we do now?" Takala forced herself to meet her mother's tear-filled blue eyes, dreading what she might hear, yet knowing she could live with whatever came.

Skye swallowed hard, tears trailing down her cheeks. "Do you think they want to see me?"

"I don't know, but if you don't face them, you're missing out. Fala and Nina just got married. They'll be starting a family one day. Grandmother acts like you don't exist, but every day I see emptiness in her eyes, like a part of her is missing, and it hurts me to see her like that. You know she kept a picture of you, in spite of the old laws."

"She did?" Skye sounded surprised.

"I found it when I came looking for you. Hid it in the old cedar chest in her room, under some quilts."

Skye looked as if she was picturing the cedar chest Takala had just described as she said, "That's where I used to snoop for things when I was a kid." A sad smile edged across her wet cheeks, and she wiped at the tears with the back of her hand. "She must hate me for what I did." Skye sounded as if she hated herself for her weakness of so long ago.

"How can you say that? Grandmother raised your children. Went against the laws and kept a picture of you, even though you'd been disowned. She wears the hollowness you left in her like a badge. She is getting old, too. I think she deserves to see you again and hear a thank-you, at least."

"But I've been abjured."

"We'll cross that bridge when we come it. Anyway, Fala is the leader of the council now, and Meikoda is a powerful member, and I doubt anyone will question their decisions."

For a moment, Skye looked torn. Years of uncertainty swirled in the blue depths of her eyes. Then she said,

"Okay. I have to go to Washington and write a report on what I know about Raithe's organization—"

"I thought Raithe found out you were an agent. What can you tell them from your last report?"

"That was over two months ago. He kept me prisoner in his den for a month."

"Something I don't understand, but I'm grateful for, is why he didn't just kill you when he found out."

"Ego. He wanted to rub me in Striker's nose before he killed Striker. I'm sure my demise was not long behind Striker's. By the way, I saw the brave thing you did by sending Katalinga to help me, with no concern for your own safety."

"Those crystals had made you weak. I knew—"

"Stop making excuses. You saved me and Striker. You're a brave young woman. No daughter of mine could be otherwise."

The proud tone in her mother's voice and her smile struck a place in Takala's heart. It swelled in her chest until she could hardly breathe. After a moment she said, "Yeah, the curse of Rainwater women." Takala teased her with a smile.

"Not a curse. An honor."

"Wow, that's what Grandmother says all the time." Takala felt goose bumps crawl down her arms. Their voices had sounded so much alike, she could have sworn the words had come directly from Meikoda's mouth.

"Rainwater women think alike. I'm just glad you came looking for me. Raithe's empire will be going down now."

"All of it?"

"Yes. He kept me tied inside the room where he held

court. I know what businesses he owns and who runs them. It's enough to destroy his web of evil."

"That should make Striker happy." At the mention of Striker's name, Takala felt that squeezing sensation in her chest, the lump in her throat closing in on her vocal cords, emotion grinding up from inside her. Then tears swam in her own eyes, but it wasn't for the same reasons as her mother's.

Chapter 24

"Takala…"

Takala jumped, almost losing the toothbrush in her hand. The name had come unbidden directly into her mind, riding the waves of her synapses at will. It was as though Striker was inside her head, communicating directly with her. It wasn't really speaking, more like a sensation of feeling, mostly fuzzy and vague. Like right now, she could feel something akin to hunger for her fading in and out.

A shiver of yearning to go to him toyed with her, a powerful longing that she found impossible to control. She grabbed the sink and hung on, feeling light-headed, fighting the urge with her whole being.

Another impression of what felt like disgust dropped on her like a grand piano. It left her cold inside. She panted and hung on to the sink, staring at her reflection in the mirror. Toothpaste covered her mouth, and her eyes looked a little demented. She was on a winding road of emotion and she'd lost her bearings. How long would this connection last? Days? Weeks? Years?

The desire part wasn't so bad. It was the yearning to be with him that followed that was so hard to bear. But even worse was sensing his disgust, because she couldn't tell if it was self-castigation for his own bloodlust or from desiring her physically or just plain aversion to her in general. After all, he had been up front about their relationship. She was the one who had wanted more. The old Takala hard at work.

This was a nightmare. How could she forget him when they shared this bizarre connection? Had to have happened when he'd fed on her blood in the warehouse. She realized the toothpaste was beginning to sting her tongue and lips, and she spit it into the sink and rinsed out her mouth.

She toweled her face and remembered when she first felt the strange perceptions over a week ago. She had hardly been able to believe they had been happening to her. She'd heard of the phenomenon before, but the truth was she didn't know anyone who had been bitten by a vampire and lived. You just didn't get close enough to vampires to find out the full extent of their powers. But she was living proof that the blood connection was real. Oh, joy!

She checked out her reflection in the mirror. Her eyes were huge, and her hand trembled as she fluffed the tawny curls hanging around her shoulders. She had to get a grip.

She steadied her hand as she applied makeup, covering the dark circles under eyes. For days her sleep had been broken. She had been on edge, waiting, waiting for what? For Striker to call her. There, she admitted it. Not one word. Not a text message or email saying goodbye. Not a "How are you doing?" Or a warning about the emotional connection. Hadn't their time together meant anything to him? She couldn't forgive him for not saying goodbye. But why would he? She had only been caught in his revenge scheme. He probably didn't care that he was making her life miserable.

She frowned at the bathroom mirror as she drew eyeliner above and below her lashes, heavy enough to hide the discrepancy in her eye color. What was she doing? She had promised herself not to pine over another guy. Was she pining?

Yes. Yes. Yes. She missed Striker's grave, piercing looks, as if he could see down into her soul, his smooth, debonair way of charming every woman in a room, including her, the smell of his starched shirts and rum aftershave. She had taken to eating bags of butter-rum candy.

Most of all she missed the way he kissed her and held her and that feeling of actually being with a man more powerful than she was, a man who knew her better than she knew herself. Yes, she missed him more than any man who had come and gone in her life.

Takala felt someone behind her, and when she turned and saw an actual person, she dropped the eye pencil in her hand. It clattered down into the sink.

"Good grief, you scared me," she said to her grandmother.

Meikoda was a petite woman, shrunken from age. The top of her gray hair only reached Takala's shoulder. She might be of small stature, but Meikoda Rainwater had a strong, square chin and the proud, confident bearing of someone who knew her own power and was comfortable in her skin. She used to be the Guardian before Fala assumed the powers. She was still a commanding shaman in her own right, so formidable that people feared looking directly into her vibrant blue eyes, a Rainwater trait of which Takala was only graced with one.

Meikoda's wardrobe usually consisted of blue-jean skirts and gingham blouses, but today she was dressed to the nines, spiffed out in a royal blue silk pantsuit. She had braided her long gray hair and twisted it into a bun at the back of her head. She even wore a set of pearls around her neck. The most adorned Takala had ever seen her grandmother, other than when she donned tribal gowns. But they were a whole different fashion statement.

The wrinkles around Meikoda's eyes and mouth stretched, revealing her eyes. Looking into them was like looking into a blue sphere of cut glass lit by the sun, magic and wisdom swirling in the depths. Takala knew better than to meet her grandmother's gaze for too long, so she lowered her eyes out of respect.

Meikoda took Takala's measure for an uncomfortable moment. Then she raised a gnarled hand and placed it over Takala's forehead—a gesture she'd done a million times, so it came naturally to her. "Something is wrong with you? I can feel it."

Takala felt the warm hand buzzing against her skin, the fizz of her grandmother's magic making the hairs on her skin stand up. "Nothing is wrong." Takala saw her grandmother catch the lie as it left her lips.

Meikoda narrowed her eyes at Takala. "Grand-daughter—" her voice turned stern "—I know you are keeping something from me."

Here we go. For this very reason, she had tried to maintain a safe distance from Meikoda since returning home. Takala didn't want to explain what was happening to her. She just didn't want to get into it with her grandmother, but it was too late.

Takala took a deep breath and said, "Okay, remember me telling you about finding Mom?"

Meikoda nodded.

"Well, I left out the crucial part about Striker Dark."

"The vampire?" Meikoda said, her eyes sparkling like she was facing a foe.

"Yes." Takala went on to explain about letting Striker bite her to get his strength back.

After the telling, Meikoda pursed her lips. "I see. You could have mentioned this earlier."

"I know." Takala didn't like the look she was seeing on her grandmother's face and said, "What's wrong?"

"Let me see your wrist."

Takala had put on a thick silver bracelet that covered the two puncture holes, and she inched it up her arm.

"Hmm!" Meikoda examined the wound, turning Takala's wrist first one way then the other, prodding it with her finger. "Did you know you can tell a poisonous snakebite from a nonpoisonous by the bite marks? The nonpoisonous snake leaves an impression of the teeth. The viper leaves only two fang marks. Here we clearly have a poisonous bite, but a vampire's venom is of a different ilk, much more dangerous. The wound is still red and puffy. This vampire has a powerful spirit. The blood connection to you cannot easily be broken. We shall have to summon the council for a combined magic spell. Fala is here now. She will join us. You will have your body back, do not worry." She patted Takala's forearm.

Takala didn't know if she wanted her body entirely to herself and Striker completely out of her life. This connection, as worrisome as it was, was all she had of him. And as much as she didn't want to, she missed him with a kind of ache that made her feel depressed and hollow inside, like a part of her was missing. And it wasn't that deprived, superficial need she used to have for guys, for Akando. This was something deeper, an honesty and warmth and sharing that she'd never experienced with anyone. Striker knew her too well. She felt raw and open with him, bared her soul with him. Her feelings for Striker went deeper, to a place that frightened her, for she knew he wasn't capable of caring for anyone. Hadn't he said that? Hadn't he admitted to not knowing how it felt like to have human feelings, to be human?

"Do not worry, my child, we will cure you…if you wish it?" Meikoda added the last four words with a heavy question in her voice.

"What do you mean? I hate what's happening to me."

"Do you?" Meikoda shot her a look that had always demanded total honesty from her grandchildren.

Takala thought that over. "Okay, I hate *some* of the things I feel."

"They are not all unpleasant?"

"No."

Meikoda smiled ruefully to herself.

"What's that grin for?"

"Never mind," Meikoda said. "You'll be free of him soon."

"Great." Takala heard the lack of enthusiasm in her voice. She quickly changed the uncomfortable subject. "I have to tell you, Grandmother, you're looking mighty fine tonight. Dressed up for Mom?"

A rare open expression swept over Meikoda's face, one of uncertainty as she looked down at her suit. "Is it too much?"

"No, just right."

"She's late." Excitement and annoyance stirred in Meikoda's normally placid voice. "They're all late."

"Oh, they'll be here before seven." Fala, Stephen, Nina and Kane hadn't arrived yet. She knew Fala and Nina weren't real keen on seeing Skye again. It had taken an hour of pleading on the phone to bring them to the reunion.

Meikoda had gone all out and made roast beef, rolls, her famous lemon cake with butter-cream icing. She and Takala had spent two days cleaning and cooking to prepare for this special gathering. With a little persuasion from Meikoda and Takala, the elders had voted to allow Skye onto the reservation for this visit, a large concession for a member who had been deemed dead to her people—but Takala was certain Meikoda's influence with the council of elders had brought it about.

Takala hoped it was just the beginning of Skye's reinstatement. But Skye would have to stand before the whole tribe and ask forgiveness from each member and those she had hurt in order to be invited back. And every member had to agree to forgive her. She would also have to give up something dear to her heart and bury it in the sacred prayer cave as an offering to the Maiden Bear. Then there would be much time spent in the prayer cave by the elders, and if the Maiden Bear accepted the offering, she would give an elder a vision with Skye's new Patomani name. It would be as if Skye were reborn into the tribe and the Book of Life. No, Skye had a long road ahead of her before she was allowed back into the fold. This was a start, though.

Takala could sense how nervous Meikoda was about the whole thing. Meikoda's dignity usually gave her an unflappable composure, but today she was a switchboard of nerves and uncertainty.

Oddly, Takala felt good about the reunion. She'd spoken to Skye several times since talking her into coming home. One way or the other it would all work out.

Meikoda tilted her head to the side, that familiar finely honed look that said she was sensing something way beyond Takala's grasp. "Company is coming, and it is not my prodigal daughter or your sisters."

"Who is it?"

"Someone for you."

"Who?"

Meikoda left without replying and headed for the front door to intercept their visitor.

Takala grew suddenly on edge. Was it Striker? She

checked herself out in the mirror. She'd curled her hair and let it wave around her shoulders, glistening dark and light gold. She wore a reserved striped black peasant sweater that fell just below her shoulders and black slacks and high heels. She had on just the right amount of makeup, covering the dark circles. Her eyes were wide with excitement and glistening, green and blue. But she'd used shiny mauve eye shadow and dark liner, which dulled down the inconsistency. Her appearance was as good as it got. She couldn't quell the excitement stirring in her belly as she hurried to see who had arrived.

Striker found himself holed up in his office. It was a pretty big space, considering the federal money crunch. Twenty by twenty, a retractable window to keep the sun out, a sleek modern desk with special crystal-powered monitors that he used to communicate with everyone who worked at B.O.S.P. His command center, the bridge of his Starship *Enterprise*. All he had to do was think of an employee or department and it popped up on the screen. To be so connected to the world, why did he feel so alone in it? In all his extensive life, he had never felt so destitute and isolated.

Yes, he had his job with B.O.S.P., and that had fulfilled him for over half a century, since Roosevelt had acknowledged that the supernatural world could become a real threat to national security without monitoring and had established B.O.S.P. During Striker's long run as director, he had seen a lot of administrations come and go, some bad, some good, and he'd always done his duty, lived for his job, kept his mind centered on his work and finding Raithe. Oddly, Raithe had been the measure for

Striker's own moral compass, and it had helped him control his cravings. Maybe that was what was wrong with him: he didn't know how to live without a foil. Or was it something else entirely?

He paced across the floor and hit a button. Part of the wall slid aside, revealing a hidden window. His office was on a concealed second floor of B.O.S.P. headquarters, and he could see for blocks.

He looked across the street-lit lawn of his office toward Michigan Avenue. He had designed the B.O.S.P. office building himself. It was a Parthenon replica, replete with granite stone sides and huge white Doric columns. The sign on the drive proclaimed Library of the Divine Spirit. His brainchild. From the street it looked like an obscure and rarely used religious research library, part of the local Catholic University campus. The cover had kept the B.O.S.P. headquarters hidden since its inception.

The shadows from the streetlights seemed to form an image of Takala's face on the lawn. That's how it was. He saw her everywhere. In everything.

He turned around and crossed the floor in the opposite direction, and her features appeared in the leaves of the philodendron plant on his desk.

He groaned aloud, the sound echoing through his office like the whimper of a sad dog. Pathetic. That's what he had become. A pathetic, mooning calf. The wrinkles in his brow furrowed so deep his forehead hurt. He reached the credenza, absently changed directions, and paced down the length of his office. His life had been so ordered, so straightforward. Work. More work. Searching for Raithe. Meeting with O'Malley, denying the vampire cravings that were so innate, desensitizing himself to life. All of that had worked until Takala.

She had resurrected the human side of him that he'd lost so long ago, the part of him that had died with his parents and Calliope. He had thought it was lost to him forever. Then Takala arrived, dredging up memories of Calliope, her multicolored eyes and same invincible spirit. Brave and loyal to a fault, that had been his baby sister. Always there for him. Qualities he'd seen and admired in Takala.

The two were so similar. Takala was a living album of images, all of them with Calliope in them. She had brought back ancient details of his sister. Even now, Striker remembered their last hurtful words to each other. Calliope hadn't liked Raithe and his friends, and she'd warned Striker to keep his distance. Striker had laughed it off. His little sister couldn't possibly be a better judge of character than himself. After all, he was the older brother. He had been so arrogant and blind. He wished he had listened to her, but he'd fallen under Raithe's spell.

It had started with all-night orgies in Rome's highest circles, all of Raithe's vampire concubines Striker had wanted. Slowly he was lured into their bloodlust hell. He wished he had listened to Calliope. She and his parents wouldn't have been killed. No matter how hard he tried, he knew he would carry that guilt for all eternity. In truth, when he was near Takala it worsened. So why did he feel so drawn to her? As if by being near her he was somehow finding redemption from the largest mistake he'd ever made in his life. None of it made sense. He should feel the opposite, shouldn't he?

It might just be the craving for the taste of Takala's blood that had awakened in him a sleeping monster, one he thought he had conquered. He'd had no choice but to drink her blood in the warehouse. If he could have refused, he would have. He could feel the blood bond it created, feel her heart beating inside his own veins, feel her essence entwined with his. The only thing he couldn't feel were her emotions, and the only explanation he could fathom was that her white magic had blocked them. Still, she would remain a part of him until he let her go.

He should let her go, but he couldn't. The need within him to keep her close was like a virus inside him. He had tried to wipe those lurid sensations from his memory, but he knew he couldn't clean Takala from his system. She was an ache in his heart, a thorn in his heel.

He wished she felt the blood connection, but he was powerful enough to make sure she didn't know about it. No, this was his agony alone.

He pulled out the vial of earth, suspended around his neck with a gold chain. He had kept it for eons. He held it up to the ceiling florescent light, examining it with loathing. He was so tired of not feeling like a vampire or a human, caught in a purgatory he had made for himself….

The screen near his desk pinged, and Katalinga's face appeared.

It drew his thoughts from the one thing he wanted: Takala. He noticed Katalinga was out of breath, and a few bloodstains dotted her leather jacket. She stood in what looked like a run-down room with peeling and ripped brown wallpaper. A dim lightbulb threw a yellow haze over the area. He could hear and see Brawn behind her, giving orders to cleaners. They were working on the memories of several large human thugs that looked beaten, bloodied and bruised. Striker had thought of breaking up the team of Brawn and Katalinga, but had changed his mind. They worked well together, despite the sexual attraction. And he was betting Brawn's feelings were more involved than Katalinga's. After being with Takala, he found himself oddly tolerant of anything having to do with affection. The thought made him grimace at the phone as he said, "Yes."

"Just wanted to let you know, mission accomplished." Katalinga's brows narrowed as she surveyed him.

She must have noticed his lack of attention to his appearance. In fact he looked like hell warmed over. He had on a pair of old worn chinos and a wrinkled chambray blue shirt. He hadn't bothered to pull his hair back before he left his townhouse, and it straggled around his shoulders. His sleep had been broken or nonexistent for days, an insatiable desire for Takala, slowly, by degrees, taking over his life.

"Well done," Striker said. As punishment for losing Takala to the bats, he had put Katalinga in charge of destroying the last of Raithe's murder rings at a house in Prague. He couldn't have chosen a better agent to handle it.

"We freed all the victims, and the cleaners are finishing up."

"No casualties?"

"None. We got here before a new shipment of teens left."

"They are home safe?" he asked.

"Yes."

Striker wondered how long they would be safe in the world. At least the highest bidder wouldn't be draining their life away tonight. "Fine job," he said. "Don't leave anything out of your report."

"I won't, sir."

"Goodnight." The phone went blank.

He felt the walls getting smaller and smaller and headed for the door. He felt antsy, his senses highly responsive, the scents of humans filling him. Takala's steady heartbeat pounded in his head.

He found himself walking, walking, the cool night air doing little to clear his mind. There was a battle going on inside him, and he was determined to win.

He heard a man and woman arguing even before he saw them. They stood in front of a bar called Fat Louie's. The man was slapping the woman while she screamed for help. People just walked past them, gawking but not helping.

In a blink, Striker grabbed the guy and threw him against a building.

He made a move toward Striker, but Striker's voice stopped him. "You don't want to do that. Go home and sleep it off."

When the guy turned and strode down the sidewalk, the woman flung herself at Striker, thanking him. "Oh, jeez, thank you so much. My boyfriend would have killed me. I'm telling you, I'd be dead. He didn't want to break up. You're my hero."

"I doubt that." Striker noticed she was about thirty, short, blonde, and smelled of cigarettes and stale, greasy

French fries. Her cheek was bruised, and a stream of blood ran down her lip.

The smell. So wet and fresh. He could sense the warmth of fresh arterial blood. Something snapped. Striker reacted without thinking. He grabbed her, glamoured her, and led her into the closest alley.

She was dazed, ready to let him do what he wanted.

He grabbed her, felt the heat of her human body next to his. His fangs snapped out. He bent toward her jugular.…

Right before his lips touched her skin, a vision of Takala's beautiful face flashed before his eyes. He paused, his body trembling uncontrollably, gripping the woman by her upper arms. "Nooooo!" He heard the scream in his own mind. What was he doing?

He stepped back from the woman and handed her a twenty dollar bill. "Get a cab home," he said.

She still looked up at him, wide-eyed, as if expecting more from him.

"Go," he demanded.

She walked slowly down the alley, head down, clutching the twenty in her fist, and disappeared.

Striker fell back against a dirty Dumpster, the smell of rotting food, filth and rat feces surrounding him. Seemed fitting to find himself here. This wasn't the lowest point in his life; that had been when he had discovered that Raithe had killed his family. But this came close. He had mistakenly believed it was blood he craved. Now he realized he had evolved beyond that.

It was Takala he wanted. A woman who could make Atlas look like a wimp. The bravest woman he'd ever known, and that was saying something, because he had known thousands of women, vampire and human alike. Not one of them had been strong enough to resist his powers of suggestion, nor irritated him as much as Takala Rainwater.

He smiled, thinking of how she had made him believe he could force his will on her. Little minx with her bag of tricks. But he admired her pluck. She tackled the snake shifter to save his life and dove into the fray with the hover demons at the airport without a care for her own life. And she had given him strength at the warehouse by sharing her blood with him. She was a beautiful, sexy enigma. Tough as nails on the outside, but insecure and unsure of herself on the inside. There wasn't anything she wouldn't do for someone she loved. She was a woman by which he would measure all females. He'd never met a woman like her, nor one who came close to her beauty on the outside and inside. She had opened him up, peeled back layers of dead skin from his heart. He felt alive again just by having spent a few days with her. What would a lifetime with her feel like?

That wasn't possible, was it? He'd ruined his chances. He had let her believe she meant nothing to him. Striker thought he could walk away from Takala, let her find a normal human with whom to share her life. That's why he hadn't said goodbye. Now he regretted it. Would she even speak to him? He didn't know, but he had to try.

Chapter 25

Takala made a face at Meikoda and said, "Tell Akando I'm not here."

"He knows you are here. He can see your car."

"Tell him I'm sick."

"It is not like you to be a coward, Takala. You have unfinished business with him. Finish it." Meikoda gave her a long, disapproving look, then left her alone at the door.

Takala fought her disappointment that it wasn't Striker at the door. She straightened her spine, threw back her shoulders, summoned her courage. She could do this. She flung open the door and stared at him. Akando stood there in all his handsome, male-model glory, tight jeans hugging his muscular thighs, long brown hair pulled back in a braid down his back, that wicked smile that could charm the panties off a woman in seconds. The porch light cast a bronze-yellow glow over his skin that added to his machismo. She found herself gasping a little at his beauty.

It was safer to keep him outside, so she stepped out the screen door and onto the porch.

"Hello." She folded her arms over her chest.

Akando reached for her, but Takala dodged his hands.

The smile turned into a guarded frown as he said, "We can't touch now?"

"No."

"Can't come in, either?"

"We spent two days cleaning the house. Grandmother wouldn't approve." Well, tiny fib there. But what was the harm in that?

His dark gaze drank her in. "Takala, give me another chance. That's all I'm asking."

She noticed a needy look in his eyes that she had seen in her very own eyes countless times, in situations just like this one, hoping that a man wasn't about to dump her. The sweaty palms, fists clenched, that sick, angst-ridden look swirling in his expression. The signs were all there. She actually felt sorry for him and gave him a polite little grin. "Please don't make this harder than it is. Let's just part as friends."

"'Part as friends.' That's something to say to me. Good grief, we've been friends forever. You've turned into a cold woman, Takala."

The old Takala might have knocked him off the porch, but now she only said, "I'm not cold. I just don't need a man in my life to complete me."

"Stop with the Oprah crap."

"It's not crap. I mean it. If I find love, okay. And if I

don't, so be it. But I don't need a man to make me feel secure." She waved her hands in a dismissive gesture and wondered if she was being entirely honest. If this was another man, say a tall, sexy, blond vampire who was older than Methuselah and dressed like an Armani model and tossed orders at her that she disregarded and made her insides melt when she was near him, she might be changing her tune. She wished Striker was standing before her—no, what was she thinking? He had hurt her. At least he'd been honest about how he felt about her, not like the jerk standing before her, waffling back and forth like a mouse unsure about coming out of his hole. That's what she had been dating. Mice!

Akando grabbed her hand. "You could find love with me again."

"We've been through all this. The cheating thing isn't going away. You don't love me. You just think you do right now because I don't want you."

"That's not—"

"That's it and you know it. It's all about the chase with you, Akando. You're still in love with Fala, anyway. You'll always be in love with my sister." She tossed the words out, and they hung between them like a heavy cloud. Finally, she had spoken the truth, something she had forced to the back of her mind because she'd had such a crush on him. Getting it out felt like a yoke being lifted from her shoulders.

He looked pensively off into the woods behind her grandmother's rancher, his jaw hardening as he ground his teeth. A huge full moon hung over the trees, bright as a torch in the night sky.

At his silence, she said, "Don't worry, you'll get over her when you meet the right girl. I'm just not her."

He glanced at her, his expression dejected, tears shimmering in his eyes. He was finally dealing with the truth, too. "I had hoped you would be," he said, his voice low and sexy as he grasped her hand.

"We both did, but we were fooling ourselves."

"You've changed, Takala. Different somehow. Wiser, more mature."

She knew she had Striker to thank for clearing her head on what she wanted from men and what she needed from them. Two different things.

"Thanks." Takala felt his sweaty palms and pulled her hand back. "Sorry, I have to go. My family will be here any moment."

"So your mom's really back?"

"Yes."

"Let me know how she's doing, will you?"

"Sure."

Akando turned, and she watched him walk away, his form disappearing into the night. If Striker hadn't opened her eyes, she might have run after Akando and nurtured a bad relationship, making it worse and lying to herself about Akando being in love with her. Now she could watch him walk away with only heartrending sympathy for him, because unrequited love stinks. She was the expert on it. Whoever came up with that saying, "It's better to have loved and lost than never to have loved at all," probably had never loved someone and suffered the heartache.

"Touching."

For a moment, Takala couldn't tell if the sarcastic

male voice came from inside her mind or out. Then she felt a familiar dark overpowering presence behind her, and her heart lurched.

Chapter 26

"This is *so* not fair. You need a bell around your neck," she teased while she breathed in the sight of him.

His hair was loose, straight around his shoulders. He had that five o'clock shadow on his face and chin. He wasn't wearing his usual suit. God forbid, no tie, and a wrinkled cotton shirt. Something was definitely wrong with this picture, but he was still so handsome it hurt her eyes to look at him. She gazed down at the steps.

"Then I wouldn't be able to scare defenseless women," he said, a definite warmth in his voice that she'd never heard before. He seemed relaxed, his guard down.

"I'm not defenseless." She shot him one of her proud and defiant looks.

"How well I know that." He stared at her, some nameless emotion swimming in the purple depths of his eyes. He pulled a small box of imported Belgian chocolates from his pocket and tried to hand them to her. "Do these do anything in the way of softening you?"

"You can't buy me with food."

"My mistake." His jaw muscles clenched until tension pulled along his shoulders, straightened his spine. For a brief flash, he looked almost wounded. He blinked once; then the walls went up again and his poker face was back in place. He shoved the chocolates back in his pocket.

As much as Takala wanted to throw her arms around his neck, she kept her distance. Why was he here anyway? She felt his emotions rolling around her head, but they were all jumbled. She wouldn't let herself hope he was here to sweep her off her feet. That was the old Takala thinking.

"So—" she forced an aloof note into her voice "—you're finally getting around to saying goodbye?"

"I am sorry about that. I had to personally oversee the destruction of Raithe's businesses."

"Make the world a safer place," she finished for him. She couldn't endure the weight of his dark eyes, and she stared down at the toes of her high heels.

"Yes." The one word seemed to separate them a mile apart.

"You've gotten a new laid-back look." She pointed to his clothes.

"It appears so." He frowned down at the shirt.

"Kind of like it. You're not all starched up."

Silence built between them, and it pulsed against her.

After a contemplative moment, he said, "I don't know who that man was."

The painfully adrift tone in his voice went right to her heart and squeezed it. He sounded so sad, and she wanted to make the sadness go away, but she wasn't certain if he wanted that or not, so she said nothing.

After a moment, he said, "Who was that man you were talking to?"

Was that jealousy beneath his voice? "Didn't you hear everything with that Superman hearing of yours?"

"Caught the tail end of the conversation."

"It was Akando."

An almost chilling smile slowly inched across his lips. "Are you two back together again?"

The old Takala would have told him the truth. The new one was a little more leery about putting her feelings out there, so she tested the waters by saying, "I don't know."

He fell silent and made a point of studying the moon.

She watched a vein throbbing in his neck, watched his fists tighten and loosen. He seemed uncomfortable, on edge.

When Takala couldn't stand the pressure of the silence any longer she said, "I'd appreciate it if you would stop getting into my head."

"What?" A blond eyebrow cocked in surprise.

"You heard me. Something weird is going on with both of us. I know it comes from sharing my blood with you. You have to make it stop."

"You can feel my emotions?"

"Yes, and it's annoying, let me tell you."

"I don't see how that's possible. I blocked them from you."

"Well, maybe you can't, and I'd appreciate you severing the connection." There. She'd put him on the fence. He'd have to fall one way or the other, and she'd know how he felt about her.

When he didn't move, only stared at her with that fathomless, unflappable expression, she couldn't stand it any longer. She had her answer. He didn't care.

She said, "If you don't, my grandmother will."

"Is that what you want?"

"Yes." The pressure moved up into her throat. She felt it building behind her eyes. Any moment, tears would flood her eyelids. "Why did you come here?" she asked, the pressure moving down into her chest.

"I guess to say goodbye."

"Okay, goodbye." The words tumbled out of her mouth. She reached for the doorknob and opened the storm door.

He grabbed her hand. "Takala, wait!"

She turned to look into his handsome face and saw fear and loneliness, so wide, so deep she found herself drowning in it. Tears streamed down his pale cheeks, but they were thick, the color of blood. She'd never seen a vampire's tears before. She didn't even know they could cry—especially one who was two thousand years old and had said he couldn't feel anything.

"Takala, I know I'm a vampire and the life I offer you will be a difficult one, but I love you."

Takala just blinked at him.

"You're the only woman I've ever loved," he continued. "You made me feel things that I thought were lost to me forever. I can't go on without you."

"You mean it?" she asked, still leery on the outside but bubbling over with joy on the inside.

"Yes."

She flung herself at him, inhaled him. He held her with a trembling fierceness; then he was kissing her, stealing her breath, making her toes turn under, her knees weaken, stoking a fire inside her only he could fuel. After a long moment of reveling in being held in his all-encompassing embrace, she broke the kiss and dabbed at the red tears on his cheeks with her fingers. "I'll get that bell around your neck yet."

He grinned and said, "I'll settle for a chain."

They both laughed. She felt his laughter resonate through her own body, just like she felt their souls were inexplicably tied together. She hugged him even tighter.

The screen door opened and Meikoda said, "Hmm. Akando, you have changed."

They broke apart. An awkward moment ticked by where Meikoda's blue eyes challenged Striker's purple ones.

Takala said uneasily, "Grandmother, this is Striker Dark."

"Oh, the vampire who possesses my granddaughter's spirit." Rarely could anyone stare down Meikoda, but Striker seemed determined. He didn't blink.

The clash of two powerful Titans.

It was Meikoda who made the concession by glancing at Takala. "Well, do not keep him standing on the porch all night. Where are your manners, Takala?" She waved a gnarled hand at Striker. "Come in, and I will read your tea leaves and tell you if you are worthy enough to possess Takala's heart."

"Yes, ma'am."

Takala and Striker walked hand in hand inside the house. They didn't see the amused gleam in Meikoda's eyes that she leveled at their backs.

* * * * *

nocturne™

COMING NEXT MONTH

Available July 26, 2011

#117 ASHES OF ANGELS
Of Angels and Demons
Michele Hauf

#118 GUARDIAN WOLF
Alpha Force
Linda O. Johnston

You can find more information on upcoming
Harlequin® titles, free excerpts and more at
www.HarlequinInsideRomance.com.

REQUEST YOUR FREE BOOKS!

2 FREE NOVELS FROM THE PARANORMAL ROMANCE COLLECTION PLUS 2 FREE GIFTS!

Once bitten, twice shy. That's Gabby Wade's motto—
especially when it comes to Adamson men.
And the moment she meets Jon Adamson her theory
is confirmed. But with each encounter a little something
sparks between them, making her wonder if she's been
too hasty to dismiss this one!

Enjoy this sneak peek from ONE GOOD REASON
by Sarah Mayberry, available August 2011
from Harlequin® Superromance®.

Gabby Wade's heartbeat thumped in her ears as she marched to her office. She wanted to pretend it was because of her brisk pace returning from the file room, but she wasn't that good a liar.

Her heart was beating like a tom-tom because Jon Adamson had touched her. In a very male, very possessive way. She could still feel the heat of his big hand burning through the seat of her khakis as he'd steadied her on the ladder.

It had taken every ounce of self-control to tell him to unhand her. What she'd really wanted was to grab him by his shirt and, well, explore all those urges his touch had instantly brought to life.

While she might not like him, she was wise enough to understand that it wasn't always about liking the other person. Sometimes it was about pure animal attraction.

Refusing to think about it, she turned to work. When she'd typed in the wrong figures three times, Gabby admitted she was too tired and too distracted. Time to call it a day.

As she was leaving, she spied Jon at his workbench in the shop. His head was propped on his hand as he studied blueprints. It wasn't until she got closer that she saw his eyes were shut.

He looked oddly boyish. There was something innocent and unguarded in his expression. She felt a weakening in her resistance to him.

"Jon." She put her hand on his shoulder, intending to shake him awake. Instead, it rested there like a caress.

His eyes snapped open.

"You were asleep."

"No, I was, uh, visualizing something on this design." He gestured to the blueprint in front of him then rubbed his eyes.

That gesture dealt a bigger blow to her resistance. She realized it wasn't only animal attraction pulling them together. She took a step backward as if to get away from the knowledge.

She cleared her throat. "I'm heading off now."

He gave her a smile, and she could see his exhaustion.

"Yeah, I should, too." He stood and stretched. The hem of his T-shirt rose as he arched his back and she caught a flash of hard male belly. She looked away, but it was too late. Her mind had committed the image to permanent memory.

And suddenly she knew, for good or bad, she'd never look at Jon the same way again.

Find out what happens next in ONE GOOD REASON, available August 2011 from Harlequin® Superromance®!

HSREXP0811

Celebrating

Blaze™ 10 years of

red-hot reads

Featuring a special August author lineup of
six fan-favorite authors who have written
for Blaze™ from the beginning!

The Original Sexy Six:

Vicki Lewis Thompson
Tori Carrington
Kimberly Raye
Debbi Rawlins
Julie Leto
Jo Leigh

Pick up all six Blaze™
Special Collectors' Edition titles!

August 2011

Plus visit
HarlequinInsideRomance.com
and click on the Series Excitement Tab
for exclusive Blaze™ 10th Anniversary content!

www.Harlequin.com

HBCELEBRATE0811

SPECIAL EDITION

Life, Love, Family and Top Authors!

IN AUGUST, HARLEQUIN SPECIAL EDITION FEATURES
USA TODAY BESTSELLING AUTHORS
MARIE FERRARELLA AND *ALLISON LEIGH.*

THE BABY WORE A BADGE
BY *MARIE FERRARELLA*

The second title in the **Montana Mavericks:
The Texans Are Coming!** miniseries....

Suddenly single father Jake Castro has his hands full with
the baby he never expected—and with a beautiful young
woman too wise for her years.

COURTNEY'S BABY PLAN
BY *ALLISON LEIGH*

The third title in the **Return to the Double C** miniseries....

Tired of waiting for Mr. Right, nurse Courtney Clay takes
matters into her own hands to create the family she's
always wanted— but her surly patient may just be
the Mr. Right she's been searching for all along.

www.Harlequin.com

SEUSA0811